To Kid

My number one fan

Seth Miller

His vision, from the constantly passing bars,
Has grown so weary that it cannot hold
Anything else. It seems to him there are
A thousand bars; and behind the bars, no world.

From "The Panther" by Rainer Maria Rilke

To My Daughter Allison

PART ONE - BOUND

There is no such thing as paranoia.
Your worst fears can come true at any moment.

Hunter S. Thompson

SMOKE

She strolls in like she owns the place and orders a dirty Tanqueray martini, straight up. Understandable if I stood behind a bar with my sleeves rolled up and a dishrag slung over my shoulder, but I'm a therapist in private practice at work behind my desk. Dark sunglasses and a scarf conceal her oval face as my mysterious nighttime interloper shuts the door behind her and I'm no longer alone in my office.

"Miss, I think you want *Dooley's Bar* across the street," I say, as I look up from the invoices I've been hunched over for the last hour.

She ignores my comment and removes her scarf. When the sable coat comes off, my Spartan office instantly fills with the sweet scent of gardenias. She sits across from me and crosses her long legs. Off come the dark shades. Not a red hair out of place. Her green sequined cocktail dress reveals plenty of curves, and my eyes shift from the woman's cleavage to her bling as she fishes a cigarette from her purse and lights it.

I recognize her immediately. That iconic face, those green cat eyes, and classic high cheekbones. Blaze Stark, mega best-selling dystopian author and homegrown St. Louisan sits before me, back in town.

Is this an elaborate joke somehow pulled off by one of my friends? I feel like a mark on that old television show my parents used to watch, *Candid Camera*.

I find the small ashtray in a drawer and slide it across my desk before she sets the carpet on fire. "I don't normally allow smoking here, but in this case, I will make an exception, Ms. Stark."

She grins briefly at the mention of her name and blows a perfect smoke ring at me through full red lips. I watch the tight little circle expand and float halfway to the ceiling before it dissipates. The act, Marilyn Monroe sensual yet so casual, takes me by surprise, and when I look back at her those striking green eyes have locked on mine.

"I know exactly where I am, Dr. Adams. I have something to confess ... I need help. *Your* kind of help." Deep throaty voice, provocative, a tad dramatic. Borderline slutty, or am I reading too much into it?

"The head shots don't do you justice," I say, leaning back in my chair.

She nods slightly. The diamonds that hang from her necklace and earlobes sparkle as she blows more smoke my way. "Have you read my books?"

"You sell door-to-door now?"

The corners of her mouth turn down and she takes another drag, then exhales smoke through her nose. "Well, have you?" she repeats, perturbed this time.

"I'm afraid not."

Her eyes widen. "Good, because they're crap."

"Crap certainly keeps the wolf from the door."

"You'd think so," she says, extinguishing the butt in the tray. That's when I notice the slight tremble in her hands as she roots in her purse again. "A plot is afoot. Someone wants to drive me crazy, or worse." She slips a pill into her mouth and dry swallows it in a motion so smooth and practiced I almost miss it.

"Someone?"

She rolls her eyes, lets the silence linger. "That's right. I don't know the identity of the culprit."

"Who would want to make you be less than sane?"

A wry grin follows while she opens her purse. "That's a novel way to put it."

I return her look with an exaggerated smile. "You would know."

She parts her lips ever so slightly. "I could use that drink now."

"Maybe you didn't notice the sign on the door."

She waves a dismissive hand in the air. "What self-respecting therapist doesn't squirrel away a bottle in the office?"

When I don't respond, she flashes an *I'm-not-stupid* look and hands me a bookmark with the cover of her novel *Bound* on the front. "When in town I stay at the Ritz-Carlton. My suite and phone numbers are on the back. I want you there tomorrow night. Ten o'clock works, but eleven is better. Call from the lobby so my bodyguard Alonso can let you in."

"Can't Alonso fetch your drinks?"

She looks at me like I just belched during her fancy dinner party. "Of course, he can. Don't be a cad."

I point to the diplomas on the wall, among them my doctorate in social work. "I'm a therapist in private practice, Ms. Stark. I see clients in the office. I don't make house calls."

She makes a face, her nose wrinkles. "For a therapist you're not very warm and fuzzy."

Her remarks hint at the answer, but I ask anyway. "Have you *met* many of us before?"

She takes in the office and shakes her head. "You really *haven't* read my books, have you? If you had, you'd realize I have an image to maintain." From her purse she produces a travel bottle of Tanqueray, twists off the plastic top, and drinks it in one motion.

Smoking, pill popping, and drinking—all verboten behaviors for clients in session, but she isn't a client, and this isn't a session. I have no idea what *this* is, but if it's an audition to be a future client she is failing miserably. "There now. You no longer need that drink. If an office poses an inconvenience for you, you're not serious about therapy." I want to leave it at that, but when she fails to respond to my comment, I repeat my previous question in her words. "Who do you think wants to drive you crazy, or worse?"

She fishes out another cigarette and taps the end quickly on the arm of the chair twice before she raises a gold lighter to her mouth. At this rate I'll need a bigger ashtray. She exhales more smoke. "It could be my husband Sam. Or my publisher Ted. Maybe Harry my agent." In sotto voce, full of menace, she adds, "Or my husband's mistress."

Warning alarms sound in my head. My gut tells me not to take the case. "If you suspect your husband, your suite would be the worst place to meet."

"We maintain homes in Manhattan, L.A., and Sun Valley. In an hour Sam jets to the West Coast for *business*." The last word slices the air between us like a sword.

"The other woman?"

She nods.

Eager to go home, I look at my wide-open schedule and pretend to search for an available time. "I have openings this Friday—at two and five o'clock. Just so you know, I employ eight other therapists who see clients here day and night. There may be people in the waiting room. You can enter by the privacy exit to avoid the waiting room, but I can't guarantee a client on their way out won't pass you. Wear the shades and scarf; they fooled me. Pick a time."

Her face lemons in distaste. "I can't risk being seen here. My image is sacrosanct. To tarnish it would devastate my readers."

"I guess that settles it then. I don't know any therapist worth their salt willing to make house calls. Now if you will excuse me, I have work to finish."

She stares at me until her head lowers. I'm about to ask if something is wrong when she looks up from her lap. She tugs self-consciously at the hem of her dress and her eyes well with tears. "What am I to do? I know it's late, but I need help. You have no idea how difficult it was for me to come here. I'm sorry to be so weak and needy." Her voice an octave higher, she sounds younger, demure. She dabs at her eyes with tissue and emits two sad whimpers. A tactical switch to manipulate me?

I offer a box of tissues. "You don't live here, so any sessions with me after you fly home would be limited to web cam or Skype. You have a home in L.A. and many people in Hollywood see therapists; there's less stigma concerning therapy on the coasts. I imagine ones there make house calls. That's my recommendation."

She bites her lower lip as she squeezes the tissue in her lap. "I asked around. You've worked high-profile cases. You had a taste of celebrity and know the dark side of fame. Two fans recognized me tonight as I left the limo. One ran up for an autograph in the parking lot before Alonso could intervene. The next fan that comes up to me could be the next Mark David Chapman. I don't want to end up like Selena Gomez."

Understandable on one level, the price of fame. Could the culprit be a deranged fan? A stalker? "You say you want help but refuse to accept it in an office because of an image you wish to maintain. You don't want to devastate your fans, yet you fear them. So, on Friday have your chauffeur drive you here in a Camry."

Her full lips press together tight and almost disappear. She stands and walks to the floor-to-ceiling windows that look down on the streets of Clayton, her back to me. After some time, she turns and glares at me with her arms crossed. A defiant posture. "That's a rather callous thing to say." The breathy, seductive voice is back.

"I'd call it practical."

She makes a face at the tissue in her hand like it's a foreign object and tosses it in the trashcan by my desk. She walks up close. "I'm Blaze Stark. I refuse to be a victim or the target of cruel mind games. Can you imagine how that feels?"

I've had my moments the last few years. "Our schedules conflict. Maybe I'm not the right fit for you, perhaps a female therapist—"

"NO!" She enters my personal space and her head tilts sideways while she strokes her throat. "No, you're exactly the right man for the job. You solved your girlfriend's murder, you helped put away that corrupt prosecutor, and last year you stopped a group of terrorists. You've taken on men of power and defeated them at their own game. I flew into town for one purpose—to hire you. I'm trapped in a bubble that's about to burst. If anyone can help me, it's you."

I made headlines three years running. My times under the public microscope were loathsome. I received death threats, people I love were hurt, one died. Over time I stopped looking behind my back and gladly faded into local anonymity. My practice grew with each round of free, positive publicity. I got lucky each time, but invariably luck runs out.

Perhaps I've been too hasty. "I *can* relate to your situation. Which Friday time works better—two or five?"

Her jaw set, she leans forward and pats the lapel of my jacket with manicured nails. "Tomorrow night. My suite."

I sigh inwardly and direct us back to the chairs where we sit. "Have you hired private investigators?"

A bitter smile. "Nobody found anything out of the ordinary. Not even photos of Sam with *her*."

I think of the travel bottle and pill. "Sometimes the mind plays tricks, misinterprets events, distorts reality … becomes altered."

A subtle shake of her head, then: "What you're thinking about me right now … you're wrong."

"Ms. Stark, you're a rainmaker in a struggling industry, one of its golden geese. Why would the business associates you helped make rich want you out of the picture?"

"You answered your own question."

"How so?"

She flinches at the loud whoosh of a wall vacuum cleaner in the hallway. "I *am* the golden goose from the nursery rhyme."

"So, someone wants you dead."

Her forehead wrinkles briefly when she stands. "Watch the news on Channel Four. You *really* don't know about me, do you? Tomorrow night, in my suite. Block out two hours; you're gonna need it." Her hand lingers on my shoulder, she turns and fans out five crisp, hundred- dollar bills on my desk.

By the time I get home tonight the news will be over. A local would know that. "Keep your money. I won't be there."

"Then donate it to charity or treat your pretty new girlfriend to a nice dinner," she says, donning the sable coat, scarf, and shades.

She has vetted me. I remember the pill and gin. "Is your chauffeur here to drive you?"

She notices the clutter in the hall on the way to the other rooms in my H-shaped office. "What's with the drop cloths, steel, and drywall?"

"I'm having renovations done. Is your driver here?"

"Alonso sits in the waiting room. See you tomorrow night, Dr. Adams."

I watch those long legs leave the way they entered. Her words felt staged like a scene from a novel, but things, clinical minutiae, piqued my weary mind. I hear muffled words in the waiting room and resist the temptation to catch a peek at the bodyguard before the door to the outer hallway opens quietly and snicks closed. Alone again in the suite of offices, I finish my paperwork, stamp bills and invoices for the outgoing mail, grab my coat, and walk to my Solstice.

As if on the heels of Blaze Stark, dust devils commandeer the streets of Clayton, loose scraps of paper twist and spiral into the cool fall air. Heat lightning rolls out of the west toward downtown. Ten minutes later a torrent of rain falls, and the wind blows so hard I struggle to keep my little red car on a dark road that rolls out before me like a slippery human tongue. The convertible top billows against the sudden onslaught of wind. I struggle to secure it but get drenched in the process. The windows steam the rest of the drive home even with the defroster on high, so I roll down a window part way. As I near my subdivision, the green lights in my rearview loom like cat eyes, following me.

RIP

When I enter the kitchen from the garage, Barney the beagle greets me with howls and tail wags. He spins and wiggles in tight little circles until I kneel to pet him. He nearly licks my face off.

I look up at my girlfriend Miranda who stands with arms folded at the doorway to the living room. "Now that's a greeting. You could learn a lot from your little guy."

"So could you. Want to know what he was licking a minute ago?"

I rub his velvety puppy ears which elicits a groan and an eye roll. "Pass."

Miranda flashes a smile. "You seemed to enjoy my greeting the other night when I came home from the Mexico job."

"I remember. You were gone two weeks." I set my briefcase on the marble countertop. "The dinner was exquisite, and I loved what you wore later that night."

"I wasn't wearing anything."

"Exactly."

She eyes my wet hair and clothes. "You decide to run home?"

"Very funny. I was delayed by a real rainmaker."

Miranda's work involves travel. She's an RN with a master's degree and works as a fantasy broker for a firm based on the left coast with satellite offices across the country, including St. Louis. She recently returned from Aguascalientes in north central Mexico, where an adrenaline junkie with more money than brains decided he wanted to be a bullfighter for a day. The company, *Fantasy into Reality*, arranged for lessons with a pro at one of the two local arenas. On his big day, after the mounted picadors sank their lances into the back of a now very pissed-off and bleeding bull, the gringo matador didn't spin away fast enough and his traje de luces became ensnared on the beast's horn. Before he could earn a single *Ole*, el toro unceremoniously dragged the fledgling matador around the ring and hurled him against the wooden wall like a piñata, shattering his right arm and clavicle. Miranda provided on-the-scene triage and accompanied her client to the local hospital. Later, the happy jet setter received a CD of his training and the ever-so-brief bull confrontation before he returned to Miami with a story to tell his friends. On the flight home, he wore his cast like a badge of honor.

I change into jeans and play fetch with Barney until he settles down with his chew toy. Monday is my late night at the office and Miranda ate dinner hours ago, so I scavenge for leftovers while we sit on the sofa and recap our days. As always, I make no direct reference to clients, including the bizarre encounter with Blaze.

I still feel relief that I maneuvered her away from the practice.

As chance would have it, I always DVR the late news on Channel Four news. The familiar face of Debbie Macklin, their anorexic-looking nighttime news anchor, fills the screen. We've known each other for years; she occasionally asks to interview me when the station wants a free professional opinion or clarification on a story with a mental health component. In exchange my practice gets a free plug. Tonight's news leads with the latest rolling gun battle on the near North Side and a deadly drive-by shooting that killed a toddler. Debbie reports that St. Louis city is again is on pace to lead the country in per capita murders. I fast-forward through the commercials, weather, and sports until Debbie's big blonde hair returns.

She smiles into the camera. "We end late news tonight with an upbeat story. An exclusive on St. Louis' own best-selling author, Blaze Stark, who returned home this week to announce the signing of a blockbuster movie deal with Infinity Pictures. The motion picture giant won the intense bidding war for the film rights to her wildly popular trilogy, *Boundless* and, as many of our viewers know, each of her novels has dominated the national number one best-selling lists for a year."

The screen cuts to a close-up of Blaze addressing a packed audience, with Debbie doing the voice over. "In video recorded earlier today, Ms. Stark treated an overflow crowd at the main county library to a spirited reading and discussion of her latest and final book in the trilogy. Tickets to this event sold out in minutes online and, as you can see, traffic backed up for miles along Lindbergh. We heard reports that scalpers sold individual tickets for two hundred dollars." The screen shifts from shots of Blaze during her talk, to the overflow crowd of costumed fans on the street waving signs, to more frenzied fans clustered around a black stretch limousine in the parking lot. The final shot is a close-up of Blaze with an older man.

Debbie returns to the screen and swivels to her co-anchor. "I wonder—is that gorgeous dress is a Dior or Chanel? With the almost simultaneous release of back-to-back-to-back number one, world-wide, best-selling novels, and her marriage to California business mogul Sam Golding, they are Hollywood's latest power couple. Mark, isn't it great to see a local girl make it big?" Before the mop of wavy brown hair next to her can stop grinning and reply, I turn off the TV and finish my Negra Modelo.

On screen, hordes of fans, hundreds dressed in similar outfits and marching down the street stop traffic for blocks. I couldn't quite make out the garb because the shots were brief, and the scenes shifted frequently. In the corner of one shot, it looked like police dragged fans off the road.

I wonder if there were arrests. At a book signing in a tranquil St. Louis County suburb.

I pick up my plate. "I'm gonna go read." Then nonchalantly: "Have you read any of her books?"

"The first two. I just ordered the third in the trilogy from Left Bank." A local St. Louis bookstore.

"Do you like them?"

She nods. "I started reading the first one and got hooked." She pauses and adds, "They resonate with me on several levels." She studies my face and grins. "Don't give me that look. Men have *Rocky* and *Armageddon*."

"I think those were screenplays adapted into movies."

She considers that for a moment. "Okay, men have Ian Fleming."

"Had but point taken."

"And Edgar Rice Burroughs."

"You're preaching to the choir, hon."

"So, what if other famous writers have panned her work. Shame on them. They haven't written the Great American Novel, either. After going through the trouble of writing books, isn't the idea to sell them to readers who enjoy them?"

A smile slowly spreads across my face. "You're right."

She can't suppress a smile of her own. "Listen to me. They may be a bit salacious and tempestuous. There's nothing wrong with a little escapism every now and then."

"No argument here."

"Blaze seems so genuine, so composed and sure of herself. I love that dress she wore. She looks so beautiful on TV. I wish I could have been there."

If she only knew.

What was it Blaze wanted me to see on the news? I felt a vague sense of unease about the crowd marching down Lindbergh Avenue but couldn't put my finger on it. I asked Miranda about the fans' outfits and what they carried.

Her answer stuns me.

Blaze's writing certainly stimulates primal nerves in her readers. Reading the look on my face, she says, "You really don't pay attention to pop culture, do you?"

"Guess not. Call me Rip Van Winkle." Then it hits me, the crowd reminds me of the vengeance-seeking mob in the movie *Frankenstein*.

BARS

I feel the walls close in on me while the elevator rises swiftly to the eighteenth floor of the Ritz-Carlton. Three years ago, a hired gun tried to kill me on this penthouse floor, to prevent me from blowing the whistle on his boss. He shot me when I sprinted down the fire escape and, had I not been able to make it to a sympathetic Secret Service agent, Missouri's next senator would have been a corrupt and amoral politician with designs on the presidency.

Maybe I'm here because it's a welcome break from the dull routine of paperwork, or the intriguing challenge Blaze presents, or plain idle curiosity. Maybe I'm exiting this elevator of polished wood and glass because Blaze dropped money on my desk. Or because I can relate to her fear of the lunatic fringe. Maybe I'm here because her writing struck a chord in Miranda, and I sense us slowly drifting apart. Perhaps it's the weird clinical hunch that struck me when I first met Blaze. Or maybe an unconscious motivation compels me here or some weird hybrid of the above. Maybe I'll find out along the way.

Walking down the wide hallway with the familiar garishly colored carpeting, I reach suite 1810 and knock. I don't believe in omens, but a chill crawls up my back because it's the same damn room from three years ago. I fight the flashbacks that want to worm their way inside me. While I wait, I scan the cover of *Bound* on the front of her business card: a voluptuous young blonde lay prone on a bed; full lips parted, her frightened face tilted toward me; her blouse partially open and her arms stretched behind her head because her wrists may have been in chains. I say *may have been* because that's where the cover artwork disappeared into the edge of the bookmark. The cover evokes imminent danger and vulnerability. Perhaps the promise of violence, debauchery, and sexual deviance.

The door opens and a huge black man in a conservative three-piece suit with muscles on top of his muscles steps into the hallway.

"I.D.," he says. It's not a request.

He scans my driver's license and searches the manila folder in my hands. He returns both.

"Turn around," he commands while he pats me down. He removes the Dictaphone from my sports coat and the Montblanc in my pocket. "You get these back when you leave."

"I tape all my clients' sessions."

"Not this one."

"Why not?"

"Ms. Stark pays me to protect her. An audiotape with her innermost thoughts on it could fall into the wrong hands. You're not part of her inner circle."

"This isn't how I work."

"Orders from the boss."

I consider leaving but for some reason I'm here. "Sounds like she's in the Mafia and you are …" I squish my nose with my thumb and scowl.

He flashes a perturbed look, like I'm a fly buzzing around his face. His brown eyes fix on mine. "You'd be amazed by the number of crazy people obsessed with celebrities."

"No, I wouldn't, but point taken. Who *is* in her inner circle?"

He stares at me and doesn't answer.

He must wear a size 50 coat and he's all muscle. "How about I fight you for my Dictaphone?"

He looks down at me and grins. "You have a death wish?"

"Not far as I know. You know of anybody here, inner circle or otherwise, with a death wish? A homicidal wish? Or someone who enjoys risk-taking behavior?"

The grin vanishes while my Dictaphone disappears into his pocket. I follow him into a large sitting room where a cozy gas fireplace throws out yellow and blue flames. A black Steinway stands near the picture window that reveals a prime view of downtown Clayton and the Arch to the east. He doesn't offer me a seat but walks to a door and taps on it. The door opens a few inches, and he speaks in hushed, deferential tones too soft for me to hear.

Blaze enters wearing a full-length white robe, her hair wrapped in a matching bath towel. "Thank you, Alonso. You may wait outside."

Once the door closes behind him, she turns to me. "Care for a drink, Mitch? If I don't have it here, room service will bring it up. It's okay to call you Mitch, isn't it?"

The sultry, provocative voice again. The way she stares at me, I feel like a piece of meat. I'm reminded of Marilyn Monroe again; she's sex on a stick and she knows it but there's more to her than just that. "No, you may not. Didn't I give enough notice that I was coming?"

She looks puzzled while she pours three fingers of a dark brown liquid into a crystal glass at an elaborate wet bar. "You did. I like a punctual man." She winks at me.

I drop her money on a granite table. "This isn't a game and I'm not part of your entourage. I'm leaving."

She puts the glass down. "No. I need you." A near whisper.

"You're dressed in a bathrobe."

She glances down as if to check. "Why, yes I am. I was in the Jacuzzi. It helps me relax."

I walk to the bar and pour her drink down the drain. "If I agree to this, you will be ready on time. You will wear proper clothing. And you will not depress your central nervous system with alcohol or other drugs."

"But it helps me—"

"Relax, I know. This was a bad idea." I turn toward the door.

"No, wait!" She points at the fireplace. "Alonso arranged two chairs and bottles of water on the table. I have an idea." She sashays into what must be the master bedroom that Alonso knocked on earlier. She emerges with her arms full and a sly look on her face. She sits in one of the chairs, covers herself with a plush comforter, and clutches a scruffy brown teddy bear in one hand. I groan inwardly when I see the stuffed animal. Those who've worked in mental health know why.

I should have insisted she get dressed in suitable evening attire, but I can imagine how long that would take a woman like her.

I ask about her current home situation and she speaks in generalities that aren't helpful.

Same for questions about her family history, her childhood and schooling, her adult years, and alcohol and drug consumption. I get the impression she's making up answers as she goes. She says she drinks when depressed, stressed, or anxious, that she may have two or three drinks a night to take the edge off.

Some colleagues multiply by three when clients self-report their alcohol consumption while others multiply by four. My hunch is that a larger number applies here.

When I ask what pill she took in my office the night before, she removes the towel from her head, produces a brush from her robe pocket, and teases the knots from her wavy red hair. She casts a sideways glance at me when her robe partially opens. The sly smile returns.

"Sit up and cover yourself. Enough with the seduction shtick. If you refuse to act like a responsible adult, I can't help you."

The smile lingers until she realizes I'm serious. She places the brush on the table between us.

I point to her. "Close your robe."

She straightens up and tugs the collars of her robe together. "There. Is this less threatening for you?" That low breathless whisper.

"Cover yourself with the blanket, please."

"But I was hot."

"Do as I say, please."

She reluctantly complies and the grin returns. "I make you nervous, Mitch. I understand. I make a lot of men feel that way. It's why I don't have women friends."

"If we are going to work together, there will be boundaries. Call me Dr. Adams and I will address you as Ms. Stark. You didn't answer my question. Last night in my office, you took a pill. What was it?"

"Xanax. I have a prescription for them." Her tone wary, as if I plan to take her pills away.

"Do you take anti-depressant or anti-psychotic medication?"

"No."

I hand her a packet from my folder. "New client paperwork. Please fill it out before we meet again. If we meet again. Make sure to include your insurance information. I will submit a bill to your provider—"

"I don't have insurance, so keep the money. My business manager sends me cash or cuts a check whenever I want. Tell me when you need more."

I've had wealthy clients go that route. "Okay. Have you been in therapy before?"

"No."

Not the answer I expect after things she mentioned during our first encounter.

"If we are to work together, you will be on time and dressed appropriately. You will not drink alcohol, smoke, or ingest drugs of any kind during session. Will you abide by these rules?"

She lowers the comforter to her lap and fans herself with the bear. "Yes."

"Please fill out the client history form thoroughly. Make sure you list all your medications and every doctor you see. There's also an information release to sign so I may obtain records from your primary care physician."

She settles into the chair and touches her lower lip with a nail.

"Who do you think wants to harm you?"

"I'm not sure. Women resent or hate me and men are intimidated by me or want to fuck me."

"What about your husband?"

A wan smile. "Sam's another story. He'd love to replace me with his young mistress. And take my money."

"According to Forbes, your husband is a multi-billionaire. Why would he need your money?"

She laughs and her eyes narrow. "That's adorable. Bless your heart. To be so naive about the wealthy. Does a rich man ever think he has enough money?" She fondles the terry cloth tie of her robe. "I didn't come from money like Sam; but I know how the game is played. To keep an aspiring young trophy wife on a stringer, expensive bait must be dangled, and the eventual promise of more. I worked hard to make my fortune and refused to sign a pre-nup. I could demand half his fortune in a divorce."

So, Blaze is nouveau rich while Golding comes from old money. "You mentioned other suspects the night we met."

"My publisher Ted. He hated it when I accepted Sam's marriage proposal. They're lifelong friends and Sam was dating Ted's sister when we met."

"Was this before or after you became famous?"

She takes a drink of water and absently twirls one end of the robe sash. The delay drags on so long I'm about to ask the question again. "Shortly before, I think. Teddy sees me as the reason his sister had a nervous breakdown and didn't marry into money. He's also a lecherous cad with a casting couch in his office who preys on actresses and female writers eager to do anything to break into the business. Ted runs Lightning Rod Press, the largest publishing house in the world."

Another surprise. "That was years ago, and you made each other a fortune."

"What can I say? Like a lot of men, he can be a vengeful prick."

It seems a bit anomalous to hold such a long-standing grudge against his biggest client. Hardly sounds like motivation for years of harassment, much less murder. She mentioned they met before she became a best-selling author. "Did Ted lure you onto his casting couch?"

She grins. "He did his best. Lightning Rod, like all major presses, doesn't accept unagented submissions. Ted agreed to have an underling consider my manuscripts as a courtesy to my husband. I'm convinced he already planned to sign me when he dangled a contract in front of me in exchange for a blow job. I threatened to tell Sam. She throws her head back and laughs. "I think that added an extra zero to my contract. Over the years, it tainted my relationship with Ted and Lightning Rod. To keep him in his place, every now and then I threaten to buy out my contract and sign with his biggest competitor."

"Does Sam know any of this?"

A shake of the head. "And I want to keep it that way. They remain good friends. Besides, Ted gives me anything I want now."

"Go on."

She crosses her legs and cerise-painted toenails pop out from beneath the robe. "Well, there's my agent Harry Firestone. He doesn't think authors should write screenplays of their own work. I disagree. He wants a *more seasoned* Hollywood screenwriter to write the adaptation for *Bound*. One of his male cronies. He wants the series to be the greatest, money-making movie franchise ever. I do, too. Who better to write the screenplay than me, the author of the most successful series of all time? Everything's in the negotiation stage now with *Infinity Pictures* and what I want should carry a lot of weight. The presumptive movie director is a drinking buddy of Harry's and a known pedophile. A pedophile is the last person who should bring my work to the big screen." She reaches for a cigarette, then stops herself. "I'm a writer, but I despise the business and this good ole boys' Hollywood club. I threaten to fire Harry every day for not supporting me. I'm most qualified to write the adapted screenplay. I haven't written one, but how hard can it be to condense what I've already written?"

"I hear they involve two different skill sets."

She crosses her arms while she shoots me with a look. "Harry thinks I should focus on my next novel. A prequel or spin-off."

"That sounds like practical advice. Maybe a dive back into writing would be therapeutic."

Her pursed lips and scowl indicate she doesn't agree.

"What about the other woman?"

She laughs. "Nothing complex there. She's twenty-two, a former Miss wherever on the prowl for a sugar daddy. She longs to see her face splashed on magazine covers while globetrotting to A-list parties. Who wouldn't? Been there, done that. It's a rush. There's always someone out there who wants what you have. Survival of the fittest also applies to the rich."

So much for money buying happiness. "Have you confronted Sam about her?"

"He denies the affair. He's lying, of course. A woman knows." She uncrosses her legs, revealing more flesh than I care to see. I tell her to cover herself and she does.

"You haven't been upfront with me. You didn't fly here specifically to see me. St. Louis is the first stop on your book signing tour and your hometown a fitting venue to announce the movie deal with Infinity Pictures."

She looks confused. "Yeah, so?"

"In the office last night, you said the reason you flew to St. Louis was to seek my help."

"I never said that."

"That *is* what you said."

"Perhaps I embellished a bit." A sly smile. "A few tears to get you here isn't a crime, is it?"

"Did you exaggerate about your fan base?"

She shakes her head. "Some scare the shit out of me."

Good thing I spoke with Miranda about this. "Your dystopian books pit men against women and contain violence toward both sexes, especially women in bondage. Your female protagonist is a recipient of, and doles out, horrific pain on a regular basis. I imagine that naturally attracts a certain fringe element."

She doesn't respond.

"Have you ever felt in physical danger from your readers?"

She hugs her bear. "I receive hundreds of love letters from fans, women and men, some with unsolicited nude pictures of themselves. An assistant throws away stacks of men-bashing hate mail from abused women around the world, who often share bizarre and incredibly cruel torture ideas for my next novel. Then there's the occasional sick gift that reaches our gates. One box contained a mannequin's head with a plastic male body part stuffed in its mouth. The box it came in had smiley face stickers on every side. Despite a cadre of bodyguards and security cameras, a few have caused scenes in public and trespassed on our properties. One scaled the security fence to our L.A. home six months ago armed with a Claymore before security apprehended him. Luckily no one was injured, and the man arrested. He told the police he planned to kidnap Hester and take her to his castle. I was in London at the time, but it's terrifying to think what could have happened."

"I'm sorry, who is Hester?"

She freezes and looks at me quizzically. "You've read my trilogy. She's the main protagonist you mentioned. You know what she's done to survi—"

"No, I don't. Last night you asked me twice if I'd read your books and I told you I hadn't."

The confused look again. "I have so much on my plate I don't know if I'm coming or going. I receive boxes of hate mail from conservative, religious groups. The language in those letters would make a longshoreman cry."

My bad feelings about this case rise and turn more complex by the minute.

She stares into the gas flames as if she's looking a thousand yards beyond. Her brows knit together. "I've kept this to myself all these years. You won't believe the story I'm about to tell you.

"At nineteen, I wanted to become a famous romance or YA writer. So, I saved my money to attend a weekend writer's workshop in upstate New York. The teacher divided us into groups of two paired me with an older man. His writing skills were more advanced than anyone else's in the class. He'd published short stories and completed manuscripts of three novels, thousands of pages. He took me under his wing, befriended me. Back then, I was a failed poet and unpublished short-story writer with no zero-confidence. I didn't know the basics of storytelling or how to write an outline—"

"I'm sorry to interrupt, but I'm guessing this had to be at least ten years ago and your speculative fiction isn't romance nor is it intended for young adults."

She smiles. "Handsome and sweet. More like fifteen years ago."

No response at my mention of the genre change. "Are you sure you want to start that far back?"

"It lends important context to my life." She takes another sip of water.

"We discussed writing between sessions, dined in the evenings, and spoke of literature. I had little to offer, so I discussed my favorite poets and authors and how their works affected me. He spoke volumes on the craft of storytelling.

He was attentive, polite, even a bit shy. At midnight we returned to our separate rooms until the conference resumed in the morning. When the workshop ended, he offered to drive me to LaGuardia in his SUV that night to save cab fare."

Her hands betray a slight tremor.

"The last things I remember are a sweet, pungent smell in the car and not being able to breathe." She pauses to close her eyes. "I woke up alone in a strange place, on a bare mattress. I stood up and vomited. My watch and cell phone were gone, along with my shoes, clothes, bra, and panties. All replaced by a thin, one-piece outfit reminiscent of a toga. I must have peed when I was out, for the toga was wet. I was dizzy, sick, and terrified; locked in a basement with a concrete floor and walls. The door was steel. I beat on it and screamed for help. No answer came; I heard no noise outside the room. For hours I heard nothing other than the rummaging sounds I made. Images of pending rape and death filled my thoughts."

I thought of the cover for *Bound* and her dressed-up fans but kept it to myself. "I can't imagine what that must have been like."

"I knew you wouldn't believe me."

"I'm listening. Go on."

"No one in the world knows this except me, my kidnapper … and now you.

"I searched for a way out, a tool or anything to use as a weapon. Nothing. Iron bars protected black-out windows set too high on the wall for me to reach. I don't know how long I paced beneath those bars. It was as if there were a thousand bars: and behind them, no world. I couldn't tell whether it was night or day. There was no clock in the basement, and I had no idea how long I'd been unconscious. A small enclosed half-bath stood in one corner of the basement. The toilet bowl held rancid brown water and the tank contained an anti-syphon fill valve, but the light-weight plastic was hardly a useful weapon. He'd shut off water to the sink. I tore the hem of my toga, but it was too flimsy to use as a garrote.

"I returned to the mattress and noticed a bottle of water and a sandwich next to it on a paper plate. After my kidnapper drugged me, the thought of food nauseated me, even though my stomach growled. I grew more terrified as each hour passed. Had my mentor been killed by my kidnappers at the gas station? We'd become friends. Surely, he would have fought them. Then another thought seized me: what if something happened to my mentor and the kidnappers and no one knew I was here?"

She pauses to look at me.

"What happened next?"

"Eventually I drank water and ate some sandwich. Then I heard floorboards above me squeak like mice. Someone *was* here. I tried to walk to the door, but my legs wobbled. It took all my strength to lay back down on the mattress before I fell on my face."

Her green cat eyes grow large. "I'd been drugged again, with some type of paralyzing agent. I saw two of everything and my vision grew blurry. All I could move were my eyes. I heard a noise and saw the silhouette of a man standing at the basement entrance. I couldn't make out his features. He spoke, but I couldn't understand the words. It sounded as if he stood at the rim of a deep well, with me at the bottom."

I thought of a Daniel Fowles novel called *The Collector* I read as an undergrad. Blaze was the female lead in a real-life version of it. It didn't have a happy ending. "What happened next?"

She rummages in her robe for a cigarette, then stops after a sideways glance at me. She fidgets with the cord. "I couldn't move, much less defend myself, and his face remained blurry after he sat next to me. He took my pulse and vital signs and scribbled in a little book. He used a light to look into my eyes and mouth. He brushed my hair, used one of those disposable mouth swabs for dry mouth, and took my temperature. He bathed me and put a fresh toga on me. There was nothing sexual about it, it felt clinical, like he was caring for a patient. I smelled lemon cleanser as he mopped my vomit. By now, I—"

Loud voices arise in the front room of the penthouse. A short thin man wearing a tailored suit and buttoned-down shirt with matching tie bursts through the door. "Blaze, my delectable darling!" he says, pursing his thin lips. "Do you have any idea how fucking hard it is to get past that gorgeous hunk of ebony man-meat you call a bodyguard? We simply must discuss tomorrow's schedule." The multiple and exaggerated esses remind me of a balloon losing air. Hands on hips, he waggles a finger at her as if reproaching a misbehaving child, oblivious of me.

"Miles, the night is young. We need to do this later." She smiles and tilts her head at me.

He looks to me and pushes frameless glasses higher atop the bridge of his tanned nose. "Sure, babe." Then he puts his palms upward, bends forward from the waist, and turns to me: "I'm begging you, please don't keep her up too late."

I stand and extend my hand. "The name's Mitchell." His handshake lingers and is firm.

He pauses, as if expecting more, then clears his throat, and turns to Blaze. "Don't forget, my dearest dumpling! I know how you get in the wee hours. Harry and Ted returned your calls about the screenplay. They've dug in their heels. Call them the second you free up. Preferably now."

He winks at me. "My, you're a handsome one." Then back to Blaze: "These are movers and shakers, sweet cheeks! Movers and shakers!" As he speaks, he performs an impromptu hip grind and looks at himself in a wall mirror, checks his gelled hair to make certain every strand remains in place. "Wish me luck! I plan to ply your bodyguard with liquor. Maybe I can get Black Beauty to change teams for one night. Perchance to dream!"

"There's the rub," I reply.

Miles gives me a second once-over. "Handsome and erudite!" He looks from his Rolex to Blaze. "Remember, my sweet lotus blossom, busy, busy, busy day ahead!"

Again, with the esses. With a final turn and flourish, he exits as quickly as he entered.

Blaze groans as I return to my seat. "That was Miles Hawking, my publicist. Pressure, pressure, pressure," she says, elongating her esses in pantomime. "Type-A's make me jumpy."

She leans forward and as the robe flairs open again her lips part. "Can I have just one teeny, little drink?" Still the breathy, seductive voice.

"No. Cover yourself. Tell me, what's your real name?" I say, as the ornate grandfather clock in the corner strikes midnight.

Her eyebrows raise, a look of incredulousness on her face. "I'm paying you for this. Are you having a stroke? My name is Blaze Stark."

That answers one question in my hypothesis. "What's your given name, at birth?"

She turns away and whispers, "Blaze Stark."

I let it pass for now. I want to go home and crawl into bed with Miranda, but I also want to hear the big reveal tonight.

"You have a full day tomorrow, so let's finish the story of your captivity and wrap up for the night."

"Where was I?"

"You don't remember?"

She crosses her legs and shakes her head, waiting for a cue.

"Your abductor bathed you, changed your toga …"

"Yes, of course. By this time whatever paralytic agent he used on me was slowly wearing off. I still had no control over my extremities, but my vision cleared enough to see the man bent over me with the medical bag—"

Your writing mentor.

"—my workshop friend." She pauses and seems almost disappointed. "You don't appear surprised."

"He drugged you in the car, perhaps with Chloroform."

Those green eyes narrow. "You don't believe me, do you?"

I sense more to come. "Please continue."

"I remember feeling terror; I cried and hyperventilated. I asked why he was doing this. I begged him not to kill me. I feared the worst when he reached into his medical bag, anticipating he'd produce a scalpel or surgical saw. He held a stethoscope and listened to my heart, then used the penlight to look in my eyes a second time. While he wrote in his notebook, I asked him why again."

"Did he answer?"

"He said: 'I know you must think me a monster, but I grew quite fond of you and couldn't bear the thought of you … not in my life. I plan for you to fall in love with me.'"

Just like *The Collector*.

"I asked if I was still in New York—"

And you were.

"He nodded. He said my bone structure reminded him of a young Faye Dunaway or Diana Rigg. I had no idea who they were, so I said nothing."

So much detail, especially after he drugged her fifteen years ago. "They were beautiful, talented actresses before your time."

"I asked how long I'd been a prisoner in his basement. His face recoiled as if I slapped him. He said I had an adverse reaction to the Chloroform, a one in a million response, but the respiratory failure and mild heart issues have almost passed."

"What was your response to his non-answer?"

"That he should have dropped me near a hospital and driven away when he had the chance. He said his medical expertise and one-on-one care were superior to that of any hospital, that he has full access to all drugs a hospital would need to treat my condition. He smiled, patted my leg, and said it's normal in my position to entertain escape, but that he's anticipated every possibility and will use restraints if he must. He suggested not to rip the new toga because they're useless as a weapon."

"He had hidden cameras."

She smiles. "In the ceiling to monitor my every move. He sounded so sure of himself I began to wonder if he'd kidnapped others before me. He said with cooperation comes access to the upstairs and beyond. He pledged to conduct himself in a gentlemanly manner from here on out. I thought he was a madman. What he said next stunned me: 'that the world hasn't treated you well to date and I offer you a fresh start, a chance for a better life.' By this time, I regained some movement and control over my legs again. He helped walk me to the tiny bathroom which now contained a hotel-sized bar of soap, toothpaste, and mouthwash. He suggested I freshen up. The water to the sink now flowing, I washed my face, finger-brushed my teeth with toothpaste, and used mouthwash."

"What did his offer mean?"

She takes a sip of water and abandons her nervous habit of reaching for a cigarette. She shrugs. "During the workshop, I may have mentioned unhappiness and frustration with my life. The fresh start in his mind was for me to fall in love with him."

Given her tentative situation and our limited time together, I feel more rushed with her than other clients. "So, your childhood was unhappy. Were you abused or neglected?"

She looks away and stares into the fire. "No, of course not. He exaggerated my teenage disillusionment to his advantage. It was part of his Svengali act, to strip away my old life and mold me to fit into his. Can I finish my story? I know you think it's late and want to leave, even though the night is young."

I smile. "Go on."

"He suggested I get dressed before he returns. I hear the snick of the key in the lock and his unhurried footfalls up the steps to the main floor. Dress into what? I ask myself. I find no clothes until I shut the bathroom door. A yellow sundress, panties, wireless bra, and espadrilles, all in my size and taste, hung from a dull plastic hook. No belt or shoelaces. There was no inside lock on the bathroom door and no mirror over the sink. I tossed the scratchy paper toga into a corner of the bathroom. An old-time plastic squeeze bottle filled with my favorite perfume now sat on a shelf above the toilet. I tensed while I dressed for scraping and shuffling noises came from the basement room we'd left. He'd arranged a folding table, checkered tablecloth, two chairs, and a small plastic vase containing a single red rose, my favorite flower. As violin music filtered down from recessed ceiling speakers, he served fried chicken and cornbread. He talked writing as if we were still at the seminar and nothing had changed. I was terrified, certain that soon he'd flip and attack me."

I know what she's about to say but want to hear it from her. "So how did you escape your kidnapper of fifteen years ago?"

She sits back, a smirk fills her face. "I didn't. The man who kept me in his butterfly collection for six months is Sam Golding, my husband."

Misinterpreting my silence, she adds in that sultry, sexy voice, "I knew you wouldn't believe me."

SCREAM

I leave her suite after one in the morning.

Before I go, I learn she's been held over another day for a second book signing and the venue is the old city library downtown; *Harry* is Harry Firestone, her agent; and *Ted* is Ted Lamping, her publisher. Both flew in town from New York to help kick off the first leg of her promotional tour before continuing to Hollywood to meet with Bud Waterman, the director for the screen adaptation of *Bound*. That didn't add up for me, but I let it pass for now. She bristled over the impromptu signing and left coast conference but wouldn't elaborate.

We agree to meet tomorrow night in her suite at ten. The bad feeling in my gut about her as my client remains. Perhaps a second session will bring more clarity. When she leaves town, the plan is for Webcam sessions as our schedules, primarily hers, allow.

On my way out the door, I hear her voice over the intercom system. "Alonso, have the limo ready at the main entrance in thirty minutes."

So much for listening to her publicist. Or returning important messages. I turn back to her. "Last night you said your books are crap."

A cigarette already smolders from her mouth. "Some authors aspire to be great novelists; many are introverts who shun recognition and write for pure joy. I have no fear of public speaking, no fears of failure or success. I write for mass market sales. Women buy more books than men, and if you tap into the right vein, the story hardly matters if you strike that sweet spot. A few years ago, a quarter of all books sold were written by three women. Their time has passed; I'm taking over."

I think about our two encounters on the drive home. Instinct tells me to drop the case; that she would be better off with a good female therapist. Why the insistence that she see only me? I know she lied to me many times. Why disparage her work if it's made her rich and famous? She says she wants to remain the best-selling writer but is reluctant to write her next book. Why the indignation about a holdover book signing with her adoring fans? Can her problem be solved by adding more security? It sounds like a few unhinged fans pose a greater threat than those closest to her. When she spoke about the movie director, her confidence seemed to wane, and she appeared to become defensive. The most obvious puzzler for me tonight is, why incorporate well-known lines from a Rilke poem about a panther into her captivity story? There was no head dropping tonight but the memory lapses persist.

I've read case studies in which kidnap victims voluntarily remain with their abductors for decades, but they most often were malleable pre-teen children and the true level of their freedom tended to remain questionable at best until their eventual reunification with family. Also, a small percentage of adult women have hybristophilia and are sexually aroused by and responsive to violent men.

Her story is so bizarre and outlandish that, coupled with my working hypothesis of her mental state, intrigues me on multiple levels.

Two things I know for sure—she's a master of diversion and a woman with many secrets—as I stealth climb into bed with Miranda.

She stirs. "Where have you been? Are you just now getting home?" she rolls over, her voice thick with sleep.

"My late client session turned into something of an emergency." Not the exact truth but I didn't want to elaborate.

She stretches her long runner's legs, yawning. "Everything okay?"

She's accustomed to my shorthand way of indirectly talking about my practice.

"Too early to tell. It's a puzzler."

"You'll figure it out, you always do," she says as her aquamarine eyes lock on me. "You have any clients today?"

"A last-minute add-on, at ten tonight."

"Again? Why so late?" she asks, propping herself up on an elbow. Her other hand rubs my chest.

"It's the only time that works."

She pauses. I can tell she wants to ask one more question and I'm confident I know it.

"Is this new client a woman?"

"I didn't say it was a new client, but yes, she's female."

She removes her hand and rolls away. "I trust you. 'Night."

∞ ∞ ∞

When I wobble into the kitchen for breakfast, she's dressed for a run.

There's excitement in her voice. "Cindy texted this morning while you were asleep. She invited us to an early dinner at Brio. Blaze Stark is held over for a second book signing at seven and Cindy bought four tickets. I get a chance to meet her! Forty bucks apiece gets us a seat and signed hard cover copies of *Boundless*."

I didn't see this coming, and I tense. "We really don't need two copies of the same book, do we? And I doubt Tony wants to go."

She lowers her chin and fixes me with a stare. "Are you kidding? Cindy said he's 'dying to shake the right hand that's attached to that body.' He wants a selfie with her."

"I don't know..."

She tilts her head at me and walks to the bathroom. "You've pre-judged her books without reading them. That's not like you. I go to Cardinal games with you, even though I don't care for baseball. You said the other day you were jonesing for the beef carpaccio at Brio and a nice Cabernet Sauvignon." She peeks around the bathroom doorway at me, smiling while she pees. "Is my guilt trip working?"

I'll be part of a large crowd and skip the signing line. Being at the same venue as a client isn't verboten, but it may be awkward for her if she sees me. "It is. I've never attended a famous author's book event. What's the de rigueur fashion for a book signing?"

She pecks me on the cheek before she leaves. "I don't know about you two sausages, but Cindy and I are dressing up."

∞ ∞ ∞

I shop for clothes while Miranda runs twelve miles. A veteran of three marathons, she'd been training for her next race last year when she almost became a casualty in a case I was working that Blaze mentioned. She endured desperate hours certain she would die, while I needed all my wits and luck to find her. She suffered an especially difficult adjustment period afterward, for it triggered long-buried memories from her college days that impact us as a couple. The issue remains unresolved, and we continue to have our up-and-down days.

I linger while we get ready. Every now and then I receive a hurry-up look from Miranda. Then a verbal admonishment. We arrive late to the restaurant.

"I hope the movies will be as good as the books, but they rarely are," Cindy tells Miranda. I'd had nothing but an omelet for breakfast so when our drinks and appetizers arrive, I almost salivate.

Looking tasty herself in a gold-over-black embroidered bodice dress and black heels, Miranda takes a sip of wine and leans forward. "I wonder which actors will get the lead roles."

Tony turns to me while the women discuss the short list of movie stars rumored to be under consideration for the parts. "If my English teachers looked half as hot as Blaze, I might be a starving artist right now writing bad copy or screenplays in a cheap loft somewhere." My friend Tony Martin had been my private practice mentor years ago in the state psychiatric system. A Ph.D. psychologist, he has such a smooth, mellifluous voice that women often turn their heads to see the man with the silver tongue. In our professional circle he's simply known as *The Voice*. Years ago, he lost his practice for three years after having an affair with a client who later committed suicide. Cindy struggled to forgive him, and the conflict almost tore them apart and contributed to her nervous breakdown. Tony sought my help last year after becoming enmeshed in a doomed, high stakes project with a corrupt engineering firm to develop a machine to treat depression that ironically helped salvage their marriage but may derail my relationship with Miranda. A second case of mine Blaze referenced.

  In an homage to my old college English professors, I sport a white button-down shirt with brown slacks and matching jacket with darker brown elbow patches. I ask Tony if he's read any of her books.

  He shakes his head, smoothing his Marlboro Man mustache with his hairy fingers. He wears a black cashmere sweater and slacks that bear his trademark rumpled look. "I'm more of a Sci-Fi or spy fan. You know me, anything with innovative, grown-up toys. James Bond is like cocaine to me, and Blaze could easily pass for the next Bond girl."

Cindy overhears us and her eyes widen. "I bet you'd like some of the toys Blaze describes."

"I'm piqued," Tony says, sipping his Red Stripe.

"You peaked some time ago, old man," Cindy says with a grin as she raises her glass to her mouth.

I linger over my chicken rigatoni after the others have finished. Miranda flags down our waiter for the bill and looks at me, perturbed. Traffic is a mess and by the time we arrive at the downtown library it's past seven and she tells me to drop them off at the entrance. She shoots me a pissed off look when she closes the passenger door. I cruise half a square mile until I finally see a car leave a spot and parallel park in its place. All the lots and garage parking are full and to describe the street parking in St. Louis tonight as utter pandemonium qualifies as an understatement. Pedestrians congest every side street and claim right of way with their sheer numbers, while helpless drivers honk and gesture in frustration. Cars are double-parked everywhere. I watch bicycle cops leave so many tickets on windshields they look like Seventh Day Adventists peppering cars with flyers. There's a Blues hockey game tonight, concerts at Busch Stadium, Peabody Opera House, and The Sheldon, plus a show at The Fox. Tonight, the epicenter of the street congestion is, of all places, the downtown public library on Olive Street.

On my hike back to the library, I fall in step with a large band of mostly teens and young women dressed in togas, carrying signs. From a side street other women dressed in racy black leather and fishnet stockings merge with our group. Some with their wrists bound, a few wear masks like Hannibal Lector wore when he was transferred to a new prison in *Silence of the Lambs*. One white-as-chalk girl who looks thirteen wears a unique mask that gives the appearance her mouth has been sewn shut, like the stitches on a baseball.

I turn to a blond girl sporting a toga with her wrists loosely cuffed in front of her and say, "Halloween's over. Why the get-up?" She turns to me and seems surprised by my question. "I'm biding my time. We will rise up. Your reign is coming to an end."

This borders on performance art.

I walk over to a young woman who carries a riding crop, dressed and built like Elvira, Mistress of the Dark, complete with black widow's peak and double D cups, and ask, "Why the whip?" She glares at me while a snarl forms on her lips. "Fuck off, old man. We rule the world now."

"Old man?" I say, "I may have ten years on you, at most." Elvira ignores me and begins to chant, "A new day has come, we have risen; you cannot stop us, you cannot silence us." Other voices join in and grow more fervent while they take up the chant. Small clusters of young men in the crowd wear post-Apocalyptic clothing reminiscent of the Mad Max movies but heavier, more suitable for harsh winters. A few men pull women dressed in togas behind them, many in chains and others bound with rope.

When we near the library, our progress stalls behind a much larger throng of young and middle-aged women, dressed in everyday jeans and coats, clustered about the base of the marble steps. Several frantically ask if anybody has extra tickets to sell. At the entrance, some of the bondage set that carry real weapons are detained. One argues with security that her Doberman with the studded collar is an emotional support dog. A commotion erupts to my right and a now screaming Elvira threatens to shove her riding crop up a guard's ass unless she's allowed to enter. She's cuffed and led away. Her ticket flutters to the ground and a mad rush for it ensues.

When I enter the city library, the only empty seats are folding chairs being hastily added to the back rows of the main room to handle the overflow crowd. Miranda, Tony, and Cindy sit about fifteen rows ahead, every seat near them occupied. In two adjacent rooms, rows of bookstore staffers sell hardcover copies of Blaze's trilogy as fast as they remove them from the boxes, while vendors hawk togas, t-shirts, coffee mugs, and other paraphernalia. Four packed bars in adjoining rooms sell mixed drinks, wine, and beer like Prohibition ended an hour ago. Bloody Marys are clearly the drink du jour, to patrons costumed or not. Blaze is indeed the golden goose.

By the time I take my seat in the last row, she's well into her talk and during a pause the audience stands to clap and cheer. I must crane my neck and peer around others just to glimpse the podium or, I can watch the dais on one of the two mounted televisions in the back corners of the great room, so when my view is blocked, I watch Blaze on a monitor. During the break I observe Miles schmooze the matrons and patrons of the library that occupy the rows nearest the podium cordoned off by velvet ropes. He sports a double-breasted navy-blue suit, pressed white pants and white shoes. If *The Village People* needed a sailor in their group, Miles would have been perfect. Older men dressed in power suits occupy the row behind Blaze and sit like birds on a wire, their eyes blinking from cellphone flashes. She sips a Bloody Mary during the applause and surreptitiously slides a pill into her mouth. Standing guard in the background, Alonso and a white body builder with no neck sport form-fitting three-piece suits that make them look chiseled from granite. The white guard's lantern jaw juts so prominently he reminds me of one of those Easter Island statues.

On the screen I notice Blaze wears another sequined green dress (her signature color to complement the flaming red hair), this one low-cut and form-fitting with spaghetti straps to accentuate two of her better physical attributes, and a hem riding a healthy four inches above the knee. More thick gold bracelets adorn her wrists, and she rocks black stiletto heels. Her wavy hair cascades past her shoulders in rivulets of fire. Tonight, her full pouting lips remind me a bit of a taller version of Tony's favorite actor Scarlett Johansson when she sported red hair in *Girl with a Pearl Earring*. She returns to the podium and waits for the applause to stop. "Thank you! You're too kind! That final reading sets the stage for the denouement scene in *Boundless*. At long last Hester reaches her personal *Alamo* with the Reaper, in the remains of what used to be San Antonio, Texas. Though she and her all-woman army are greatly outnumbered against the Reaper and his screaming marauders, the battle rages throughout the night against the castle lord who took everything from her in *Bound.*" She pauses to smile. "As to whether they make it over the wall between what used to be Mexico and the United States—and what awaits them if and when they do—I will let you experience on your terms. Novels are my living, breathing babies—it took a year and thousands of hours for me to incubate, nurture, and grow this, my third child! I hope you love her as much as I do!" She wipes a tear from her eye. "You may have figured it out by now, but I pour everything into my books and I'm unabashedly passionate about my work! The world needs more female heroes; mine just happen to live in the post-apocalyptic year 2057."

"We love you, Blaze!" shout two young women in togas.

She points toward them. "I love you, too! I have a favor to ask, the best way to thank an author is to write an on-line review. It doesn't have to be long-winded or consume much time, just be honest and let your heart do the talking." She wipes away more tears. "I look out at this crowd and see so many fresh faces, so many young, strong, and brave women. You are our future! You all have stories and I pray you tell them one day! If you will indulge me again for a brief break to fix my face, I will be happy to take questions."

Raucous applause, foot stomping, and chants of 'We love you, Blaze!' rock the library while she leaves the podium in search of her drink. She may have slipped a second pill into her mouth, but from this far back it's hard to tell and by the time I turn to the screen I miss it.

Miles steps to the podium and thanks the downtown library staff and Left Bank volunteers. He offers special thanks to Blaze's faithful hometown readers for demanding the impromptu hold-over signing. He finishes with two surprise announcements—that *Bound* has just become the best-selling book of all-time and casting for the movie version has been finalized (resulting in a concussive explosion of screams and squeals). He grins, patiently waiting for the din to fade before he reports that the names of the actors will remain a well-guarded secret. For now. No mention of the screenplay.

Blaze returns to the dais and fields questions. Several star-struck young girls praise her trilogy and gush that she is their hero. They toss her softball questions like when and where she writes during the day, does she have a music playlist while she writes, which people inspire her, and her personal favorite writers. She answers every question with aplomb and bright smiles.

An older woman in a faded red cashmere sweater stands, a hardcover copy of *Boundless* clutched in her tiny hands. "I'm a retired high school English teacher and my grandchildren love your books, so I decided to read them. I understand why dystopian books are so popular with young people, given the phases they are going through, but I found your first two novels violent, at times gratuitously so, and laden with stylistic flaws and grammatical errors. Aren't you concerned about the objectification of women, the cruelty, the constant war depicted between the sexes in your grim vision of the future and the impact that can have on our children?"

Scattered boos gather into a crescendo until Blaze holds out her arms, the air in the hall around me thick with mumbled utterances of *bitch* and *hag*.

I feel like I've stumbled into a rabble-rousing political debate.

"Don't get me wrong," the tiny woman says sheepishly as she glances at the hardback now clutched against her chest like a shield. "I understand the power and influence books can have, but I question the healthiness of these."

More jeers rain down.

Blaze raises her arms once again, pleading for quiet. "Do not boo this woman! She is a sister with a legitimate question. We must treat her with respect!" She smiles at the concerned grandmother. "I will address your concern with questions. Is the violence worse than that found in *The Handmaid's Tale* by Margaret Atwood? Are my scenes more brutal than the real-life story of Malala, or Joan of Arc? More incredulous than the life of Mother Theresa, or Florence Nightingale? Life truly is stranger than fiction and let's not forget that my books are stories. They are not real. Any beautiful or horrific act that man—or woman—can imagine, has already been attempted. My characters lie, cheat, steal, rape, plunder, betray, and murder in a post-apocalyptic future in which everyone reverts to their animalistic states ... or they die in unspeakable ways. Many of my characters display unparalleled loyalty and bravery under tremendous pressure. Thrust into a world threatened with extinction, where less than one percent of the population has survived, the females I created must be tougher and smarter than men or they will not survive. The bonds these women forge transcend the barbaric new world created by the male leaders who caused World War Three. To me, that is the message, the steak and potatoes of my trilogy. I hope that addresses your concern," she says, flashing another smile while the grandmother takes her seat.

She ignores other raised hands. Is she flustered? "The world needs more strong female characters, and we are witnessing a literary shift of tectonic proportions. Talented female authors have fueled this new artistic revolution. The motor's running and, thanks to you, dear readers, I plan to take you full throttle into the future!"

Another eruption. She waves to the crowd. "Thank you, St. Louis! You're totally rad!"

Totally rad? Do kids even say that anymore?

I sit hunkered down on the metal folding chair, now feeling like I'd time warped into a high school pep rally a couple of decades ago. I feel a sudden urge to be at the bar when I observe something odd among the men seated behind Blaze. It wasn't the oldest one seated farthest away and dressed in a dark blue power suit, with an immense belly that protruded over his belt. He smiled at all the right times and hung on Blaze's every word like she invented them. Nor Miles Hawking, seated closest to Blaze and who now stood clapping, reveling in his element as head cheerleader. It was the man in the middle who caught my attention. Late fifties, with thinning curly brown hair, wearing a tweed jacket with elbow patches like mine. He sat frowning; eyes closed during the applause as if in discomfort. He projected a strange vibe, like he'd rather be anywhere else but here. When I noticed him earlier, he sat stock still, bleached of color and emotion. He looked ill as Blaze fielded questions.

She takes another sip and motions the crowd to sit. "My publicist tapped his watch—that's my cue! We've covered so much how I first became interested in storytelling, what inspires me, and the passions that drive my novels. We discussed *Bound* and *Out!?!* and I read passages from *Boundless*. I must give thanks to some very special people before we end. The first man took a chance on me, he saw something in my writing that others didn't; he and his staff lovingly tended and cultivated my manuscripts. That incredible man is my publisher Ted Lamping. He flew from New York to be here with us today. Ted, stand up. Take a bow!" Orange-tanned and rotund, Ted stands briefly and acknowledges the crowd, flashing a toothy smile as if to say the number one publishing house in the country has struck pay dirt again with Blaze. "The next man many of you met before my talk, the world's best publicist, friend, and mighty mouth—Miles Hawking!" Miles stands and blows kisses to the crowd, then one to Blaze and a sly wink Alonso's way. He and Blaze hug. When she returns to the podium, she holds a hand to her heart. A close-up on the screen shows more tears well in her eyes. "I don't know about you all, but I believe in angels. The last man I want to introduce to you saved my life. No one will ever know how much I owe him, how much I love him. I haven't found the right words in any dictionary or language to do this man justice. My perfect husband Samuel Golding! C'mon, Sam! Don't be shy!" He doesn't stand or acknowledge her but bows his head and offers the briefest of waves. At first, I consider his behavior churlish, or maybe he's embarrassed, but he looks like he could fall off the chair as the blood seems to have left his face.

    She turns back to the podium. "I want to thank each and every one of you. The St. Louis crowds on this kickoff tour leave me awestruck. Now I want to meet every one of you back at the signing table. A hundred million worldwide readers can't be wrong! Eat your hearts out, critics!" She raises a book in both arms and the room erupts. More chair banging and chants of 'We love you, Blaze!' nearly cause my ears to bleed.

    Miles takes the podium and lowers the mike to his level, while Alonso escorts her toward the rear of the main room. "Please allow Blaze a few moments to reach the table. We have another wonderful overflow crowd today, but I assure you Blaze will stay and sign one book for each of you.

She has also graciously agreed to have one picture taken per group. When you entered this beautiful old marble gem of a library, you received a square card. In a few minutes, those of you with a red square (for Blaze's hair!) with the number one on it will be first in line. Then green cards marked two, followed by blue with the number three, and last but certainly not least the yellow cards. Thank you all for coming and anyone who wishes to mingle and talk while you wait ... I'm all yours!"

More screaming and applause.

Miranda turns around to look for me during the final applause; she's smiling, caught up in the energy, and when our eyes meet her smile remains but softens. She raises a blue card and three fingers. I hold up my yellow card and make a drinking motion. She nods and turns back to our friends. I turn my head away when Alonso and Blaze approach my row, their eyes focused where Blaze will set up.

The bar farthest from the signing table beckons me and I wait behind women in jeans and some in togas or S&M outfits. I buy two drinks du jour and hope their tangy, cold bite can somehow numb the ringing in my ears. Miranda and the others eventually find me. Cindy can't contain her excitement; Tony inserts himself into line while Miranda shoots me with a curious look at the two glasses and takes one.

"I can't wait to start this when we get home!" Cindy shouts over the din, holding her copy.

When I ask her the significance of the Bloody Mary drink, a woman's scream pierces the air from the main hall, startling everyone.

As the shouts intensify, the bar crowd surges toward the great room of the library.

Blaze kneels over a fallen man and cradles his pallid head in her lap. "Somebody call an ambulance! My husband's having a heart attack!"

"Come with me," Miranda says, handing her copy of *Boundless* to Cindy. She grabs my arm. We leave our drinks on a server's tray and I follow her lead. We fight through a wall of onlookers to reach the couple on the floor.

"Stay away from him!" Blaze shouts, pushing Miranda back so hard she nearly falls.

"I'm a nurse. Get out of the way. Now." She shoves Blaze aside and I look down on an unresponsive Sam Golding. She checks for a carotid pulse, straddles him, and begins chest compressions. She looks to me. "When I count thirty, tilt his head back, pinch his nose, and give him two quick breaths of air."

The room spins as swirls of people move in and out of my vision, Lights and voices flood my senses. It feels like I'm on a Merry-Go-Round at night. I watch Alonso yank onlookers back; he carries some away to give us more room and air.

"Now!" she calls to me.

We complete three sets of compressions and breaths in this rhythm before Miranda says, "Okay, get ready to switch. Straddle him, do a set of thirty compressions, each two inches deep. Count them off if you need to. Switch."

I exchange positions and follow Miranda's instructions. She blows in two breaths each time I reach thirty. Two young women dressed in black leather get in my face, ordering me to let the woman do it until they suddenly depart up and away as if taken by the rapture. Thanks, 'Zo and Easter Island guy.

We repeat two more series before the ambulance crew arrives.

When we began, Golding's head was pallid and his neck a grayish purple. Despite our efforts, I come to believe we're breathing air into a dead man.

During the compressions, his body often breaks wind.

When I straddle him, a host of eyes land on me. During the final break between compressions, I look up and see Blaze's tear-streaked face, her green eyes glaring at me, cold and dead as those of her husband's. If looks could kill

My sport coat is soaked through from delivering CPR when the EMTs arrive. Now I realize at some point Sam's bladder emptied for I smell urine on my hands and pants. I recognize the lead EMT. His name is Curt, and he apologizes for not making it sooner because of the uncooperative crowd of people which he rightly called a mob. By now the gawkers have been removed from the main alcove, kept at bay, and a perimeter set up, thanks to Alonzo, Easter Island guy, a few responding police officers, and select library staff. Those who remain near the body are Miranda, me, Blaze, Miles, and Lamping. The crew quickly removes his shirt and Curt triages him. They confirm no measurable vital signs, which evoke sobs from Blaze. Curt's brow furrows before he speaks softly to her. "Ma'm, was your husband on insulin or other injectable medications?"

She wears a blank, unfocused gaze common of shock or trauma victims. A type of dissociation. He repeats the question before she responds *no*.

Miranda moves in for a closer look at his chest after Blaze does the same.

Blaze crosses her arms over her chest while she fails to fight back tears and repeats her words when Sam fell. "My husband had a massive heart attack. He has—had—a heart condition." She breaks down and Miles prevents her from falling. She cries into his blazer; her muffled words question how she's going to live without Sam.

The crowd whoops and cheers from the nearby library alcoves when the EMTs load Sam onto a gurney, thinking he will be okay. Lamping and I spot it first, then Blaze, but Lamping is closest and grabs Sam's phone before Blaze can break free from Miles. It must have slipped from his suit pocket and lodged beneath his flank during the frenzy. Lamping sees the screen and freezes, his mouth open.

"That's my husband's phone. Give it to me!" Blaze tries to take it, but Lamping pivots away from her long enough for me to read the screen.

He hands the phone to Curt while Blaze continues to protest.

"I'm sorry, Ms. Stark, but I'm going to have to keep this for the time being. Someone will inform you when you may pick up your husband's possessions."

The younger EMT requests my name and number. I hand him my business card.

With the crowd controlled, Alonzo and Easter Island guy (whose name we learn is Tony) return with six more bodyguards.

'Zo turns to Curt and points to an emergency exit door behind us. "We have to get Ms. Stark out of here now while we can. The mob outside is growing and they're agitated. We have a route to her limo cordoned off from the public. Any questions you have can wait. She has a suite at the Ritz in Clayton."

Blaze glares at us the entire time the entourage spirits her from the scene. Blaze clings to Alonzo. Lamping follows the group, but at a safe distance.

The fans push their way toward the exits to follow Blaze.

The main alcove reopens, and staff and volunteers rush over to hug Miranda and shake my hand. I receive pats on the back.

I remove my soaked sport coat and go from hot to shaking cold. The staff offer drinks and chairs. Miranda solemnly sips water, a trace of sweat on her forehead. Her eyes never leave mine. Cindy sits crying next to us.

Tony stands with his mouth open and hugs Miranda. "I want you in my foxhole. You were amazing." Then he turns to me: "You were okay."

I wipe a napkin across my brow, feeling small and insignificant.

What a way to die.

During the frenzy of CPR, I saw stars. Lights from the flashes of cell phones, bystanders taking pictures during the life-and-death struggle. I recall the buzz of nervous laughter, the snickers of young people each time Sam broke wind. I recount the looks of excitement and curiosity as a fellow human being lay in his death throes, helpless. The blasé attitude of these people aside, my thoughts keep returning to Sam's phone and Blaze demanding it immediately. I wipe my hands and face with napkins and notice the damn things have her likeness on them.

I ask for and receive three fingers of Jack, neat.

"Mitch, Mitch. Are you okay?" Miranda asks, touching my arm, which snaps me back to the present. "You were gone there. Tony was talking to you. You've been acting funny all day."

"I'm sorry. That was my first time doing CPR." I want to keep my thoughts private.

All I want is to leave this place and crawl into bed, even though I know I won't sleep.

On our way to the car, a chill wind blows over the front steps of the library and darkness shrouds the line of local news vans grouped nearby like vultures ready to feed. I walk with one arm around Miranda, looking down at my feet. Tony and Cindy trail us.

Miranda turns slightly to me. "You're not going to make your appointment. You should call to cancel."

My ten o'clock, with Blaze. There's obviously no point in calling, but Miranda doesn't know that. "I'll reschedule."

Miranda looks confused by my reply. "She must be waiting for you at the office." "Later." I'm too tired for explanations I can't share.

We fall into a stunned silence while we trudge down the marble steps when a familiar voice calls out. "Mitch! Mitchell Adams!"

I look up and see waiflike Debbie Macklin, blond Channel Four news anchor, rush straight up the long steps toward us, a cameraman in her wake. She thrusts a mic in my face. "What was it like in there? This, you, and Blaze are all over the Internet and Facebook." She turns to Miranda. "Twitter feeds have gone viral about you two giving CPR to Blaze Stark's husband."

"No comment," I say.

"C'mon, Mitch. It's me. For old times' sake, can you describe what you're feeling right now?"

I've seen and heard this inane question asked far too many times to make distraught people spill their emotions for the audience. "A man died in there. Go chase the ambulance and while you're at it, go fuck yourself."

"Hey asshole, watch your filthy mouth," the burly, flannel-shirted cameraman says, the red camera light on me.

I take several steps toward him before Tony horse-collars me, pulling me away and down the steps. "Let's go home, Champ. It's not your night."

We drive Highway 40 west back home in silence. After we drop off Tony and Cindy, Miranda and I sit on the deck around the gas fire pit. Few stars are visible on this chilly, windblown night. We often gather around the pit, alone or with friends, and chat deep into the night, debating and offering solutions (often alcohol-fueled) to the world's myriad problems. Tonight, we sit in deafening silence and stare into the dancing flames that reflect off the cobalt-colored glass shards in the pit. Miranda changed into jeans and a heavy coat and I my old college pullover hoodie.

An owl hoots deep in the dark woods of the common ground. I drink Crown Royal straight up while she hugs her knees.

"Did you call your client?"

"I texted." This wasn't a total lie. I texted Blaze to ask if I could help while I changed clothes. I received no answer.

"Let me ask you something else."

I wait for her question.

"Did you see it, too?"

"What?"

"The look on her face."

"What do you mean?" I ask, even though I have a good idea what she's about to say.

"Blaze. She fought me. Most people are in total panic mood but grateful as all get out to find a pro on the scene to initiate CPR. She looked pissed when we tried to save him."

I raise the glass to cover my face. "Huh. I didn't notice."

She studies me. Did she also notice the look of shock and anger in Blaze's eyes upon seeing me help perform CPR on her husband?

"That man was dead before he hit the floor," she says, sipping her hot chocolate. "It probably *was* a massive heart attack like Blaze said, but something felt … wrong." She looks to me for affirmation.

Instinct tells me to deflect, to suggest an alternative. "I was caught up in the moment, focused on your instructions. She was in shock. People respond to crises in their own unique way. It doesn't necessarily make what they do wrong."

She reaches her hands closer to the flames, studying me. Finally, she says, "You're right, it was probably just my imagination." Her skepticism feels leveled at me from across the fire pit.

"What was so important about Golding's phone?"

My face warms to the lie I'm about to tell. "I don't know. I couldn't read over Lamping's shoulder."

The owl calls again for its mate, more persistent this time.

She exhales and clears her throat. "I know it's been a hellacious night, but what got into you back there with the reporter and cameraman?"

"She pushed my button, but it's my fault. I lost it."

"You let them bait you. Were you really going to fight him?"

I didn't want to withhold the full truth again. "I don't know. Maybe. It happened once before."

"Really?"

A few years back, I punched a pimp who orchestrated the brutal beating of one of my clients. I didn't know a camera recorded it all back then and the video aired on the news for three days. This time was different; I saw the red light and still wanted a piece of him. My nerves were frayed, maybe it was being so close to the presence of death, I don't know. Maybe it was something else.

"You're not going to tell me about it, are you?"

"What else is there to say? I'm not proud of it."

She sips her water. "It's a side of you I haven't seen before."

"You sound disappointed, but someone needs to call people out when they're wrong. Given the circumstance, I'd do it again. She damn well knew how I was feeling on those steps; she took the low road for a sound bite."

She purses her lips. "But it was the cameraman you wanted to punch."

I shrug my shoulders. "It was between Debbie and me. He inserted himself in the middle of it. Like I said, I'm not proud of it."

She folds her arms across her chest. "Your job, this side of you scares me."

The owl hoots, this time from another tree farther away, and receives no reply.

Maybe it was the brush with death, exhaustion, her disappointment in me, too much alcohol, the cold darkness, or a combination of the above, but I resurrect our unresolved issue. "Your fear goes back to last year. You still blame me for the kidnapping."

She diverts her eyes, then looks at me. I see a hardness in them. "It *was* directly related to your job, Mitch. I thought I was going to die like Kristin, or worse."

I leave my glass on the fire pit ledge and drink straight from the bottle. An image appears in my mind of Kristin Gray, the first woman I ever loved, dead on a morgue slab, killed by a former client. She knows about Kristin from the news years ago. From a darkness inside me I say, "What were the odds of that happening again, a billion to one?"

Her eyes lock onto mine. "But it happened, Mitch. So, the odds were a hundred percent."

That same darkness in me raises our other unresolved issue. "Were you ever going to tell me that you can't have kids? I had to hear it from Danny, your kidnapper?" My tone harsh, the words come out clipped. Drunk and angry, I feel lied to, betrayed, and mad at myself.

Her welling tears shine like diamonds in the glow of the fire. "You're right, I should have told you before we got this far. I was afraid you'd leave, like the man before you did." She ignores the tears when they roll down her cheeks. "She *knew*. How could Danny possibly have known that about me?"

I've explained this to her before. Danny was an expert at Psych Ops, and one of her fortes was intelligence gathering. She was an adept emotional terrorist and said it to throw me off-kilter while I tried to hunt her down. I saw no benefit to answer Miranda again.

She pulls a tissue from her coat and blows her nose. "We hadn't really discussed kids before—"

"There was the time in the paddleboat at the boathouse this summer. We talked about being only children and how nice it'd be some day to have two about the same age, so they'd always have someone to play with."

She wants to sit next to me, but I wave for her to stay on her side of the pit. "I wasn't sure about us then."

Months ago, she told me about a trauma from her college days—three men in a van from the Gateway University basketball team, abducted and raped her, then left her for dead in Forest Park. She required surgery but omitted the fact that the damage had left her barren.

"I flashed back to the inside of that van when you became so angry tonight. I've tried therapy but it only helps so much. You say you're not proud of your behavior, but admit you'd do it again."

The owl keeps hooting but receives no reply.

As we continue to talk in circles, I finish the dregs of the Crown Royal. "That's right. If the situation warranted, I'd do it again for you or anyone I care about, and especially for people who can't speak for themselves."

"It's been a long day. I'm going home." She puts the leash on Barney and the Prius backs out of the driveway while I go inside to root in the fridge for greasy leftover pizza.

I call Blaze's suite and get a busy signal. I watch the tape of tonight's Channel Four News on the DVR. Debbie with her big blond hair announces tonight's lead story. "Death struck swiftly and with no warning at the downtown city library this afternoon. Entrepreneur Sam Golding, the west coast business magnate and husband of St. Louis' own best-selling author Blaze Stark, suffered what appears to have been a massive heart attack. EMTs pronounced him dead at the scene, despite the best efforts of a local nurse and Dr. Mitchell Adams. Our viewers may remember Dr. Adams, a clinical social worker in private practice, who's appeared on our station many times as a professional consultant.

"Ms. Stark is rumored to be undergoing precautionary tests in an undisclosed local hospital after she collapsed outside the library. Sources say she appeared uninjured in the fall but is under close observation."

While Debbie speaks, the screen cycles through a montage of pictures with the couple in happier times, publicity shots of Blaze, and of the many businesses Golding owned or controlled. I find it difficult to picture this uber-wealthy businessman as a kidnapper in his younger days but looks can deceive.

Debbie returns on screen. "Channel Four chose not to air the dramatic videos of the failed CPR attempt that went viral on Facebook. The posts were later removed out of respect for the families. Mr. Golding had a mild heart condition, but anonymous sources close to the family say his death came as a complete surprise to his family. The thoughts and prayers of fans around the world go out to their families."

The segment ends with a close-up of the smiling magnate dressed in a business suit with Debbie's somber voice-over. "Mr. Samuel H. Golding, dead at age 53." His age comes as a surprise, he looked ten years older.

My thoughts grow darker and more cynical. Debbie spoke as if she and the station took the high road, but she arrived on those steps with the help of social media. I know all the major stations scan police radio channels and monitor all potential sources in the race to be first with breaking news. I shut off the television and return to the fire pit with a beer and a cardboard pizza box.

My foul mood lingers while I eat cold pizza. My level of anger toward Miranda surprised me more than her leaving. We seem to be drifting apart and the more I dwell on it the angrier I become.

I try Blaze's penthouse again, even though reports say she's in a hospital. More busy signals. The phone's likely off the hook. I consider calling Miranda but don't.

I replay the chaos of the evening in my head as new thoughts come to mind. Her public persona is diametrically opposed to what she confided in private. On the surface not that unusual, was her emotive performance simply an act to sell more books? Did that façade extend so far to call Sam the 'perfect husband who saved my life' if he's the one trying to kill her? Did her reason to fear for her life die on that cold marble floor? Tonight, there was no slutty Blaze, no young and demure Blaze. Only *public Blaze*. I have hunches, but that's all they remain for now. Replaying the entourage's exit, I thought I detected a level of intimacy between Blaze and Alonso. Does it extent beyond the protective bodyguard/grateful client relationship?

And the biggest question, something else I withheld from Miranda tonight out of respect for my client's privacy, the message on Golding's cell, typed, but not yet posted to his Facebook page: *I think my wife intends to kill me.*

INTIMIDATION

I wake with a hangover, shave, shower, dress, and drive to my office by ten the next day to meet with the therapists in my practice. We review changes to insurance guidelines, and spitball ideas on challenging cases to those who ask for help. Afterward, I try Blaze's penthouse number. This time Miles Hawking answers.

I tell him my name and ask about Blaze.

He doesn't answer until I remind him of the night we met.

"Sure, sure. Bright blue eyes. The handsome man in the cashmere sweater. She usually doesn't go for the cerebral type. Our beloved Blaze bravely keeps her head high and her spirits up. Even in the darkest times, she rises to the occasion like Hester."

No mention of the effort to save Sam.

He's unaware of my relationship with Blaze, so I play the jealous card and ask if she's seeing other men besides me.

"This isn't the time to discuss this, Cowboy, but I think you already know the answer."

"Did she leave any message for me?"

"Wait a minute." After a moment of silence, I hear papers shuffle. "Yes, there is an envelope here with your name on it. She wrote, 'For services rendered.'" He lowers his voice an octave and says, "Way to go, Cowboy." Then a brief pause: "Ever play for the other team, hmm?"

He's incorrigible. "No, I'm content being the pin rather than the cushion."

"Such a waste. If you want to get what you've earned, it'll be here in my hot little hands. Don't wait long, once the docs clear Blaze it's off to the next stop on the tour."

He's right; there's nothing to keep her in town once she discharges from the hospital, but I think the death of your spouse would put a book tour on hold.

He misreads my silence and says, "Don't take it personally, Cowboy. That's life in the big city."

I ask what hospital she's in, but Miles refuses to say before he hangs up.

Blaze and I had discussed ongoing sessions via Webcam after her departure and she seemed eager to continue treatment. How can it be that the husband of my only client dies suddenly, and she no longer needs me?

At lunchtime a stranger enters the waiting room asking for me. The portly man wears a dark power suit, sports a bright orange tan, and a nose so red and bulbous he reminds me of WC Fields.

"What can I do for you, Mr. Lamping?" I ask Blaze Stark's publisher.

He seems surprised I remember his name. "A moment of your time."

We sidestep boxes and stacks of construction material that line the hallway to the suite of offices. I get a brief whiff of sawdust and see a flash of steel blade when we pass a room. He opens his mouth but is interrupted by the banshee whine of a power saw and the pounding of hammers in the room behind where my desk sits.

He waits until the noise stops. "What the hell are you building in here?"

"A little reconstruction is all."

We enter my office, and he walks straight to the floor-to-ceiling windows of my ninth-floor suite, as most people do the first time. He looks at the view and asks if I've ever been to the Big Apple.

"Several times. Great city, love the restaurants and night life. Saw the Cards beat the Yankees."

"I own the top floor of The Majestic, overlooking Central Park. Ever been there?"

I offer him a seat next to mine, which he takes only after I sit. He helps himself to one of my business cards on the desk and places it in a suit pocket.

"I didn't make time for your hotel or the Trump Building during my visits. I did jog through the park and tour The Dakota, for the old-world architecture, but I doubt you're here to chit-chat about hotels."

With some difficulty he crosses his legs and emits a soft wheeze. "I want to talk about yesterday."

I wait for him to continue.

"Thank you for trying to save Sam."

I nod. "I'm sorry for your loss."

He shakes his head. "The thought of him dying on that floor, while those costumed idiots laughed and giggled and took photos of him made me sick. I wanted to bash their damn skulls in." He tugs at his collar, closes his eyes, and takes a deep breath. "Sam was a good friend and those are rare." He removes a speck of lint from a pants leg. "He could remain loyal to a fault, especially with the wrong people."

"You have someone in mind?"

"Take a guess."

"I'm not big on guessing games."

"His wife."

"How is Blaze holding up?"

He ignores the phone that vibrates in his vest pocket. "I don't give a rat's ass."

I'm not sure he knows I was able to read Sam's phone last night, so I act surprised. "She *is* your top-selling author of all time, right?" The golden goose.

He makes a face as if he bit into some foul thing. "Mine is the final word on all major company decisions. I greenlighted the *Boundless* series and yes, it's made us a fortune. I wish Sam never met her. I wish I never met her."

I wait for him to continue.

He leans back and the leather chair squeals in protest. He fashions a steeple with his hands and massages both sides of his nose before yielding to a sudden sneezing fit. "Goddamn Midwest pollen. I know you saw her two nights ago. What did she talk about?"

"I cannot confirm or deny that."

"The two of you met for hours in her suite at the Ritz. Why?"

"I cannot confirm or—"

He pounds the armrest with his right hand. "Bullshit!" His bejeweled pinky ring whacks the wooden arm rest. "I have to know!"

I stare at him. "HIPAA exists, even for those who live on the top floor of The Majestic, Mr. Lamping." The Health Insurance Portability Accountability Act is the backbone of patient/client confidentiality of medical records.

Red-faced, he closes his eyes, as if to calm himself. "Sam and I were life-long best friends. His parents were domineering, fifth generation doctors who mapped out his life for him before he could crawl. If he wanted to inherit a multi-billion-dollar empire, he had to become a physician, but he fell in love in college—with writing. Thus began the battle for his soul. He was introspective and genteel, qualities his parents strove to eradicate. During his undergrad years he walked a tightrope between chemistry, anatomy, physics, and advanced writing classes. He wrote in his spare time; he had zero social life."

"Did you ever read his manuscripts?"

He shakes his head. "I offered the services of my staff to critique, but he insisted no other person would lay eyes on his work until every paragraph, every sentence was perfect. He toed the parental line and completed med school while living on a meager trust fund, just enough to pay the bills and survive. He now stood to inherit the family business when his parents died, but he was miserable practicing medicine. His parents pushed him to marry another physician, or at least someone from old money. Jesus, it's like doctors are inbred or something. Sam drew the line here;

this wasn't part of the deal he agreed to with his parents. I offered to fix him up with all sorts of women—sexy ones, introverted female writers, hookers, high society women—but he wasn't interested. He didn't have time. His passion was writing, so he doctored by day and wrote by night."

"Why are you telling me this?"

"Because you're listening." He raises those bushy black eyebrows and stares out the window. One leg bounces so rapidly I think he's about to wear a hole in the carpet. "A sick game is afoot. Whatever she has in mind, it's not going to end well."

"Blaze?"

Perturbed, he nods and fixes his eyes on mine. Sweat dots his upper lip. "She materialized from nowhere one day in my office, clinging to Sam like a parasite. More like the ground split open and she crawled up from the depths. That same day, he announced their plan to marry. This was about two months after his mother died, leaving him the sole owner of the family fortune. He decided to hang up his shingle and let underlings run the business. He surprised me when they became regulars in the Hollywood scene after the marriage. Blaze unleashed the social animal in Sam, once released from the watchful eyes of his parents and all those nights writing. Jet setting. Endless vacations. Parties on his yachts."

"Did he stop writing once he turned socialite?"

Lamping hikes up a sock. "I'm getting to that. Behind him stood three large cardboard boxes on a handcart. I assumed he'd finally readied his manuscripts for submission."

"But you were mistaken."

Another nod. "He hesitated and finally said his manuscripts were no longer timely. When I asked to let me be the judge of that, he said he destroyed his outlines and the flash drives." He made a face. "The boxes supposedly contained his fiancée's work. He said they were the next big thing. I politely asked about her bio—no writing experience, nothing self-published. I'm thinking straight to the slush pile with a quick form letter to her and my sincere apologies to Sam."

Lamping pauses to look at the floor, then produces a handkerchief to wipe his face and brow. "I wouldn't have believed it in a million years." An exasperated snarl.

"The *Boundless* trilogy?"

He pauses so long I almost repeat the question.

"Yes." His face turns crimson until he regards me again. "The fact you sat there and listened to my story tells me she's your client."

"It proves I'm a good listener and your story interested me. Nothing more."

He searches my face. "Whatever she told you is a lie. Especially if it's about me."

"How did Sam and Blaze meet?"

He snorts. "I asked him that the next time we were alone. He stonewalled me. I asked if he knocked her up and he grew incensed at me. I said to make damn sure he's got an iron-clad pre-nup in place, but he became defensive and clammed up. He said I should be happy for him, that he found someone to love who was a fellow writer.

"I hope they find proof in his phone that she played a role in Sam's death. Did you see his final words that he typed on the screen?"

I decide to act like I didn't and shake my head.

"Huh, from the look on your face I thought you had. 'I think my wife intends to kill me' is what he wrote. Pretty damning testimony. I hope she fries for this."

"Assuming he was the one who typed those words. We don't know that. And Sam could be mistaken. Do you have any proof? Or is this based solely on your disapproval of their marriage?"

"You are quite the devil's advocate. Don't fall under her spell. I know she's guilty of something, I just can't prove it."

I recall that Lamping left the library at a safe distance from Blaze. "Did you accompany the group in her limo?"

"Hell, no. She was livid when I handed over Sam's phone to the EMT. I called a cab, returned to the Chase, and contacted the company trouble-shooter."

The Chase Park-Plaza is a famous local landmark and hotel in St. Louis.

"The trouble-shooter?"

"A corporate fixer. Isn't it obvious? I began to wonder if Sam had written the *Boundless* trilogy and that Blaze had somehow coerced him into stealing it. I had this creeping suspicion early on, as did some trusted employees who knew Sam. Her responses to my editors seemed amateurish at best, like she wasn't familiar with her own work and couldn't understand the reasons for recommended changes. As time passed the feeling lessened when sales took off."

"You seem frightened of her. Why?"

He runs a hand through what's left of his hair. "You know what a changeling is?"

I nod. "You're saying fairies switched Blaze at birth? Like Peter Pan or something more sinister, maybe evil trolls?"

"Don't be absurd," he says in exasperation while twirling his ring like a fidget spinner. "She's *like* one. She's a chameleon, what you see is not what you get. She's cunning and manipulative. I wouldn't be surprised if she murdered him."

I had questions, specific ones, but couldn't ask them without breaking confidentiality. "You said you have no proof. What's your feeling based on?"

The look on his face mirrors his frustration. "Maybe we can pool our information and figure it out together. What did she talk with you about?"

"I cannot confirm or deny anyone is my client. Did anything happen recently that makes you think Sam's death might not be an accident?"

He leans back and the chair squeals again in protest. "We arrived early for the signing in the same limo. The five of us milled around together in a staff meeting room when Blaze asked Sam to follow her. She smiled at him, but something about her demeanor seemed off, so I followed at a distance. They walked into the men's room together. She had her purse with her. They stayed there fifteen minutes.

Why?" He shows me a picture on his phone of Blaze and Sam in front of a men's room—not of them entering or leaving it together.

I return the phone to him. "Maybe she, or he, felt like a quickie."

He rolls his eyes, and his orange hue deepens. "The EMT found needle sticks. She could have injected him then."

"Why would Sam agree to an injection he didn't need?"

He shrugs. "Sam has—had—a very mild heart condition. Arrhythmia, very common. No coronary artery disease or history of heart attacks. We see the same cardiologist and Sam just received a clean bill of health two weeks ago."

"How do you know this?"

His beady eyes narrow. "Sam told me."

"The autopsy will reveal the cause of death. If you have reason to suspect foul play, contact the police."

The fidgeting with his ring increases. "It's not that easy."

"It is if you're acting in good faith for a lifelong friend. What are you not telling me?"

He shifts his considerable weight. "She lobbied to cremate him before rigor mortis had even set in. Sam was California born and bred; his family still lives there. He always said his final wish was to be buried in the Golding family crypt in L.A. Doesn't that tell you something?"

"Not necessarily. My parents paid in advance for a cemetery plot decades ago. When cremation gained in popularity, they opted to change plans rather than take up land in a cemetery. If those were Sam's wishes, they'd be outlined in his Advance Directives."

He points a finger at me and shifts his weight. "That's another thing. I was his durable power of attorney until she came along. She convinced Sam to tear up his directives and write a set of new ones, naming her his DPOA."

"That's common when people marry."

"She's pushing for immediate cremation, even though the new DPOA specifically states he wishes to be buried in the family crypt. I told the Medical Examiner this, along with my suspicions about Blaze."

I can almost see his teeth grind. "I ask you again, what did she talk with you about?"

"You won't like what I have to say. I cannot—"

Angry, he stands with great effort, so I do the same. "If she's your client, watch your ass."

"Not that she is, but why do you say that?"

He smiles, a smirk grows on his lined face. "That's the thing, you won't know what she has in store for you until it's too late. Consider yourself warned."

I've had enough drama for the week. Lamping wasn't going to leave with what he came for, which explained but didn't condone the undercurrent in my attitude. "Intimidation tactics and vague threats don't work on me, Mr. Lamping."

"You may be a big fish in a little pond here, but you're in the big leagues now, son. I investigated your background, what you've accomplished during the last few years likely gave you that big head. Whatever she has in mind, it will end badly for you."

"You've read too many thrillers, Ted."

A look of dread replaces the bully and bluster persona. The air seems to go out of him all at once until he regains his composure. "Maybe I have, but we're both in one now."

This is a turn I didn't foresee. "What power does she hold over you?"

He stands there frozen, biting his lip.

To mention Blaze's claim of a casting couch would break confidentiality. I soften my voice. "Maybe I can help. It's what I do for a living."

He paces the room, opens his mouth but just as quickly closes it. He walks to the door and mumbles what sounds like 'slush pile' to himself. "Don't believe a word she says. She isn't what she seems. Eject her from your life while you can."

Before he leaves, I ask, "Who were the people that arrived with you at the library?"

He seems taken aback by the question. "Blaze, Sam, that little fruit Miles, and her bodyguard, a big ex-football player named Alonso."

"If Blaze is what you claim, why sign her to a contract? It didn't stop you from making piles of money publishing her books."

He laughs. "I didn't know the full extent of how evil she was until it was too late. Prepare for a reckoning. I am. You've been warned." He leaves the door wide open on his way out.

A prime apartment in The Majestic goes for about twenty million. I can only imagine what an entire floor cost. Lamping may be a big fish in a big pond, but today he sounded like a scared man with a dark secret and everything to lose.

∞ ∞ ∞

For dinner I marinate a flank steak and cut veggies while I dial Miranda's cell. She picks up on the first ring, but I can barely understand her due to background construction noise and poor reception.

"Got a job from the boss today during my run. I'm at Lambert, hurrying to reach my gate. I can barely hear you," she says, raising her voice to a shout.

So much for dinner together. Now isn't the time to talk. Keep it simple. "What's the job?"

"A married couple wants to get up close and personal with great white sharks through a steel cage. I'll be gone four, maybe five, days."

I hear a muffled voice from a speaker announce a gate change. "Where's the location?"

"Martha's Vineyard, where the movie *Jaws* was filmed."

"Isn't the water off Massachusetts cold this time of year?"

The interference worsens. Her voice cuts in and out. "No doubt, but that's why God made neoprene wetsuits."

I switch the kitchen TV to Channel 4 for the news and remember we have an upcoming concert at the Fox Theater. "I'll give our Saturday tickets to Tony and Cindy since you'll be gone."

As I speak, loud noises from Miranda's side of the line fill my ear. "What? It's getting harder to hear—"

Nothing about picking her up, but she was in a hurry and likely left her Prius in short-term parking.

"Have a safe trip. I—" is all I manage to say before the line goes dead. I don't know if she heard me. She was only about ten miles away, but the distance between us feels to be increasing.

CONFESSION

The next morning, I make an educated guess and drive to Gateway Hospital. I inform the silver-haired volunteer at the front desk that I'm one of Blaze Stark's doctors. She says I must sign in because the patient is on black-out status and then directs me to the right bank of elevators after I receive a visitor badge and the suite number. Alonso Jefferson stands guard at the entrance to her private suite, dressed in a charcoal gray pinstripe suit and purple tie. He frowns when he sees me.

"How's she doing?"

"She's resting. Ms. Stark doesn't want to see you." His eyes seem to betray a fire behind his outward Zen appearance.

"Not good enough. I'm going to have to hear that directly from her."

He mulls it over.

"I don't want to have to kick your ass, 'Zo, but I will if I have to. C'mon, tell her I'm here and let me in. If she tells me she no longer needs me, I will leave and spare you the embarrassment of taking you down."

That brings a smile to him. "Wait here," and he slips into the suite. Minutes later, he returns with a manila folder. Inside is a brief hand-written letter from Blaze telling me

I've been fired. There's also an envelope marked 'For Your Discretion.' It contains several thousand dollars.

I push the envelope into his heavily muscled chest. "She gets my discretion for free, forever, as a client. You may be able to protect her from the outside world, but you can't protect her from herself." I weigh my next words carefully. "If I'm right, she's sick and needs my kind of help. She's going to fall apart, and soon."

His jaw muscles flex. "She's a proud and stubborn—"

"Sam's death will cause her to deteriorate, which will worsen her condition. She needs to talk about it."

We stare at each other, neither of us willing to back down. "Look, I'm sure she pays you well to protect her, but covering for her doesn't help. Let me ask you something—how many lies did Blaze tell the crowd at the book signing? I just met her, and I heard a bunch."

He stands blocking the door, weighing my words.

"I imagine there were too many lies for you to count. Let me in."

His angular features soften. "What do you mean, she's sick?"

"I can't discuss it with you, but she needs my kind of help."

His resolve seems shaken. "I will talk with her, but for now you need to leave." He closes the door in my face.

∞ ∞ ∞

Back in the Solstice, my cell phone barks (my new ringtone, Barney).

"Where you at?" a familiar baritone voice asks.

"Leaving Gateway Hospital."

"Meet me at the Castle on south Lindbergh. Worked a double murder all night and I be Jonesing' for a sack of belly bombers," says JoJo Baker, a black bald city homicide detective. Years ago, he tried to collect enough evidence to charge me with my girlfriend's murder, until I identified the real killer. Since then, we've forged a strange symbiotic partnership—whenever I need an *in* with the police Baker is it, he complains all along the way but eventually receives accolades for a nice collar. JoJo is a creature of the night, most at home on the meanest streets of north St. Louis city. He's a throwback to the seventies in garb and talk, though he never lived a day in the decade.

His muscular body takes up most of one side of a white plastic booth as he pops a cheeseburger slider in his mouth. He chose a corner booth with views of both entrances. He grins when he sees me.

"Cool Breeze. Long time, my man," he says when I slide into the booth across from him. He's dressed in his trademark black leather jacket, black jeans, and matching boots. He produces a flask from a pocket and splashes a healthy dose of Jack in his coke.

"I see you're having the breakfast of champions. How's Simone?"

"Sexy and satisfied as always. Miranda?"

I don't want to get all into that, so I say, "Fine. Why am I here?"

He places another slider into that yawning mouth, chews it, then licks his fingers. The smell of onions lingers in the air while staff chatter in the background about work schedules and take drive-through orders. "Heard you was in that circus at the library, giving CPR to the dead rich dude."

I grab the last belly bomber and a ketchup packet from his plastic tray. "That's right."

His eyes fix on mine. "You and Miranda just happened to be there?"

"She's a fan. I tagged along."

His ears perk and he shakes his head. "Oh shit, I know that matter-of-fact tone. You involved somehow. With him or her?"

I groan. "All I know is that he died of a heart attack."

A wiry trio of young males in doo-rags make a noisy entrance replete with curses but fall silent when they see Baker. They nod to him and fall in line to place orders.

He turns back to me. "May not be natural causes after all. The stiff took no injectable meds, and the M.E. found several fresh needle sticks in his abdomen."

Lamping saw Blaze and Sam enter the mens' room together.

He watches me hesitate ever so briefly in mid-chew as he reinserts one of his ever-present toothpicks into the side of his mouth.

"All I know is he's dead."

He works the toothpick to the other side of his mouth. "He your client, or is she?"

I don't answer.

"Why were you two at the library again?"

"For the signing. Like I said, Miranda likes her books."

His eyes narrow. "A little birdie also tol' me the widow-to-be put up a fight when you and Miranda began CPR."

I fold the empty slider box and add it to his overflowing tray of empties, hoping to wrap up this conversation. "It was verbal and very brief. She was in adrenaline shock. You know people can act strangely under stress."

"What interaction did you two have when the cavalry arrived?"

"There wasn't time; it was chaotic. EMTs whisked him away on a stretcher while Blaze and her entourage followed the body. Nothing unusual about that."

"But you found somethin' weird. I see it in your eyes," he said, still fishing.

I keep my mouth shut and swallow the last bite of greasy slider.

"She said nothing to you while the ambulance was in route?"

I shake my head.

"And you've had no further contact with her since that night?"

"No." Technically the truth.

"Did you have contact with any of her people since that night?"

"No." I make a show of wiping my hands with a napkin while I lie.

"You gonna stick to your bullshit story that one of them ain't your client?"

I hold his gaze and say nothing.

His demeanor hardens. "Dammit, Breezy. If it gotta be this way, okay. Lemme give you somethin' else to chew on beside my last damn slider—"

The opening notes to the theme song of Shaft sound from his cell. "Speak," he commands. He listens for some time, agrees with the caller, and says thanks before turning back to me. "Sharp new ME. Got some kinda head on her shoulders. Her bumper be awful damn fine, too. Looks like your dead rich dude may be a murder after all, Breezy. In the library, but not with a knife or rope or candlestick. Possible OD. Maybe potassium chloride." He pours the rest of the Jack into his soda and eyes me again. "If one of 'em was your client, I hope for your sake it's the stiff. Before I find out on my own, there anything else you want to tell me about Blaze Stark or that night?"

I consider what I can say. "This is pure speculation, but before he died Golding didn't appear interested in his wife's speech. He didn't seem to want to be there, or maybe it was the imminent heart attack. He looked pale, uncomfortable, and ill at ease."

Baker grunts while I rise to go. "Thanks for nothing. I'm gonna pay a little looky-loo call on the new widow, but you already know that. Call me if your memory improves. About anything."

I am bound by my code. "Nothing else to say. I was in the last row during her talk and couldn't see much. When he fell, we were on the other side of the library, at one of the bars."

What he says next stops me in my tracks for a moment. "I know what Golding typed in his phone before he died."

I don't respond.

He raises his cup and grins. He regards me like a stranger, or something worse.

∞   ∞   ∞

While shopping at The Galleria that afternoon, I'm surprised by a call from Alonso Jefferson. He says Ms. Stark has been released from the hospital and has changed her mind. She requests to meet me at ten tonight in her suite. When I accept, he thanks me and sounds relieved.

That evening I endure the same full-body pat down and confiscation of my phone and Dictaphone from 'Zo.

"I need that to help prove my theory about her diagnosis. I also want to videotape our sessions."

He shakes his head. "Ms. Stark left very specific instructions. No audio or visual tapes."

"I will discuss it with her. Next time you're gonna have to buy me a drink if you continue to grope me like this."

He makes a harrumphing sound. "You like that little Miles dude?"

"I don't know him well enough to like or dislike him," I say, to pull his chain. Then: "I get your drift, I'm not *like* him."

"Didn't think so."

He ushers me into the same posh fireplace suite, but this time Blaze sits waiting, dressed in demure black blouse and slacks. No bling. Not a cigarette, drop of alcohol, or pill in sight. She puts down a Star magazine and looks up at me, like any client would in my waiting room.

"I'm so sorry for your loss. We did everything we could."

She smiles briefly and motions to the chair next to hers. "You and that pretty blonde—Miranda?—were amazing." She gives a brief shake of the head. "My, how that woman took charge." There's a slight quaver in her young-sounding voice.

"She's a pro at CPR. How are you holding up?"

She exhales, a tiny moan that seems laced with pain, or fear? "I have a confession to make. I need your kind of help. I've resisted it my entire life; I try to forget the past with alcohol and pills and—" She hits her head sharply with her fist. "How could I have been so stupid to marry the man who kidnapped me?"

It's been years since a client intentionally struck herself in the head with such force, aside from disturbed children and chronic psych patients in the state system. "Maybe we can find some answers and solutions. I'd like to record our ses—"

"I murdered my husband," she says as casually as the first night when she strolled into my office and ordered a dirty martini. I've had clients say they killed years ago and done time for it, and some who spent years in mental institutions because they acted on voices during a psychotic episode that commanded them to kill. I had one murderer confess during an active homicide investigation and that client almost killed me. I recall the fear in Lamping's eyes and his words of warning. For one of the few times in my life, I experience a brief loss for words.

"Why are you telling me this?"

"At the time I was glad he was dying. I enjoyed seeing his head hit the marble floor—"

Miranda's intuition was right; Blaze fought us out of fear we would revive Sam.

"Later that night, I felt like I couldn't breathe, I vomited, and my whole body shook. Even though he abused me for years, I felt awful about what I'd done." The tears come and she lowers her eyes. "I don't have to remind you that abusers instill a high level of guilt in their victims."

"I thought the cause of death was a heart attack."

Her ears perk at my words, a brief flash of suspicion? but those green eyes never blink. "Where did you hear that?"

"You told the EMTs he had a heart condition."

She regards me warily. "For months I've laced his drinks with anti-freeze."

I keep the surprise from my face. I can't dispute this without admitting I've talked to the cops. "Do the police know?"

She stiffens, her brows knit as she hugs herself. "No."

"What led you to do this?"

She cracks open a bottled water and winces at the sound. "I did fall in love with Sam months after he kidnapped me. You probably call it Stockholm syndrome, but it was love. He is—was—an Alpha male accustomed to being in control, but when my star rose, our marriage soured."

"When we met last Monday night, you said you didn't know who was trying to harm you. You mentioned four people as suspects. Now you admit to poisoning your husband for months after years of abuse from him. I'm confused—why the list of suspects?"

Terror fills her face. "Don't you believe me?"

She folds her hands in her lap ever so demurely and her chin lowers to her chest.

"Blaze, can you hear me?" I nudge her shoulder, but her face remains lowered.

There's no response until she straightens and meets my gaze. The sultry smile and breathy voice return when she realizes my hand is on her arm. "You're out of your chair, Mitch. What about those boundaries you spoke of when we met? If this is part of therapy, I won't argue … or tell."

I sit back down. "You blacked out for a moment and didn't respond to my voice. That's why I want to record our sessions."

Unconvinced, she grins. "That's absurd."

I cross my legs. "Have you ever experienced fugue states, more commonly called lapses in memory? Have you opened your eyes and found yourself in a strange place, with no idea how you got there or how long you've been there?"

The sultry grin widens. "Fugue, what a great word. Sure … when I drink too much."

Wanting to test my working diagnosis, I repeat my earlier question. "You admit to poisoning your husband over a period of months, but when we first met you said you didn't know who was trying to hurt you."

She applies red lipstick and looks confused. "I never said that."

"You did, two minutes ago. Before your head lowered to your chest."

She takes a tissue to blot the lipstick. "You must be mistaken. I knew Sam was the culprit all along."

My kingdom for a video recorder.

"You don't recall telling me this in my office Monday evening?"

She levels her eyes on mine. She raises her voice. "I would remember. I said no such thing."

I uncross my legs. "Tell me why you knew it was Sam."

"Little things at first—household items moved from where I'd left them, packages at the front door I hadn't ordered, and bogus phone messages in Sam's handwriting from people who never called."

All explainable by memory lapses.

She pauses for a deep breath and to adjust a bra strap under her blouse. "Then the hang-ups began. Followed by voices, whispered and garbled on the line, so soft I couldn't tell whether they were male or female. Then I began to distinguish certain words like *die* and *pain* and *suffer*. Then the voices mocked and ridiculed me. Most of the calls came when Sam was away, but some occurred when he was in another part of the house. I asked the police to put a trace on them, but they said the calls were made from burner phones. One day, I found a noose hanging from a foyer chandelier in our Malibu home and a week later a chauffeur found my Bentley running in the closed garage."

"Alonso?"

A shake of the head. "A different driver. Someone had drawn a smiley face in the dirt on the driver door window next to the words *Get In*. We have state-of-the-art security systems with multiple cameras throughout our houses. Not even the servants are aware of them all. Not a one recorded anything unusual, other than shadows off screen. Whoever did the deeds knew the exact location of the blind spots."

Why would she confess to murder by spiking her husband's drinks with anti-freeze if Baker says the cause of death was lethal injection, possibly potassium chloride?

"Sam kidnapped you. Did he force himself on you sexually then or after you married?"

"He was a perfect gentleman when he held me captive. The last two years when the marriage soured, he raped me several times when I angered him. To show his dominance."

"Any other examples or recent threats of physical violence?"

She pauses, thinking, while I wait.

"Before the kickoff tour, he took my phone and locked me in the basement. He was gone two days. I assume to be with *her*."

"When did this happen?"

She bats her lashes. "I'm not good with time, maybe a week ago."

"Did you report the rapes to the police or tell anyone? Alonso, a girl friend, a neighbor?"

She picks at a manicured nail. "He threatened to kill me if I did. So, no."

"Are you currently having thoughts to harm yourself?"

She frowns and says no.

"Are you currently having thoughts of harming anyone else?"

She stares at me and slowly shakes her head.

"I'm gonna need a yes or no on that."

"No, of course not."

Scenarios leap to mind, each more bizarre than the one before. "As your therapist, I want to help you do the right thing so you can move forward—"

Her eyes grow wide for an instant. "Are you going to turn me in?"

"If you keep this to yourself, the guilt you have will destroy you. You're already showing signs of this. Sometimes it takes courage to do the right thing. The courts will take into account the abuse you suffered by his hand. The answer to your question is no. I will not report this, but I strongly urge you to contact the police and tell your side of the story."

If she was planning to harm herself or others, I'd be forced to report it. It's called Duty to Warn.

She appears to mull it over but doesn't answer.

I improvise off Baker's information. "When the coroner finds glycols, the chemical substance in antifreeze, in Sam's system, you will be their prime suspect. The D.A. could seek a first-degree murder conviction since this was premeditated."

She asks four more times whether I'm going to call the police and my answer remains the same. She promises to give it a lot of thought. I schedule another session with her early in the morning before she flies to the next signing. She again refuses my request to tape our sessions.

When I exit the Ritz-Carlton after midnight, Baker's souped-up black Cadillac pulls into the circular courtyard in the no-parking zone near the main entrance, twenty paces from my Solstice. I retreat behind a corner of the building. Another person exits the Fleetwood with Baker, a thin black woman dressed in jeans and a jacket. Too short for Simone. I hurry to my car when they enter the lobby, hoping he didn't make my sporty red car.

What I remember most from that night with Blaze is the smile in her eyes when I say I'm not going to the cops. It sounds crazy, but those eyes seem to follow me again in my rearview as I drive.

QUESTIONS

There's no answer the next morning when I dial Blaze's suite from the hotel lobby. I leave a message that I'm downstairs. We have a brief window before her flight, so I inform the concierge at the front desk about my appointment and learn she's already checked out.

I return home, change clothes, and go for a run to clear my head. It doesn't work, for I still feel churlish when my thoughts focus on Miranda and Blaze. I finish my run around noon when my cell barks, but it's neither woman.

"Hey, JoJo. I had a hunch you might call." I put him on speaker.

"You *really* mixed up in the shit again, Breezy. Like that sticky baby shit that don' ever wanna wash off your hands."

I remove my sweaty shirt and towel off. "Meaning?"

"You damn well know. Now open the fuckin' door, it be freezin' out on your porch."

Baker has this annoying penchant for calling when he's at my front door. A foul wind has blown all day as early fall leaves tumble and skid down the street. The sky turned to slate early, and the sun remains hidden. I let him in.

"Lookin' buff there, Breezy. I'm here to tell you your client killed her husband."

I put on a clean shirt. "Which client is that?"

He makes certain I notice the exasperation on his face. "Blaze Stark, famous writer and babe, the one with more money than Jay Z and built like Beyonce."

"You know I can't tell you whether she's a client of mine."

Baker works overtime on the toothpick in his mouth. "See? That's my concern. If she not a client, then you musta lost your mind and you hittin' that." He leans closer and smiles. "Pearl necklace sho' look good on that sweet thing and there's just enough cushion for the pushin'. I bet she be a fuckin' Bengal, saber-toothed tiger 'tween the sheets. Prob'ly maul 'em all up, with you in 'em."

My guess would be more like a panther. "Don't go bad cop on me. It won't work. You always pounce on the simplest explanation." My eyes narrow to slits as my thoughts return to earlier times. "Like with me when we met."

He returns my glare with one of his own. "Ancient history, man. You were an exception. I followed the evidence, but the killer planted it. Usually, the simple explanation is right on the streets. Even the ones paved with gold." He pauses but twists the knife one more time. "For you and Miranda's sake, tell me you ain't hittin' that."

For the second time this week I feel like punching someone much bigger than me. I comb my hair with a hand. "Why are you here?"

"Your client just confessed to the murder of her husband." The toothpick shifts to the other side of his mouth.

"I cannot confirm or deny she is my cl—"

"—but your little red Solstice sat parked outside the Ritz in Clayton after midnight. Saw the plates last night. And Miranda out of town…"

I cross my arms and stare up at him.

"You also signed in at the hospital and visited her. C'mon Breezy. This is me. She your client or are you slipping her the bone?"

"You're the detective. Figure it out."

He emits a groan. "This is wack. Get me a damn beer and whatever white people food you got. I'm comin' off an all-nighter."

I grab two Rolling Rocks and sandwich fixings from the Sub-Zero as he removes his black leather coat and sits at the kitchen table. He stretches out his long legs. "This is it? No leftover barbecue?" He grunts. "Times be tough all over. Where's your better half off to?"

My mood sinks another notch. "I forget. This is all I got." I twist off a beer top. "You said she confessed. What did she say?"

Baker squirts hot sauce on the roast beef and adds a pickle and two slices of Swiss cheese before he pauses the sandwich construction. "So now you want me to spill the beans?"

I take a pull on my beer. "We worked our asses off to revive Sam. The situation was intense. I think I earned the right to be curious. You don't want to tell me, that's fine." I take another swig. "You're the one who drove all the way out here to West Jesus, as you call it."

I'm in a Mexican stand-off. We want to use each other and I'm at a dead end.

He takes a drink and adds crunched bits of Old Vienna barbecued potato chips to the top of his sandwich.

I make a face. "What the hell are you doing?"

"Gives it a nice crunch. Try it sometime. Don't be so damn pissy."

He takes a healthy bite and wipes crumbs from his mustache. He pauses, as if he lost his train of thought. "Yeah, okay. That's cool, we'll play it your way. When I told the new widow that preliminary lab reports point to a suspicious death, she confessed."

While he speaks, I watch the condensation slowly weave down my bottle. "How much time did that take?"

He looks away briefly. "This morning, about ten hours."

I know first-hand how grueling and intimidating his interrogations can be, and I also know that a quarter of suspects confess to crimes out of fear, lack of legal counsel, verbal intimidation, sleep deprivation, or lack of access to food, drink, a restroom, or some combination of the above. Given the right amount of time and pressure, a vulnerable suspect can say anything to get out of the hot seat. Especially one with a mental illness. I find myself peeling off the label of my beer bottle.

"Ten hours, with you? Downtown?" That explains the no answer at her suite this morning.

I think of the woman who accompanied Baker into the Ritz last night but can't admit I saw her. "Was her attorney present when she confessed?"

He shakes his head and rolls his eyes. "My new boss insisted she tag along. Anything that smells of face time with the press and she all over it like a fly on shit. We Mirandized her. She even declined her phone call until after she confessed. We did everything by the book, and she still wanted to talk with us. I could see the relief on her face; she said she felt like a weight had been lifted afterward." He takes another swig. "Her attorneys didn't know whether to shit or piss when they arrived. They gave us some mild static for show on behalf of their client, but they seemed more pissed at Blaze."

"Wouldn't you think a smart, wealthy person like her, who also writes books in a genre not that far removed from detective novels, would know to clam up until her lawyers arrive?"

He thinks about it and shakes his head. "Seen it happen before. They need to unload that guilt."

I finish my beer. That doesn't sound like Blaze. "Did you notice anything unusual about her? Her mood? The way she spoke?"

Baker's grin widens. "Whaddaya care? Unless she your client."

"I'm curious. You're one intimidating dude. Was she emotional or an ice princess?"

Baker constructs a second sandwich and pops another beer. "She may be rich, she may be smart, but there is somethin' *off* about her. Like we were playing some weird game of cat and mouse, only at times it felt like she was the cat. It's hard to explain. There were times when she was scared shitless, rockin' in the chair, and cryin' for her teddy bear. She made a comment about being held prisoner for months and abused. The boss thought she might be having flashbacks to past trauma. Then there were times she got all flirty flirty with me and demanded my boss fetch her a martini." His grin returns. "That was *fuckin'* funny and she kept on her about getting that drink, too. She'd had a few when we brought her to the station. She may have been jonesing'. Lab work is pending. After dawn, she started yelling for some chick named Bloody Mary that was gonna break her out of here and tear us all new assholes. First writer/murderess I've dealt with. She's entertaining as hell. What's your take on this?"

He wants my opinion on her sanity. "What did she say about killing her husband?"

He eyeballs me while he crunches chips in his hand and grunts. "You answer my question with a question. Said she killed him because he abused her for years. That he locks her in a cage when he wants to be with his mistress. Sometimes he drugs her, and she wakes up in a train with a bunch of old men wearing masks. Not the choo choo kind of train. Says he puts a bottle of sleeping pills on her nightstand with a note that says *kill yourself*. She felt certain he'd kill her before she worked up the courage to do somethin' about it."

I let the silence linger between us, hoping he'd answer my question without my having to ask.

He wipes his mouth and looks at me for some time. "Lifestyles of the rich and shameless."

Hoping for the best, I say, "You said one minute she was rocking and crying for her teddy bear, then later turned flirty and demanded a martini. That seems odd."

He studies me carefully. "Duh. She flipped. Like she two different people."

I slowly tear my beer label into tiny pieces. In his layman's way he's corroborating my initial diagnosis. "What you describe sounds like D.I.D."

"What the hell is that?"

"The DSM 5 diagnostic criteria for multiple personality disorder, dissociative identity disorder. Some practitioners don't believe it exists; I had my doubts until I treated someone with it a few years back. This client convinced me, no one could be that accomplished an actress to fake all the personalities. Childhood sexual abuse is considered to be the primary reason for a schism or fracture to develop in the victim's mind. The personality splits as a primitive way to survive the horror. If true, the stress of your interrogation may have caused the personalities to cycle faster."

He finishes my food and finds his toothpick. "Dunno. You the damn shrink. You tell me."

I avoid his eyes while I concentrate on the beer label. He's doing more than fishing for information; he's trying to suck me into the case by piquing my curiosity.

Baker's excitement level rises. "When she ain't acting bat-shit crazy, she knows murder is a crime, but here's where it goes off the rails. She admits to the murder but says she did it by puttin' anti-freeze in his drinks for months. No mention of needles, no potassium chloride."

He expects an answer; I feel his eyes study me. "You happen to know anything about that?"

"No. You're the detective. How do you explain it?"

He wipes his mouth with a napkin and frowns. "You answer with another damn question." He rubs his shiny bald head. "I can't. If she is nuts, could one personality kill her husband and the other not know, and why would she give the wrong cause of death?"

I don't have a ready answer. The worst my former D.I.D. client did was make superficial cuts to her abdomen. "Most D.I.D. patients hurt themselves, not others."

"Most, not all?"

"That's what I remember from my research of the illness. One of the personalities almost always represents the abusive figure from the person's past. When the abusive personality lashes out, it usually results in self-cutting. Some D.I.D. patients die early, either from suicide or under questionable circumstances. One prone to disassociate can also exhibit fugue states—"

"In English, professor."

"Memory lapses. Hours, entire days, even weeks, can be lost when the dominant personality takes control. Other personalities often include a childlike character (often the client as a child prior to the abuse), an angry violent one who doles out punishment (a replacement for the real-life abuser), and a promiscuous one. There can be many others. If true, it sounds like you've witnessed childlike and provocative so far, but not the aggressive one. Yet."

He shakes his head. "Fucking weird shit you deal with, Breezy. Don't know how you do it without losing your marbles."

"I've been known to misplace them at times. Is the tox report back yet?"

He shakes his head. "Too early for ethylene glycol levels. She claims to have mixed equal parts anti-freeze and scotch in his drinks. Nobody in their right mind would drink that shit after one sip. M.E. did find sky-high Potassium levels."

"Have you ever run into a case like this, with a confession but a wrong modus operandi?"

He drains his second beer. "Only with chronic confessors, which is why we keep key aspects of the crime scene from the public. There's more of them than you think. They visit police departments once news breaks of a murder or high-profile crime, but when questioned their story falls apart."

"Do they fit a profile, aside from obvious feelings of guilt?"

He tilts his neck until it cracks. "They mostly loners who feel better after confessing. Most get off on the attention. Seen one who finally admitted he wanted to return to the joint but didn't want to hurt nobody. Ended up robbing a liquor store to get sent back."

That's not Blaze. "Do they tend to be female?"

"You might think so but no. It about fifty-fifty."

"Huh," I say, hoping it ends here.

"Some crazy shit, ain't it? That's right up your alley. I could use your help."

Receiving no reply from me, he sighs and opens a small ratty notebook. He produces something from his shirt pocket I've never seen him use before—a thin pair of black framed readers.

He reads the surprise on my face. "Not one word to anyone, Breezy. I still be a black Ninja warrior."

"The world as I know it is coming to an end."

"Shit, these are like X-ray glasses on Superman, they help in crime fightin' is all. Ain't a man on the planet can whup JoJo Baker."

I think of Alonso Jefferson and mention him.

"The bodyguard? He's a big strong boy, but I don't think he ready to die if the shit ever hits the fan. Fighting's more mental and technique than pure muscle."

I regard the readers perched on the end of his nose and smile. "Never thought I'd see this day is all." I stifle a laugh.

He clears his throat and focuses his attention on the notebook. "As I was about to say, Muthafucka, anti-freeze got three active poisons: Ethylene glycol; methanol; and Propylene glycol. Poisonin' is found by readin' glycolic acid in the blood and with evidence of accumulation of calcium oxalate crystals in the kidneys. We see some intentional ODs with it in the homeless and depressed. It's a bad way to die. Symptoms sound just like what you witnessed—irregular heartbeat, coma, blue lips and fingernails—"

"What does your bodacious ME say about the Potassium Chloride levels?"

Baker eyeballs me over the top of his readers before he reopens the notebook. "It's tricky. Potassium is an abundant ion in the body. Potassium Chloride is a chetal halide salt (whatever that is) that's odorless, dissolves in water, and tastes like salt. It's mostly used in makin' fertilizer but it's also one of the three lethal injection drugs states use to kill prisoners, at least Missouri did before they ran out of money and before one brother on death row took too long to die." He grunts and shakes his head. "The ACLU called it cruel and unusual punishment. Tell that to the victims' families."

He returns his attention to the notepad. "Too much Potassium Chloride causes hyperkalemia in the body, which happens most often in acute and chronic renal disease. For someone with normal kidneys, like our boy Golding, a much higher dose is needed, enough to overcome the normal excretory mechanisms of the body. Overdose leads to cardiac changes, muscle weakness, ascending paralysis, cerebral anoxia, nausea and vomiting, sudden heart attack, and death. Much like what you and Miranda saw."

"You said potassium chloride poisoning is tricky."

"Because it's harder than a mother to prove intentional OD by Potassium Chloride—"

"Why?"

He again refers to his notebook, which looks the size of a bubble gum wrapper in his hands. "Only extra-cellular potassium can be screened in the lab, yet 98% of the body's potassium is intracellular and can't be measured in OD situations, unless the killer be stupid enough to leave the syringe and empty vials of potassium chloride at the scene."

"Which we know didn't happen, right?"

He smiles. "ME found a large, concentrated, dried amount of it on his shirt opposite the injection sites. That's what led her to check the levels."

"So, what you're saying is Sam or someone else did the injecting. And that person either got cold feet, or—"

"There was a struggle." Baker presses me again for information about Blaze and grows more frustrated each time I stonewall him.

His look hardens. "Cut the bullshit, Breezy. You been playin' me all along. Your voice was on her answering machine this morning before ten, requesting to be let in. You sounded urgent, like time was crucial. And the night before you left her suite after midnight. If she is your client, you got some weird ass hours and I think she's playin' you. Or, if you have lost your mind and are hittin' that, I gotta treat you as a person of interest in a possible murder. The woman already has stacks of money and is about to become richer than Oprah."

I keep my mouth shut and he leaves with a full belly but nothing new to scribble in his notebook.

∞   ∞   ∞

No word from Miranda that day, so I take a long bike ride and work the heavy bag that hangs from a joist in the unfinished basement. That evening, I phone consult with one of the therapists in the practice who's befuddled by an especially treatment-resistant client. When we finish, I hear Debby Macklin's voice in the living room. I forgot I left the television on in the background and raise the volume.

"Tonight, there's more stunning, late-breaking news about St. Louis' own Blaze Stark. Just a day after the sudden death of her husband Sam Golding, tragedy strikes again. Publishing icon Ted Lamping, the man who signed Blaze and helped make her famous, was found dead this afternoon inside his Chase Park-Plaza suite. Police are not releasing details currently, other than to classify it as a wrongful death. A Channel 4 source close to the investigation who requested anonymity said there was evidence of a break-in. The motive is unknown at this time and police have not ruled out the possibility that Mr. Lamping happened upon a burglar. A spokesperson for Lightning Rod Press reports the entire New

York-based firm is shocked and in mourning, that the Lamping family is in seclusion and trust that their privacy will be respected during this darkest of hours. Mr. Lamping is survived by his—"

I shut off the TV, replay my office conversation with Lamping, and try to make sense of it while goosebumps travel up my spine. I wish he'd opened up when I gave him the chance. St. Louis ranks number one in per capita murders, but I'm not a big believer in coincidence. The detectives will withhold key pieces, so I leave a message for Baker to call. I recall what Alonso said about me not being part of her inner circle; her rapidly shrinking inner circle. Where was Blaze when Lamping died?

I feel like I know nothing about Blaze and Golding, so I start with his biography. The only child born to a family of wealthy physicians/business moguls, Golding was California-born and –raised like Lamping said. A third-generation pledge at UCLA, he studied English and creative writing there and worked for the school newspaper. Scattered throughout the archived college articles, he writes of his aspiration to become a famous novelist, par for the course for many writers, I imagine. He published short stories in various sci-fi magazines while an undergrad, creating no significant wave in the genre. The older, published male writer jives with Blaze's kidnapping story. I find back magazine issues with his stories, pay for them, and print them for review later, in case Lamping's suspicions are justified. I find no novels written by him, no trace of a nom de plume. He graduated summa cum laude with a B.A. in English. He worked briefly as a paramedic until his acceptance at Stanford Medical School, where he earned a degree in plastic and reconstructive surgery. Young, handsome Dr. Golding sets up his shingle in Hollywood and soon becomes the top plastic surgeon to the stars. Television appearances, talk show circuit. After his mother dies, he inherits the largest medical supply company in the US and becomes an instant multi-billionaire. The bio describes Golding not only as an entrepreneur but an ardent contributor to environmental causes, world hunger, and *Doctors without Borders*. The final section touches on his marriage to Blaze near Bora Bora aboard one of his yachts and of their rapid ascension to Hollywood royalty. I wade through a seemingly endless montage of paparazzi shots with a host of other celebrities around the globe until my eyes blur and find nothing significant.

    Blaze, however, was another story. Her bio, such as it is, reads in reverse—it begins with page after page of glowing praise for her trilogy and brief oeuvre. No shortage of glitzy red-carpet photos of her in chic designer dresses and production ones of her decked out in various togas and more risqué garb gleaned from her novels. She plays the parts well, but the more I read, the more confused I become. Did her captivity spark the idea for her trilogy? Was her writing a coping mechanism? I find endless blog posts, most rather vapid for my tastes, and clickbait links to sites to buy every sort of Blaze merchandise imaginable, plus one for those seeking information about her worldwide book tour. No mention of a future novel in the works. It takes a lot of online digging, but my assumption proves correct, the name is a nom de plume. Buried deep in an appendix, I find this hidden nugget: Blaze was born Karen Jackson in St. Louis and attended high school at Smithson. No mention of parents or any other early history; as if she emerges from the sea fully grown, red hair flowing in a breeze as she steps off a half-shell and onto a red carpet. Ala the birth of Venus. I conduct other online searches for where she was born in St. Louis and the names of her parents but run into dead ends.

I know Smithson only by its reputation—a private, high-end, Catholic college prep school for girls in an affluent section of West County.

Still no word from Miranda, so I grab a book and drive to Smithson, where a beefy security man stops me before I drive onto the campus. I request to see the principal about an alumnus, Blaze Stark. He makes a face and radios ahead to the main office where another guard escorts me through a metal detector, several locked doors, and down a long corridor with a floor so polished it looks wet. We pass a control room filled with stacked banks of surveillance cameras that cover the grounds, classrooms, and meeting areas. When I mention this is a far cry from my old high school, the guard says all employees are trained to deal with active shooter situations, trespassers, and protestors. At last, we reach the principal's office where he directs me to wait in a plush chair.

Half an hour later, a tall, slender woman in her mid-fifties appears. A handsome woman with a firm handshake, she points to the seat in front of her desk. "I am Mrs. Fielding. I apologize for the wait, Dr. Adams, but you are here without an appointment."

On a shelf behind her stands a bizarre statue of a robed figure holding his decapitated head in his hands. I tear my attention away from it and look into her steely blue eyes. "That's quite alright. It's not the first time I've waited to see the principal."

That brings a polite smile from her before it quickly fades. "What brings a clinical social worker in private practice to our halls to make inquiries about Blaze Stark?"

She kept me waiting to Google me? I can't explain my relationship to Blaze without a lie or breach of confidentiality.

I paste on a sheepish grin and glance down once at the floor, honing my lie. I show her Miranda's copy of *Bound*. "My girlfriend and I met her at the signing this week. I'm a big fan and—"

Her gaze hardens and she squirms a bit in her chair. "You read that damn bio, didn't you?"

This is unexpected, so I run with it. "That's right, but there's no mention of her in Smithson's online list of notable alumni."

"Easily explained, Dr. Adams. No one named Karen Jackson, or Blaze Stark for that matter, has ever attended Smithson during the time this … *writer* would have been of high school age."

"I take it you're not a fan."

She ignores my remark. "I plead with those who run her website to fix this inconvenient error, but it hasn't happened yet."

"Inconvenient error?"

She looks beyond me and out her office window before her eyes return to mine and narrow. "Since the release of her books, we have young and zealous fans trespass, often when class is in session, determined to visit the rooms where *Blaze* attended class, to see which locker was hers, to sit in her desks. Some try to abscond with mementos. We endure nighttime break-ins and property destruction, which has forced the board to add extra security. It's been quite the nuisance for staff and students."

"I bet it's been a boost for recruitment."

A faint smile appears at a corner of her mouth. "Well, there is that." She clears her throat. "It's too bad you wasted your time coming here, Dr. Adams." She tilts her head and crosses her arms. "I must say you aren't the typical demographic drawn to Ms. Stark's tawdry attempts at writing."

"Well, you know what they say: there's no accounting for taste."

Her lips press together. "You're the second person this week to come snooping around here with questions about Blaze Stark."

"Who was that?"

"A most disagreeable, hirsute, runt of a man. He reeked of cigarettes and Old Spice, he reminded me of a weasel. He had little sense of propriety and insisted I give him access to our past student records dating back to year one. He had no court order, so I sent him on his way."

"What's his name?"

"The card indicated his name is Mr. White. It proclaimed his expertise in finding lost things. No first name or business address. He refused to tell me the name of his employer. When I asked if he was a private investigator, he flashed a crooked smile and said, 'you might say that.' He insisted I was hiding something about Blaze Stark and when I contacted security to escort him out, he said he'd return later for the truth. After the men removed him, I called the number on his card to file a complaint. The number was a strip club in New York. The man never heard of a Mr. White, but he encouraged me to come because today is Lady's Night.

"Now if there is nothing else, I'm sorry to quash your dream of visiting the high school of your hometown heroine, or whatever the true reason may be for your visit. If you will excuse me, Dr. Adams, I have a school to run."

I have an idea who 'Mr. White' works for.

I direct my eyes back to the statue, wondering how many underclass girls freak out the first time they lay eyes on the headless figure. "No need for the apology, Mrs.

Fielding, but unlike St. Denis behind you, I won't lose my head over it."

∞ ∞ ∞

I drive to my favorite restaurant, *Manno's Café*, and nurse an extra dirty martini straight up, at the bar while I wonder what I've learned. I sift through the lies and find nothing of substance.

I spear a blue cheese olive from my glass and glance back at the pictures of celebrities that line the dark walls when you enter the restaurant. Some are local sports stars, actors Jon Hamm and Kevin Kline, and the latest addition, Blaze Stark.

The bartender stands nearby, looking dapper in a black tux while he mixes a cocktail. "Have you met all the local stars on the wall of fame, Bobby?" Bobby's worked here since the place opened.

He thinks about it while he organizes his workstation. "Most of them. Hamm and John Goodman are my favorites." He expertly cuts a thin curl of lemon for a Kir.

"Blaze Stark's on the wall of fame now. You ever meet her?"

He receives more drink orders and reaches for highball and martini glasses. He rattles the ice well with a scoop, turns back to me and shakes his head. "My granddaughter wishes I had. No, I don't think she ever ate here. A close look at it reveals it's a publicity photo. It arrived in the mail and the boss told somebody to hang it. If she'd eaten here, Paul would be in the picture with her."

Paul is the owner.

He places a cherry in an Old Fashioned. "Good looking woman. Reminds me of a redheaded Marilyn Monroe. Terrible thing about her husband the other day."

I order a second drink after he's fulfilled the table orders. "You think St. Louis has had a representative share of famous people for its population?"

"When I was young St. Louis produced quite a number of stars. St. Louis was a big deal when my family emigrated from Sicily. Did you know St. Louis ranked among the top ten most populous US cities for a hundred years until the 1970s? For decades it was the fourth largest city in the country."

I know this but let him continue while I sip my drink and give him a nod. Bobby makes the best dirty martinis in town.

"Today, St. Louis ranks sixty-second." He cuts more limes and lemons. "With the murders and violent crime, corrupt politicians, and no decent mass transportation system, residents move to the counties and businesses threaten to leave for greener pastures unless the city offers them massive tax breaks. Local celebrities these days are mostly sports stars or rappers." He places drinks on a round tray for a similarly dressed waiter before he turns back to me. "Did you know St. Louis claims Tina Turner, Miles Davis, and Jackie Joyner-Kersee, but none were born here? Tina was born in Tennessee and moved to St. Louis when she was thirteen. Miles and Jackie were born across the river in East St. Louis, Illinois."

I take another sip and turn to Bobby. "Miranda's a fan of Blaze Stark. I read her bio—it claims she was born in St. Louis and attended a college prep school in West County. Funny thing is, the school has no record of her ever going to class there."

He dries his hands and sips a ginger ale. "What do you care?"

"I don't really. I thought it was odd."

He glances at the wall. "That reminds me of Shelly Winters over there, the actress who won two Oscars in the 50's and 60's. She was born into poverty across the river. Her later bios list St. Louis as her birthplace. Why, because her mother was from St. Louis? Maybe she felt ashamed of her humble beginnings, especially after East St. Louis went to hell in a hand basket. Maybe her publicity staff thought it didn't fit her glamorous persona. Who knows the reason?

"Want anything from the menu, Mitch? The rack of lamb is extra good today."

"No, thanks. I was on my way home and felt like a drink. Good talking with you as always, Bobby." I place a five on the counter for his tip. He'd given me an idea. I add another name to my persons of interest list.

DUPLICITY

Miranda flew back a day early and brings in the newspaper from my front lawn. Barney howls and wiggles and dances in circles when he sees me. She looks shell shocked while she places the Post-Dispatch on the kitchen table. "I don't believe this."

Looking at the lower half of the front page, I read the headline. "MISSOURI LEGISLATURE MOVES TO MAKE ANTI-LGBT LAWS PERMANENT." I look at her and say, "This isn't news, hon. Most of Missouri lies below the Mason-Dixon Line and wishes it was still 1955."

"Turn the paper over," she says, while Barney rises on his haunches for a treat.

I already know, of course. The front-page banner headline announces, **BLAZE STARK CONFESSES**, while the crossline headline reads:

SAM GOLDING MURDERED!

Shock waves echoed around the globe today as mega best-selling author Blaze Stark stunned the world by confessing to the murder of her billionaire husband, businessman Samuel H. Golding. It was initially believed Mr. Golding died suddenly from a massive heart attack during his wife's book signing at the downtown St. Louis Public Library two days earlier. Efforts at the scene to resuscitate him failed and Ms. Stark was rushed to a local hospital for observation after she fainted in the arms of a bodyguard as she and her entourage hurried to follow the ambulance.

The city Medical Examiner has yet to file a report that lists the cause of death. Details are sketchy as to what prompted St. Louis City Homicide detectives to question Ms. Stark, but an anonymous source has confirmed her confession. Any motivation for the murder at this early juncture is pure speculation. Ms. Stark remained in police custody when this story went to print.

The rest of the article describes Blaze's trilogy, her meteoric rise to fame, and chronicles Golding's life as a billionaire philanthropist and socialite.

"I thought something was off when she put up a fight with me, but I had no idea." Miranda says, removing her coat. "Did you already know this?"

If I was a betting man, I'd put good money on Alonso being the one who caught her. I nod. "It's a shocker."

She looks at me funny, as if waiting for me to comment further, which allows me to segue to the latest news, the break-in at the Chase-Park Plaza hotel and Ted Lamping's murder.

Her mouth falls open and she slides into a chair. "He was her publisher, right?"

There's no mention in the article of the detective's name on the case. "The head honcho for the largest house in the country, Lightning Rod Press."

"What the hell is going on?" she says.

I rub one of Barney's long velvety ears when he sidles up to me, a bright smile on his puppy face while he smacks my leg with his tail, steady as a metronome. He jumps into my lap to offer kisses, and I move my head from side to side to avoid his dog breath. "It's too early to know. We'll have to wait and see like everyone else."

Miranda makes a huffing sound and shakes her head. "They seemed like the perfect Hollywood couple, even with the age differential. I don't believe she murdered her husband, and why would she kill the publisher who made her rich and famous?" Barney jumps off me and returns to her, whimpers, and jumps in her lap, his large brown eyes stare into hers and his right paw gently settles on her mouth. The little guy reminds me of an empath; he knows when people are upset.

"No one is connecting Blaze with the Lamping murder. So far it sounds like a break-in."

We form opinions, often strong ones, about celebrities we identify with or have an emotional attachment to, based on their public personae or other traits. When that person falls short of our expectations or turns out to be the exact opposite in real life, it's easy to feel let down. Like O.J. Simpson, Kevin Spacey, or many politicians. "We don't know the facts."

She scans the paper again. "I wonder if JoJo is working the cases." She asks whether I know.

Detective Baker. I turn away and act like I didn't hear. When she repeats the question, I say, "He's the best. It may depend on his caseload." I feel backed into a corner, my half-truths and non-answers crossed the border into little white lies a while back.

She eases Barney from her lap and reassures him with head pats and a tummy rub. "I need to change out of these clothes and shower. The connecting flight was delayed, the plane was late reaching the gate.

She kicks her shoes to the floor. "Both deaths occurred in the city, JoJo's jurisdiction. Will you call and ask him?"

I inwardly groan. "If they are his cases, he won't be allowed to comment on active investigations, especially with such high-profile players."

I remain in the living room as she recounts her abbreviated trip to Martha's Vineyard. A combination of bad weather and second thoughts from the husband after his first up-close encounter with a ten-foot white-tipped shark cruising through the murky waters toward the steel cage was enough thrill for him. I hear the zip of a zipper while she undresses. She asks how my client is doing and I call out *okay* once I hear water run in the shower.

The doorbell rings. Barney the protector barks and jumps at the front door.

Through the peephole I see Baker and the thin black woman from the other night outside the Ritz-Carlton.

I open the door a few inches. "Now is not a good time, JoJo."

He hits me with that glare. "Now *is* the time. You feel me, Cool Breeze? The time is now," Baker answers, pushing through the doorway with the woman following in his wake. "This is Detective Chief Lorraine Harris. She has something to ask you."

"You should have called," I say to Baker. "Miranda and I "

Det. Harris steps forward and offers her hand. She sports a closely cropped Afro with subtle bronze highlights and wears a tailored business suit. No jewelry other than a plain gold cross around her neck. She is maybe five four and a hundred pounds but packs a firm handshake.

"I apologize for the intrusion, Dr. Adams, but the face-to-face was my idea and it's urgent. I remember your work with homicide a few years back on that counterfeiting case. Justice was served, at significant personal peril. The city and prosecutor's office are grateful—"

I walk down the hallway and shut the door to the master bedroom. The water continues to run. "I don't mean to be rude, Detective Chief, but as I was trying to say, I have company. You need to leave and call me later about this."

His arms folded, Baker frowns and looks curiously at me before glancing at his boss.

The water in the bathroom shower turns off.

"We're here, Dr. Adams," Harris continues. "This will only take a few moments of your time. Blaze Stark is in custody and has confessed to the murder of her husband. Detective Baker informs me you've had several meetings with her. She wants to see you and insists she will talk only with you. Her team of lawyers think it could help keep her calm. She's been acting … bizarrely."

She awaits my response.

Miranda appears at the doorway, dressed in a sweater and jeans.

Her hair wet, she sees JoJo and her eyes widen. "*She* must be the one you saw those late nights. *She's* the reason for the sudden interest in her books and why you acted so strangely the day of the signing. You didn't want to go because you were afraid she'd see you, or were you afraid she'd see you with *me*? What's going on between you two?"

"You know I can't discuss her, Miranda. Isn't that answer enough?"

She looks as if I slapped her in the face. She turns to the detectives, her voice rising. "What kind of therapist sees a client in her hotel suite until after midnight and then lies about it to his girlfriend?" She turns to me. "I don't know you anymore."

"I told you I was seeing a client." I think of other replies but none that will defuse the situation.

Barney puts a tentative paw on her knee, looks up at her, and whines.

"C'mon, buddy. We're leaving." She puts on his leash and they hurry out the kitchen door to the garage. I want to follow but don't. We watch her silver Prius back down the drive and into the street.

I stare at Baker, who stands working a ubiquitous toothpick in his mouth. "Sorry, Breezy."

Harris bites her lower lip and starts to speak, but I wave her off. "Blaze wants this?"

She clears her throat and shifts her weight. "The only words anyone has had her voice since her arrest are *I need to see Mitch Adams*."

I close my eyes. My thoughts want to remain on Miranda, but I must compartmentalize her for now. She needs time to cool off and clear her head. "My focus is on what is best for Blaze. I will not help you make a case against her. You already have her confession. Has she met with counsel?"

I catch Baker rolling his eyes and Detective Chief Harris nods. "The biggest Hollywood lawyers money can buy. A team of seven swept in and she hasn't said another word, apart from your name. Her dream team wants her freed, claims she poses no flight risk, and has no priors." Chief Harris shares her layman's view of Blaze's mental state which coincides with Baker's; along with the discrepancy between the initial toxicology report and the claim she laced his drinks with anti-freeze, which indicates Baker acted on his own when he first contacted me about Blaze.

"Is there anything to connect her to Ted Lamping's murder?"

Baker looks to his boss, and she gives him the nod. "Too soon to tell. She isn't talking. We're working the scene for prints, clues, and interviewing staff. Trying to establish a timeline. Early post-mortem lividity tests based on liver temp suggest time of death between six a.m. and noon. M.E. might be able to cut the time frame in half when more results come back." He lowers his voice. "No sign of forced entry; we believe he knew the killer well enough to let him—or her—into his suite before the shit went down."

"How did he die?"

Baker's face sours briefly. "Knife attack. Twenty-eight stab wounds. From the blood splatter and forensic re-creation, we speculate that the first strike occurred in the kitchen, a deep gash in the back, at an upward angle which indicates the perp was shorter than the deceased, then both Achilles heels were severed, which felled him. From there, he crawled toward the living room and front door. Splatter there indicates at some point he turned on his side and tried to reach for the phone on a glass table. At this point, he sustained multiple wounds to the hands and forearms—"

"Defensive cuts."

Baker nods. "Followed by deep gashes to the thighs and genitals. This was not a cold, calculated murder, but a frenzied one. From the shape of the wounds, the M.E. speculates the murder weapon was a butcher knife and the one the suite provides is missing. We're running fingerprints and DNA at the scene but it's way too soon for results."

A crime of passion. Did Blaze lie about being a victim of Lamping's casting couch? Would she do anything for a chance to become famous? What about those who spent time on his couch and didn't get published?

Baker refers to his notebook. "Based on what we know, it looks like robbery. No trace of his wallet, credit cards, watch, or jewelry. His cards are being monitored for fraudulent use."

Harris speaks up. "Detective Baker contacted Mrs. Lamping and close family members to determine whether the deceased had any known enemies but drew a blank. She said he wears a platinum Rolex and a heavy gold wedding band, both are gone. He often carries thousands in cash on him." She shifts her weight and clears her throat. "Her fans are creating problems at our downtown office. Peaceful protests at first, people with banners calling for her release, but last night turned violent, with officers injured by bricks and broken windows up and down the street. Today we're making arrests for peace disturbance and unlawful assembly. We've confiscated guns, knives, crossbows, even pitchforks. Protests in LA have reached the point the governor may call out the National Guard."

She pauses. Harris seems all business and keeps her cards close to the vest. "Detective Baker says you get to the truth. From what I've heard, I agree."

"If she's not speaking, what makes you think she's acting bizarrely?"

A penciled eyebrow raises. "One minute she's childlike, later she shows her breasts to the guards, waggles her tongue at them, and points to her crotch. She alternates between laughter and tearfulness. She behaves like she's several different people."

Does two plus two always equal four?

Cops are trained to suspect the spouse first. Did Baker cross the line when he extracted a confession from her? Having worked with him over the years and been on the receiving end of his prodigious intimidation skills, it's possible.

A Faulkner quote gnaws at me: the past is never dead; it's not even past. I want to learn more about my client before she became rich and famous and changed her name. Why would she invent a fictitious early past for her website by using a fake name? She's worked hard to bury it and will fight my efforts.

I escort Baker and Harris to the door and open it. "I'll see her today at one. Blaze and me in an interview room. No one listening in, no one observing. I do not report to you, nor will I help you build a case against her."

"Deal." Harris thanks me and she's first out the door. Before Baker follows, he says in a soft voice, "Miranda will be back. She doesn't strike me as the jealous type. Thanks, Breezy, and I'm sorry, my man."

I speed-dial Miranda but it goes straight to voice mail. I leave a brief message for her to call. Barney's toys that were in the kitchen are gone and when I look in the garage, the door to the driveway remains open. On the convertible roof of my Solstice sits the spare electronic garage door opener and a set of keys. Spare keys to my townhouse. Then it hits me, and I squat down in the empty space her Prius occupied moments ago. We'd transitioned smoothly from friends to lovers, to preliminary discussions of building a new home together and kids … to this. I press the button and the double door rattles on its hinges and closes with a bang, leaving me alone in darkness.

INTRODUCTIONS

The next morning, I shower, dress in slacks and a cashmere sweater, and eat toast with jam before the drive downtown to the St. Louis Metropolitan Police Department. The wind kicks up and scatters leaves across Ladue Road while I head east to connect with Highway 40. I try Miranda again, with the same result.

The Metro PD is a sandstone-colored building marked by blue reflective glass windows. In sunny weather it's an attractive edifice but with today's slate gray sky it appears cold and depressing. A small group of protestors across the street march in a circle and wave signs demanding Blaze's release. Most wear togas over their coats that make them look like chubby beige ghosts on strike a few days before Halloween. The lone place to park is on their side of Olive, so I do and cross the street. As I lug past the steel barricades with my camera and tripod, a protestor calls out my name and word spreads through the group. For some reason my appearance energizes them and the *Set Her Free!* chants intensify. A veteran officer wears a frown and stops me at the front entrance under the POLICE HEADQUARTERS marquee.

"Thanks for stirring up the Walking Dead for us."

"Dr. Mitchell Adams, here to meet Detective Baker."

He looks unimpressed. "I need some ID." While he inspects it, he says, "Oh yeah, I remember you now."

I turn my head across Olive. "Are they causing problems?"

He cocks his hat farther up on his head. "Last night the bad actors crawled out of the woodwork. I'm on the ass end of a double shift and last night here got tense. My partner got hit in the face with a brick. Another cop suffered a bad bite from a Doberman in a spiked collar. We arrested a dozen on weapons charges. They're freaks in a cult. They chanted "kill the pigs, cut their throats, spill their blood, boil their fat, spike their heads" all night while others shouted for us to release Hester, whoever that is. Damn chant still rings in my ears. They're not people, just a bunch of sickos." He looks to me, expecting a like reaction, I guess.

I remember the dog and owner being turned away at the library. "The part about killing the pigs is a rip off from *Lord of the Flies*, if my memory of high school English is correct, and the other words and the name Hester are from her novels. Millions across the world read her books. The ones across the street take it too far and role play characters. They're rabid fans, but I don't think that qualifies them as a cult."

He scoffs as he hands back my driver's license. "If they had jobs, they wouldn't have time to read. It takes all kinds to fuck up the world. And the city gets to pay for the property destruction, our overtime, and extra manpower. We'd all appreciate a quick resolution to this, Doc. She confessed, after all." His sarcasm is clear as he leaves to screen a man dressed in a courier jacket and hat rolling a dolly loaded with cardboard boxes toward the entrance.

I go through the metal detector line and my Dictaphone and video-camera are confiscated. I complain about it to the desk sergeant who makes a call while I sign in. He hands me a visitor badge and instructs me to keep it on while I'm in the building. Baker arrives while I stand arguing with the cop.

Baker acknowledges the cop and grabs the recording devices. "Follow me."

As we round a corner toward a bank of elevators, he says, "Need a refresher on your people skills with authority figures, Breezy?"

"Tired of my Dictaphone being confiscated is all."

He returns the equipment to me and asks whether I've heard from Miranda.

When I don't answer he says, "Her lawyers are moving heaven and earth to spring her—no priors, claims that the evidence is circumstantial, and the confession was coerced, blah blah."

"They're right. What you have is circumstantial; you can't prove she injected him."

We round a corner. "Not yet. You gonna be in room one. A guard will bring her in and re-cuff her to the table. You know the drill. I gotta work the Lamping murder and there ain't much to go on."

We ride the elevator in silence, and I follow him, while my thoughts return to last year when I was detained and interrogated here after a group of terrorists kidnapped Miranda. We—Miranda and I—haven't been the same since.

As he leads me into room one, I say, "Before this begins, I want your assurance that no one will be listening or watching. That's the law. Violate it and she walks."

The toothpick in Baker's mouth shifts to the other side, setting his bushy Fu Manchu in motion. He smiles. "You got it, Breezy."

"Anything else unusual with her since this morning?"

"Dunno. Been at the Chase interviewing potential witnesses. Your client been in solitary, per her lawyers' demands. I hear somethin' I'll let you know. You want anything—water, soda?"

I shake my head.

"Prisoner should be here any minute." With that, he leaves.

I situate the tripod in a corner of the small room so the angle of the video-camera will record her facial expressions. Fooled once years before, I check under the table for listening devices when voices approach as I'm about to search the drop ceiling tiles.

"Well, if you're out of Tanqueray for a martini, I want a double decaf espresso," Blaze calls over her shoulder to the young cop as she enters. "Get me that gin and you just might get lucky tonight. This hotel has the worst service in town." Her leg chains force her into short, choppy steps, but she puts some hip action into it when she sees me. Dressed in faded orange scrubs, she stands seemingly unfazed by her situation. When she notices the camera, she frowns as the cop removes a shackle and affixes it to the bolt in the table before he leaves. Her chair is bolted to the floor while the one between the table and door—mine—is not.

I focus the video camera on Blaze when she says, "I said no recordings."

"You lost that right when you landed here."

"Did you rat me out, handsome?"

I adjust the volume and direct the speaker toward her. "No. I think our next sessions could help your case. Ignore the camera while we talk."

She leans forward and the leer returns. "The cops were convinced of my guilt before they walked through my door and began their interrogation. My lawyers say you and that big black detective are pals. Am I wrong to trust you?"

I notice a slight tremble in her hands.

I lean forward to meet her eyes. "You were aware of my history with the department the night we met; you knew of my past collaborations with Detective Baker. I heard you were struggling with confinement; your mood was all over the map, and that you refused to speak with anyone but me, yet you entered this room chattering."

"You heard wrong. Cops lie."

"Why would they lie about that?"

She shrugs. "What about that girlfriend of yours? The pushy one at the signing."

An odd deflection. "What about her?"

"What does she know about me?"

"Nothing about you that isn't already public knowledge."

She shoots me a suspicious look and tugs at a loose string on her jailhouse top with fingers that can barely reach the fabric, given the shackles. I allow the silence to linger before I speak, this time in a softer voice. "I've been where you're sitting; it's scary and intimidating."

She exhales and nods while her fidgeting causes the shackles to rattle. "But *you* didn't confess."

"That's true. What exactly did you tell the cops?"

She yanks the string free. "I don't remember. The cops waved a signed confession in my face, but it's not my signature; it's loopier, like that of a child's. All I remember is he fell to the floor in front of hundreds of fans. In the parking lot by the EMT van it hit me that Sam was dead, that his heart stopped. None of this makes any sense."

"Describe the events of the day that led up to the second book signing."

The string now wrapped tightly around a finger, the chains rattle when she places her hands on the scarred metal table. Her chin drops to her chest and as her wavy red hair covers her face, I notice telltale brunette roots.

When she straightens, Blaze sounds younger, demurer. She smiles self-consciously and asks why she's in chains. I tell her and she begins to cry.

I can't pass her anything tangible, not even a tissue, so I offer words of reassurance while she rides out the tears.

When she's finally calm, I ask her name.

Blaze stares at the cinder block wall beyond my shoulder. "Sarah."

"How old are you?"

"Nineteen."

"Sarah" is presenting herself to me as a DID client, not Blaze. This is common with DID clients, who more usually make themselves known to treatment after self-mutilation or a suicide attempt. Integration is the entire process of helping the DID client recover. The personalities must share the hidden traumatic memories and the DID client must ultimately take ownership of the memories, facts, and feelings that caused the initial fracture. Fusion occurs when two personalities combine and no longer see themselves as separate identities. The trick is fusing the violent personality and client, for the abusive personality played a key role in helping the client survive the original trauma.

"It's nice to meet you, Sarah. I'm Mitchell. I'm here to help. Is there anyone else with you?"

She blushes. "The adults are Blaze, the writer, and Desiree, the party woman. You've met them both and they really like you. Especially Desiree, she thinks you're quite handsome."

"Are there others besides you, Blaze, and Desiree?"

She bites her lip and looks up at the ceiling. "The only other ones left are Boo and … him." She shudders at the last word.

"Who's Boo?"

"She's nine, has blond hair she wears in a ponytail. She likes to draw and read."

"She sounds nice. Who's *him*?"

She wants to hug herself, but the chains prevent it. "I don't know. I've only seen his shadow fill the wall; he scares me. Blaze says he wants to kill us. She calls him the Midnight Man because he usually comes at night."

"What happened to the others, Sarah?"

She looks up into my eyes, her lower lip trembles. "Midnight Man."

"How many are gone?"

"Judith and Laurie. The three-year old twins."

Fusion with the childlike personalities. That's good. "What happened next that afternoon?"

"Sam freed us from the basement, and we took a limo with Sam, Ted, and Miles to the library for the signing. Miles ordered food delivered from the best local restaurants, we ate, then discussed the tour and the screenplay for *Bound*."

"Were you and Sam alone together at any time before the talk?"

She shakes her head. "I don't think so."

"What about Blaze and Sam?"

"I don't know."

"Or Desiree? Or Boo? Or Midnight Man?"

"I don't remember."

I allow the silence to lengthen.

She scratches at the table surface with the edge of a chipped fingernail before she puts the nail in her mouth. A tiny twitch forms below her left eye and she fights to control it with her fingers. "I have blackouts. I remember fragments. After we met that night in your office, Desiree wanted to party, so we drove across the street to the Dooley's Bar you mentioned. We wore the scarf and shades while we drank. Men bought us drinks, some approached. Next thing I remember I woke up in a strange bed with a woman I'd never seen before. I have no idea how we got there or what we did."

"You share information with Blaze and the others."

She nods. "Sometimes, but never with … him."

"Where was Alonso during this?"

She sniffles and lowers the hand from her face. "Blaze says celebrity comes with a heavy price; that at times the walls close in on her, she can't breathe, and she needs to lose herself in a crowd and just be … another woman at a bar." She cracks a mischievous smile. "We gave Alonso the slip. Went to the ladies' room, used the crowd as a shield to sneak out the front, and took an Uber to a downtown club."

"I'm confused. You said the next thing you remember was waking up in a strange bed, but now you recalled an elaborate effort to ditch Alonso and go to a club. Which is it?"

She hesitates. "I guess I remembered it once you mentioned Alonso."

"Okay. What do you remember when you woke up?"

The eye twitch returns. "The lights turn on. Alonso puts his coat over me, gathers our clothes, and carries us to the limo. I don't know how he found us."

"Then what?"

"He drove us back to the suite. Miles was beside himself with worry. He teased us that he was going to install a chip in me, so he'd always know where we are. Then he told us about the holdover book signing and he chastised us for not calling back Blaze's agent Harry and Bud, the director for *Bound*. Miles brewed his famous hangover tea and ran us a bath. He's like the mother we never had …"

"What was your mother like?"

She shakes her head, appears ill at ease. "Blaze made us promise never to speak about her."

"Thanks, Sarah. I'd like to speak with Blaze now."

Her head drops to her chin and when she looks up the sultry smile returns.

"Welcome back, Desiree. I just met Sarah."

She grunts and crosses her arms. "Some welcome, I'm still in jail." She leans forward. "She didn't bore you with her sob stories or run her mouth, did she? She needs to zip that lip, or someone will do it for her."

"Will that be you or Midnight Man?"

For an instant her bravado fades at his mention. "She better hope it's me."

"As I told Sarah, I'd like to speak with Blaze, please."

Her head drops for an instant and Blaze returns. It's not unusual for the personalities to cycle faster under stress.

"Welcome back, Blaze. The Social Security Number you provided on the new client questionnaire belongs to a Karen Jackson, with your listed birth date."

Her cockiness returns. "Did you actually think Blaze Stark is my real name? I was born in St. Louis; Karen Jackson is my birth name. Far too ordinary a name for a writer and I'm no plain Jane.

"Buried in a footnote on your website is a claim that you, or Karen Jackson, attended high school at Smithson, a glitzy West County prep school. They have no record of you as a student there, under any name."

She stares at me in silence, so I continue.

"As writers go, you're a rock star with a rabid fan base. I'm not the first person to visit Smithson and I won't be the last. For me to understand you, and help you better, we need to discuss your past, however difficult."

No response.

"You can continue to run from your past, but it will catch up with you. How long do you think you can hide from it?"

She strokes her palm with the index finger of her right hand, staring at it as if the answer lay within. "Did you know that Smithson receives a sizable anonymous donation every year? Enough to cover all damages and provide five scholarships to low-income teens. I donate millions to a number of worthy causes, here and in LA."

Her movements cause her chains to rattle, and she shuts her eyes for a moment. Frowning, she shakes her head and grimaces. "This place is worse than hell. There are dangerous people here. Some of them are guards."

I wait for more.

She tries to stand but the shackles prevent it. She sits back down quickly and wrings her hands. The rattling noise echoes in the small room and serves to ratchet up her anxiety.

"Let's start with your birth name. It's not Karen Jackson or Blaze Stark."

She straightens her posture and grins. I detect a faint twitch under her left eye. "Face this reality, to you and the rest of the world I will forever be Blaze Stark."

"Okay, you're Blaze Stark. Tell me about your childhood."

"I went to great lengths to wipe every vestige of it from the earth, why would I discuss it with you?"

I lean back. "Your past holds the key to your fugue states and will shed light on the level of responsibility for your actions. Don't you wish to be free of Midnight Man? He served his purpose, but it's time for him to be fused."

It looks like she wants to agree, but says, "Your records could be subpoenaed in court. I will tell you about my childhood, but only off the record. You must promise never to repeat this, and never chart a word of this."

"Agreed. Tell me about your parents, Blaze."

Her eyes shift to the camera. "Do you swear this will never reach the court?"

"It will not."

"Turn off the recording devices."

I do so. "I will convince you to change your mind about this. It could help win back your freedom."

"No notes, either. Just listen. Repeat this to anyone and I deny it." She emits a heavy sigh. "My birth mother was a drug addict and prostitute. The fleeting memories I have revolve around me taking care of her on those rare occasions she was home. I pretty much raised myself. I never knew my father; I learned later he was one of her johns. She fashioned herself some kind of actress; she had a stage name, but to my knowledge the only appearances she made were on her back for money. The last year …" She turns away and wipes away tears. Her chest starts to heave. "I can't! I can't say it! I'm not ready!"

I cross my legs. "Take your time. Deep breaths, in and out. Whatever happened back then, your mother isn't here now. I can help you face it. We can come to terms with it together."

I wait in silence for her breathing to normalize.

Five minutes later, she faces me. "They never found the ones who … She overdosed when I was eleven and Tiara, a neighbor lady, took me in. If not for her, I would have been thrown into the foster care system."

"Where was Blaze Stark born?

"The truth? You will never repeat this?"

I nod.

"East St. Louis, Illinois. I lived there with Tiara and her son for years until she found a better job in St. Louis City. Then we moved to the near north side. When you're poor, you move out of the frying pan and into the fire."

Her eyes shift to the shadows that continue to pass underneath the door to the hallway, some quickly, others slower. "How old were you when you moved across the river?"

She shoots me with a cold stare until her head drops to her chin. It remains there for a minute. I notice her shoulders hunch and as she waggles her head, I hear the vertebrae in her neck pop. Her face contorts into an angry mask as she cracks her knuckles. I ask what's wrong. Her breaths become raspy, through her mouth. When she doesn't respond, I walk around the table, place a hand on her shoulder, and lower my face to ask if she's okay.

Before I can say a word, she rises and wraps the shackles tightly around my throat. I struggle in vain to get a finger between the chain and my neck before she chokes off my air. Her nostrils flare and a raised vein in her forehead pumps overtime as she forces my head toward the table. If the chain held more slack, she could stand and choke me out.

She's suddenly so strong, all I can manage is to whisper her name.

Her voice is so deep I swear it's a man's. "I am Bedlam. The others call me the Midnight Man. It's time … for you … to die." She tightens the chains as she talks. I drop to one knee and kick the chair out from under me. The video camera crashes to the floor, but still, no one responds. When she tries to climb on my back for better leverage, I deliver a hard blow to her stomach with an elbow, and her grip on the chains loosens. I free my throat from the shackles and suck air into my screaming lungs. Unable to speak, I stagger to the door and pound on it until a silhouette appears on the other side.

Two guards enter. Blaze sits unmoving, head slumped, eyes shielded by her hair. While I stand coughing with one hand on the wall for support, a guard warns Blaze he will pepper spray her if she tries anything during the transfer back to her cell. The other uncuffs then recuffs her hands tightly behind her back before the shackle attached to the table is removed. I wipe a trickle of blood from my raw neck. My vision slowly returns, and I see my Dictaphone in a corner. The plastic housing atop the mini cassette is broken. The video camera wasn't as lucky.

Her features now calm, Blaze slowly turns her head toward me and says in a high, squeaky voice, "You need to be careful of Midnight Man. He's mean."

"Who are you?"

"Boo. Next time you see him, run!"

A guard asks what happened. It hurts to swallow; I clear my throat several times before I can speak. "I was out of line. I pushed her too far. We're not finished. Please re-shackle her to the table."

I knew damn well this could happen. I expected the violent personality to surface at some point, but I was careless.

The first guard frowns. "You have five minutes. I will remain outside the door."

Five minutes? I might need years. "I need more time."

"Not when a prisoner turns violent, Doc. You're lucky I have a few minutes to spare." He exits and his silhouette remains on the other side of the door.

Blaze remains slumped, unmoving.

The V in my cashmere sweater is now a flap, ripped almost to my belt. I hand comb my disheveled hair and tug the hem of my shirt back into my slacks. My throat feels like I swallowed sandpaper. "Who am I speaking to now?"

She lifts her head ever so slightly but doesn't make eye contact. "Sarah." Almost a whisper.

The demure young girl. "I'm sorry Midnight Man hurt you."

"Me too. He told me his name is Bedlam."

"He lies and he's mean."

"I'll say. How do you deal with him?"

She shrugs briefly and twirls her hair with her right hand. "I'm a protector. I help protect us from him. You have any gum?"

I smile and shake my head.

She blushes and looks to the floor. "Blaze the writer is a protector, too. She trusts you, even though she may not show it. She's scared. We all are."

I knew from research and my prior D.I.D. client that the communication between personalities isn't always fluid.

"Are you really here to help us?"

"I will do my best. I promise we'll talk again, but I need to speak with Blaze. It would help me help you."

Sarah lowers her head.

The guard taps on the window and announces my time is up. I raise a fist and demand more time. A wry smile blooms on Blaze. "I see you've met Midnight Man. How'd that work out?"

"It could have gone better."

She stretches her legs as best she can and nods. "He threatens vile acts of brutality. He's marked Sarah for his next victim. He's already culled the younger, weaker ones."

Midnight Man/Bedlam made his appearance soon after Blaze mentioned her drug-addict mother and immediately when I asked how old she was when they moved to Missouri. I steadied myself against the prospect of an encore appearance.

"Tell me about the time you spent living with Tiara after your birth mother died."

Blaze rubs her reddened wrist. "She's a kind woman. She made sure me and her nephew made it to school and church, she cooked us healthy meals, bought us decent, if not trendy, clothes. At night we'd kneel and pray for my mother." A cloud looms over her, she hesitates. "I'll never pray again."

"Why, what happened?"

She scratches at her wrist with a nail. "Tiara met a man from church. The first months passed without incident, un—"

The door opens and the guard enters. "Time's up."

I ignore him. "What happened, Blaze?"

She sees the guard and cringes in terror, screaming, "Don't touch me! Keep your hands off me!"

I press the guard for more time when another appears. "The prisoner's gotta get back to her cell. You need to leave now Doc."

I gather my broken equipment and a guard ushers me into the hallway. I think Blaze mistakes the first guard for someone else—but they prevent me from calming her. I hear her screams as (I assume) they unshackle her from the table. The second guard frowns and orders me to walk to the elevators before they escort her from the interrogation room.

Back at the entry desk on the first floor, I ask for Detective Baker and the desk officer says he left the building. I call Baker and leave a voice message. One of the protestors spots me in route to my car and a group breaks off from the pack and besieges me for news of Blaze.

"All I can say is she's a fighter and she's keeping her spirits up."

"This is bullshit, man. When is she being released?" says the woman who noticed me leave Metro PD.

I maneuver through their circle, unlock my car, and place the broken camera on the front seat. "I don't know. Blaze appreciates your support and well-wishes, but the last thing she wants is more violence. She thinks it best that you all go about your daily business, return home, and pray for her."

The crowd hesitates until someone from the back shouts, "Worthless man!" and another close to my Solstice cries out, "He's one of them! He works for the police!"

Several of them pound on my car and begin to rock it until I peal out onto the relative safety of Olive Blvd. A water bottle bounces off the convertible top and explodes on the street.

On the drive home I check my backlog of text messages and one sends chills up my spine, it's from Ted Lamping, the morning of his murder.

THE FIXER COMETH

My Barney the beagle ringtone barks as I near home. Caller ID indicates *Unknown*, but I pick up anyway.

"Dr. Adams? Louis Gianelli. We need to meet somewhere private that serves food, preferably Italian, preferably now."

Lamping's text mentioned Gianelli. "Who are you and why should we meet?"

"I work for the late Theodore Lamping. His last order was to contact you. He said you're a bastard to work with, which makes you my kinda people. We said that if we work together we can help learn the truth about Blaze Stark."

Lamping's text doubled down on his fear over Blaze's instability and obliquely addressed other issues. "What makes you think I have anything to do with her?"

He grins. "Don't bullshit a bullshitter, Doc. You're trying to get inside her head and I know your session downtown today didn't go well. How's your throat?"

I do my best to hide my surprise. "Are you a private investigator?"

"Licensed in several states. I possess information of interest to you."

Likely the other visitor to Smithson. "If we meet, bring your Missouri P.I. license. Be prepared to do all the talking."

A chitter of laughter followed by a snort. He did sound a bit like a varmint. "Yeah, yeah. Lamping told me about you."

I weigh my options and find them limited. "Where are you?"

"In my car, in a lot at West County Mall."

If so, both of us are west of The Hill, famous in St. Louis for Italian food. "Massa's in Chesterfield. Be there in fifteen minutes or I'm gone." Feeling churlish, I hang up before he can respond.

Ten minutes later, I pull into the rectangular lot in the mostly abandoned strip mall off Highway 40. A few older men sit hunched around the bar at this off-peak time and both back booths are open. I grab the one farthest from foot traffic, ask Melanie for two menus, and order a Tanqueray and tonic.

Soft music filters down from overhead. Right on time, a smallish man briskly enters and I hit the play button of my spare Dictaphone that rests in a front pocket of my slacks. A man of indeterminate age sits down across from me in the dim light without a word.

"Nice car you got there, Doc. Always liked the fire red Solstice convertible option. 2.0 liter 14 Ecotec engine with a dual scroll turbocharger. Hang on to it a few more years and it'll be a classic. Too bad GM scrapped the entire Pontiac division in 2009. Fucking recession the year before put the kibosh on that."

His features include a head of wiry black hair and a square jaw, his head bobs from side to side and he adjusts his tie in a nervous habit when he speaks. Now that I see him up close my guess is he's in his fifties.

Melanie appears and he orders a shot of Four Roses and a beer. He turns quickly back to me. "I blame that stupid—"

I hold out a hand. "Driver's and P.I. license, Mr. *White*." They look legit.

His knowing smile broadens and the chitter returns. "The stuffed-shirt principal with the creepy statue didn't take a shine to me. Hey, we all need to have a little fun in our job, know what I mean? Don't see how you can in yours, unless you score a little strange on the side every now and then, know what I—"

We both miss Mel's Ninja-like approach and her uneasy throat clear. "Do you gentlemen know what you'd like to order?"

I order the pasta special of the day with a house salad while he chooses lasagna, another shot, and a beer.

When Mel leaves, I turn back to him. "This isn't Porky's. Behave yourself. I'd like to keep coming here to eat."

He drains his first drink. Another series of head bobs and a tie pull. "What? What'd I say?"

"If you want to discuss Blaze Stark while we eat, be my guest—"

He places two hundred-dollar bills on the table and slides them toward me.

I look at him, waiting.

"Lamping said you were a hard nut, but I like you already. I want you to be my shrink." He glances at the bills then back to me. "Will that cover my first session or do you need another? Am I now your official patient?"

My eyes narrow. I've got to find better clients. "What's your problem? ADHD, personality disorder, killer, sociopath?"

The grin returns. "That's a good one, Doc." His smile quickly fades. "They might all fit, on any given day. Never could sit still in school, lousy student." More tie fidgets and room scanning. "If I'm your client, you can't repeat anything I tell you in confidence, even to the cops, right?"

This spastic little man begins to make *me* feel anxious, no easy feat. "True. Unless you plan to harm someone or yourself. Again, why do you need my help?"

He leans forward, elbows on the table. "I'm a sex addict and I've done some awful shit to women—"

Mel appears and places his drinks and our salads on the table.

He winks in response to her look of shock. "Thanks, darling!"

She executes a 180 as if the building is on fire.

I watch her make a beeline for the owner. I put down my salad fork, no longer hungry. "I like this place. I don't want to be banned from it."

He turns back to me, oblivious to my concern. "Am I your client now, Doc?"

I'm curious where this is headed. "If I agree, you will make an appointment with me, in my office, before we leave this restaurant."

He downs the second shot and adjusts his tie. "Yeah, yeah. I've done some bad things in my line of work. I want to, how they say, make amends to people I've wronged."

"I doubt your sincerity. Give me a for-instance."

"Am I your client now, Doc?"

Against my better judgment, I nod.

"Good. On occasion, Lamping reimbursed me with more than money."

"Meaning?"

More head bobs and looking around. "He supplied me with select female writers for sex."

Blaze was apparently right about the casting couch. "Why would they have sex with you?"

He doesn't seem fazed by my bluntness. "Lamping had sex with them first in exchange for moving their manuscripts off the slush pile, even some that were pure garbage if they were hot enough. Lotta vampire, paranormal, and romance shit. Those who played ball got signed to minor contracts; those who expected more, like a signing bonus … he shared." He sips his beer. "I always thought writers were mousy little wallflowers. Who knew they're twisted and kinky in the sack?"

I drain my gin. "Back to Blaze."

The owner places our entrees on the table and acknowledges me with a friendly nod. He folds his arms across his chest then glares at Gianelli. "Will you need anything else this afternoon, sir?"

"Yeah, yeah. Another Four Roses and a beer. Oh, and more fresh parmesan. Look, if I spooked the waitress, I apologize. I'm a playful guy is all. I don't mean anything by it. Send her back with my drinks and I'll make nice."

"Nothing for me, thank you," I say with a polite smile.

The owner returns to the bar, and I redirect Gianelli.

"Yeah, yeah. Lamping insisted Blaze sleep with him for a contract, even though he thought the books would sell. Lamping kept that nice piece of ass for himself. Nobody else fucked her."

"How do you know this?"

"He told me."

"That's hardly proof."

"One of my unwritten jobs was to deal with any blowback from these wannabe writers when things didn't pan out the way they hoped, which happened all the time."

"How did you handle them?"

"No rough stuff or threats, Doc. Lamping would shine them on with referrals to other publishers and if that didn't work, he'd have me pay off the ones who complained.

"Lamping knew Blaze was cuckoo for Cocoa Puffs from day one and when her career took off, she grew more demanding. He said there was a definite method to her madness. Lamping never dreamed her books would take off the way they did, so he agreed to an escape clause in her contract in part because she was nucking futs. Pretty devious, if you think about it. Firing him to sign with a rival publisher was a valid multi-million-dollar threat to future earnings and movie deals. Somehow, she also learned about Lamping's *arrangements* with other wannabe female writers and threatened to blow the whistle. She had his balls in her purse."

"Charming. If true, that gave Lamping motive to murder Blaze, not the other way around."

He shrugs his shoulders while he shovels lasagna into his mouth and nods approval. "I dunno. You're the shrink. She's crazy, ain't that enough?"

"Not usually. What else do you know?"

He sops up sauce with a chunk of bread. "Lamping often had me tail her and the husband."

"Why?"

He looks at me like I sprouted a second head. "To find dirt on her … and out of concern for his now dead friend … but mostly for the dirt."

"And?"

Another head bob and look around the room. "Bupkes. At first, I thought she and that mountain of a bodyguard were bumping uglies cuz they seem so close, but audio and visual surveillance turned up nada in the boudoir.

"He also wanted to know if someone else actually wrote the books that made her famous."

"Because?"

"He suspected the dead husband wrote them." Gianelli eats faster than anyone I've ever seen and has no qualms about talking with a mouthful. He sops up more sauce with a hunk of bread and shovels it in his mouth.

I sip my water. If Sam was the author, he could have blown the whistle on her any time. Could she have agreed to keep silent about her kidnapping and marry him in exchange for the sole rights to the trilogy? "Did you discover who wrote the books?"

He shakes his head. "I found nothing that pointed to him writing them and no proof she didn't."

"How did they meet?"

More adjusting of his tie and head bobs. "No clue. According to close mutual friends of Lamping and Golding, she materialized on his arm the day Sam announced their plans to marry. Many friends view her as a gold digger."

"I read somewhere they married aboard one of his yachts near Bora Bora. You know anything about that?"

The varmint sound re-emerges as he scans the quiet restaurant. "Funny thing about that. A JP and two witnesses. The boat crew. No Golding family members, Lamping wasn't invited, and no family or friends of the bride attended. Almost sounds like a shotgun wedding for the rich and shameless, but who's holding the gun in this situation?"

It's a bit odd but akin to an elopement for people with money who don't want a big ceremony. "Did you find anything about Blaze's early years?"

Another twitchy head shake. "She's a ghost. Her legal name is Blaze Stark, changed from Karen Jackson, but she's covered that paper trail so well that Karen Jackson is also a ghost."

He grunts and lowers his voice. "One day by chance, I happened upon information in her trash that may have included a bank statement. She pays for flowers to be sent the first of every month to a pauper's grave here in the city, near the airport. Nice arrangements, they cost a pretty penny. I offered the cemetery staff a sizable bribe for information between the two, but they kept their mouths zipped. Place's all overgrown with weeds, headstones missing, but not this one. She pays someone to keep it nice. Lamping had me tail her the day she flew to St. Louis to start the book tour. The bodyguard drove her; he stayed in the car while she placed the flowers at the grave and paid her respects. She didn't stay long and didn't get emotional. Karen Jackson is the name of the stiff on the tombstone, but I got nowhere with that. The only thing they have in common is the same birthday. That's it; you're up to date."

"When was the date of death on the Jackson tombstone?"

He slides a cemetery brochure with writing on it across the table to me. "It's all there—lot number, exact inscriptions on the marker."

He pushes away his plate and drags a napkin across his mouth. "What about you, Doc? This is supposed to be a two-way street."

I shake my head. "I said, be prepared to do all the talking."

I make a writing motion to the waitress for our check.

Melanie sidles over to me with our bill, while the owner watches from the bar. I pay the bill while Gianelli motions the waitress to his side of the booth. "I apologize for any vulgarities you might have heard earlier. None of it was directed at you nor was it meant for your ears. I wasn't raised in what most people would call 'a healthy environment.' I did not mean to offend you, darling. Please accept this peace offering." He presses two hundred-dollar bills into her unsteady hands and her eyes widen while she warily thanks him.

In the parking lot the sun breaks through the cloud cover and threatens to make it a nice day. I make his ride instantly when I turn toward the lot. My first guess was a Hummer on steroids, but since they were discontinued a decade ago, we walk toward this monstrosity of a Ford SUV that takes up two parking spots and towers over the other vehicles in the lot, dwarfing my little convertible Solstice.

I turn to him and crack a grin. "Did you drive this thing to visit Smithson?"

He nods and squints into the sun. "That stuffy principal wouldn't let me see the registry of students."

"I take it your considerable charms failed to melt her defenses."

More tie adjustments and a grin. "Maybe so, but I used another means to get the registry. Another dead end."

I hand him my card and he looks puzzled.

"Your next appointment with me. In my office. Be on time. Perhaps you'll know more by then. We have a lot to discuss: your fear of women; how you treat them; and the significance of this canary-yellow mountain of an SUV with red flames painted along its engine and oversize tires tall as your waist."

"My new Ford F650 Power Stroke V8 Turbo Diesel with TorqShift. Ain't she a beauty?"

"I had you pegged for an orange Hummer."

"Nah, I traded in my black one since the bastards stopped making them. A hassle to find parts."

"Tell me you don't tail clients in this."

He makes a face. "Course not."

"How do you climb in? You repel up with a rope or should I throw you into the air?"

"Very funny. It's a mid-size truck with tricked-out tires." He climbs onto the running boards and stretches out fully for a grab bar near the cab, then opens the driver door with a grunt before he contorts his body to climb inside. I feel a twinge in my back watching his gyrations. The window powers down.

"How did you approach people at the cemetery about Karen Jackson?"

The engine revs and a jet of black diesel smoke belches from the vertical exhaust pipe. Sunglasses shield his eyes. "Showed 'em my P.I. license and that I received a tip that foul play may have been involved. Asked about any unusual visitors and who's paying to keep the site maintained so nice, but no takers. Their pat answer was Karen Jackson had no family and they knew nothing of how she died."

"Try not to run over anyone while you're in town."

He revs the engine. "Keep me in the loop. We can help each other."

"Keep your appointment."

As I watch the diesel belch from his tailpipe, I tell myself it's time to press the bodyguard. He may hold an important key to this puzzle.

Lamping's final message rings in my mind: *You will receive a call from my fixer. He's a rather loathsome person but a fearless investigator willing to do whatever it takes. If I die soon, it will be by her hand. I've made mistakes, but don't deserve to pay for them with my life.*

BOUND

I drive home and go for a long run. I speed dial Miranda, but her phone goes straight to voice mail, so I leave a brief message for her to call. Back in my quiet home, I change out of my sweaty clothes and startle myself when I step on a squeaky chew toy Miranda left by the bed. I feel a sharp pang for her and Barney. My toe brushes against something part-way under the bed. Miranda's copy of *Bound,* the first in the trilogy.

Feeling sorry for myself, I make a Tanqueray and tonic and sit down, staring at the book cover.

The one with the blonde victim in a toga. She lays on a mattress, with a forlorn and helpless look, and now I see her arms are shackled but I couldn't tell that from the smaller bookmark Blaze handed me the night we met. Not having anything better to do, I crack open the book and skim over fifteen-plus pages of rave reviews, mostly from other famous female best-selling authors and major newspaper reviews before I reluctantly read the prologue.

The concussive blast knocked me backward into the air, hurtling me toward the cliff and the roiling ocean below. If my body hadn't slammed into the scarred trunk of a dead elm, I would have fallen to a non-descript death on the jagged rocks below, another hapless victim of the plasma and radioactive bombs that have rocked the world for years. Large objects cartwheeled through the air; deadly shrapnel whistled past me with heavy thumps. Chunks of wood and stone and concrete rained down like meteorites, pockmarking the scorched earth. The magnitude of the explosion deafened me. White hot pain stabbed my head and when I touched it, my hair was on fire. I reached out with one hand and threw dirt on my hair, afraid that if I let go of the trunk in my disoriented state I'd fall to my death. It took many fistfuls to put out the fire and I gagged on dirt chunks.

When my hearing returned, the explosions had stopped. My ribs bruised and sore, I still clung to the tree stump, to be certain the shelling had ended. There'd been rumors for weeks over the emergency warning system that the war, at long last, was near an end. Also reports of how the country had devolved into utter lawlessness at the hands of warlord mutants and vague rumors that a brave new world run by freedom rebels may be forming somewhere out west to fight the mutants. My eyes stung from blood that trickled from my scalp. I screamed in pain when I tried to stand—a section of rebar had torn through my lower calf, pinning me to the ground. My screams echoed across the shore below when I finally freed my leg. I removed my shirt and wrapped it over the bloody wound. Topless, I hobbled up the first steep flight of flagstone steps for the uphill walk to our house to find my parents, fiancé, and little sister.

No peeling church bells announced the end of the war, no singing birds, nothing but an eerie quiet. Then I heard the tiniest sound grow above me on the upper flight of steps, at first like the unsteady, incessant footfalls of an animal, possibly wounded, inevitably making its way toward me. The odd noise grew louder as it tumbled down the steep steps. I was temporarily frozen by the macabre thing, which came to rest against my shoe, staring lifelessly up at me with one blue eye ... the head of my sister's favorite doll. The one she carried with her everywhere. Blood smeared across its shattered cheek; its eye fixed on me. I thought I heard the head ask: *why weren't you with us when the bombs exploded?*

I lurched up the flagstone stairs as fast as my wound allowed, screaming, "Kathy! Mom! Dad! Daniel!" Then I reached the back yard—the closest plasma fireball that struck left a crater fifty yards across and eight feet deep, exactly where our home had stood. Everything reduced to a hole of smoldering, twisted metal and wood. The swing sets had fused together into a deformed sculpture, forming a hideously twisted arch, the red plastic seats dripping like blood onto the very spot my father had told me to return to if catastrophe ever struck, but that didn't matter now. Nothing mattered.

I lost my mind that night, whether I ever regained it is another matter. I gathered the bits and pieces I could find of my mother and father, sister Kathy, and my fiancé Daniel. I gathered their remains together in a pile—one of my mother's green eyes had fused to her shattered spectacles, Kathy's tiny foot still in a worn sneaker, and the various scattered and unrecognizable internal organs and bones. Beneath a mound of shattered floor tiles, I found Daniel's right hand severed neatly below the wrist. I held his hand one final time under the stars of the eastern seaboard sky, like so many nights before. I tried to imagine his face in my mind's eye, but the talking doll head kept appearing, angry and accusatory, shouting: *Why weren't you here?* Our diplomat parent's vision and leadership had provided initial hope for an early end to the war. I foolishly thought their efforts, among those of others, would change the world, and form a new world order out of chaos. When diplomacy failed and before the government and banks collapsed, father had the foresight to withdraw our life savings and bury the money. Prior emergency broadcasts spoke of many dark days ahead, that money was the key to survival for money bought safe houses and protection. I stroked Daniel's cold and gray hand with mine, trying not to look at it as a shooting star briefly lit up the clear night sky. Flies buzzed between the torn tendons of his wrist and into my nose and mouth. Biting me, they promised rain. Using a splintered two-by-six board, I dug shallow graves for the remains of my family and Daniel. As the rain began to fall cold and hard on my naked chest, my last acts were to plant Daniel's right hand in the dirt, extend his right middle finger to the empty heavens, and place my engagement ring on the first knuckle of his index finger. This is where diplomacy gets you in this world. I didn't yet know I would bury my given name in that crater of blood along with them; but I knew I would never be the same. As I turned to dig where Father had buried our life savings, screamer engines grew louder in the distance. Mutants! There was no time to run from the crater so I quickly covered myself with dirt and mud the best I could and positioned a nearby section of 4 by 8 roofing plywood over the rest of me, close to where I positioned Daniel's hand. I held my breath and closed my eyes when I heard the mutants talking softly at the crater's edge. I panicked at the thought of Daniel's arm sticking defiantly out of the rubble. How could I have been so stupid? One laughed and told the others to look in the pit. They've seen the hand! A mutant, still laughing, climbed into the crater and jumped on the plywood; his weight crushed my chest and pushed my face sideways deeper into the muck. Something inside me snapped under that plywood. I didn't care if the wood shattered under his weight; I didn't care if they found and tortured me. I took the pain without making a sound. With one eye, I looked on while he removed my ring and urinated on Daniel's arm. Some of the piss landed on the plywood and dripped through a knothole onto my cheek. Another mutant ordered the others to search the area because the arm didn't get planted there on its own, grumbling that the rain washed away any tracks. At last, the mutant stepped from the plywood and with a grunt climbed from the crater to help in the hunt.

Tonight, I had to become someone else if I hoped to outwit the mutants in the crater; and I would need to become someone else to survive this brutal new world. The old me died in that crater. A fragment from a book appeared in my memory. I vowed to myself if I managed to crawl from this hole alive that from this day on my name would be … Hester Payne.

I waited for hours shivering in the mud until I felt confident the sound of the screamer engines had faded and no mutants remained behind.

Hester emerged from that hole and took what weapons the mutants left behind in the rubble (a partially buried hatchet and kitchen knife). She ran west, half-naked and muddy and bleeding from shrapnel cuts; her jeans stained red with the blood of her loved ones, she looked for survivors and a place to hole up for the night.

This is her story, at least what I remember of it ...

I close the book, surprised by the quality of the writing. The doll's head bouncing down the steps toward her makes for an effective post-apocalyptic opening image and it speaking to her holds the promise of a twist, but the prologue devolved into gratuitous violent descriptions, written in an overly dramatic hand that introduces a traumatized protagonist who *loses* her mind on page two and her personality seems to split or disassociate. Like Blaze. Writers sometimes infuse bits of themselves into a character—did Blaze do this or am I reading too much into it, in the hope of finding a back door inside her head? The pronouns in the last paragraph are confusing. Whose tale are we about to hear—Hester's, as told by the yet unnamed young female protagonist or the unnamed heroine? And is it reliable? If the other pages follow suit, this promises to be an unrelenting, bloody, intense thrill ride for the reader. I'm not impressed but then again, I'm not her demographic target audience. I'm about to forge ahead when Barney barks on the table. Caller ID indicates Branson, Missouri.

A hesitant voice on the other end. "Hi," Miranda says.

I say *hi* back.

A tentative sigh from her. "I get why you didn't tell me Blaze is your client, I'm over that, but I can't shake the feeling that something horrible could happen to you again, or me, or both of us, because of your practice. I know it's irrational, but I—we—almost died last year. We got lucky, Mitch. It's almost as if trouble seems to follow you, even though I know you're not to blame." There's a pause and then: "I miss your face."

Her go-to remark when she's out of town and misses me evokes a sad smile. "I miss your face. When you return, we need to talk this through."

"I don't know if I'm ready for that. I need more time."

I rub a hand across my throat. "There's nothing in this case that poses a credible danger to me, or you. My client is in jail."

"What if she makes bail and wants to see you? I keep thinking she had an ulterior motive from the beginning to see you. Like Danny and her agenda with Tony."

The thought has crossed my mind, since she recanted her story about flying here specifically to see me. "I respect your intuition, but I don't see it."

She clears her throat. "The writer in The Post anticipates Blaze will enter a not-guilty plea. How can she do that after confessing to murder?"

"Easy. She can seek a leave of court to withdraw her earlier confession and enter a not-guilty plea for many reasons. Some defect in the confession such as abuse or coercion by the cops, she could claim it wasn't voluntary due to lack of sleep, drugs, or alcohol, she could claim her Miranda rights were violated, her lawyers could have discovered some new exculpatory evidence, or her team plans to pursue not guilty by reason of a mental disease or defect. Her confession is still admissible unless the court excludes it, when that happens it's usually due to police misconduct. The court could also refuse leave to allow a change of plea, but this usually happens when the case has been pending for a while and the defendant seeks to change the plea shortly before sentencing.

"I'd like us to sit down and talk when you return."

Silence on the other end. Then: "I'm still sorting things out in my head. Don't rush me Mitch, please."

The silence between us drags on so long I wonder if she's still there until she says, "In the same article the writer predicts Blaze will be released on bail soon."

"I imagine her legal team is pressing for it."

I want to talk more about us but let her set the pace.

"What are you going to do if she wants to see you?"

"She's still my client. If she wants to see me, I will."

I hear a quick intake of breath on the other end. "You probably think I'm being overly anxious or paranoid."

I finish my gin. "Not at all. Many people are unaware of the weird challenges people in our professions face. We have tough, but rewarding, jobs."

I hear the faint clink of ice cubes on her end. "Is the Post accurate when they write that it may be two years before the case comes to trial?"

"*If* this results in a trial that sounds about right. The St. Louis city wheels of justice move slowly, same as everywhere else, even when a high-profile celebrity gets caught in the crosshairs. I'm surprised that her dream defense team hasn't filed a motion for a change of venue to LA." Everything I share with her is public knowledge.

"Why do you think they haven't?"

"I'm considering every possibility, believe me. Her fan base in LA would be larger and more out of control than the group here. I'm speculating here, but I don't think she wants it."

"I wonder why," she says, in a lowered voice tinted with skepticism.

I break the lull in the conversation. "You on a job in Branson?"

"My phone died. I need to buy a new one when I return. I'm calling from my hotel room while it charges. A rural Missouri family adopted three severely developmentally disabled kids and one is about to enter hospice. His parents are saints on earth who want to honor Tim's wishes to visit Silver Dollar City and Table Rock State Park with his family and several close friends while he still can. This little boy is a sweetie; he's so sick but always has a smile on his face. This one's getting to me; I think he may crash soon."

"It sounds rough. How many days?"

"Another week, if he doesn't overdo it. I may have to be the heavy and cut the vacation short if I believe he needs more emergent care than I can provide. Luckily his parents are on the same page. They want him to be at home when he dies, not in an unfamiliar hospital."

This time, she reverts the subject to us. "The kidnapping flashbacks worsened when I heard Blaze is your client. I sleep like shit every night and wake in a sweat, gasping for air. Now I dread falling asleep. I have an appointment with a new therapist when I return. I know you love your job and that it's an important one, but I want you to drop the case. I know it's irrational and I feel like a bad, selfish person for asking, but I'm scared for you, and I'm scared for us."

I'm about to answer when she says there's an incoming call on her room phone.

She returns in a few seconds. "Timmy needs me. I gotta go. No sleep break for me. Bye."

Damn! The line goes dead before I can say another word.

I mull over her words while I refill my glass, this time with less tonic, and fill a plate with smoked cheeses and sea salt and pepper crackers. I wonder if this marks the beginning of the end of our relationship. I wonder whether there's enough gin in the house.

To take my mind off the truncated call, I crack open *Bound* again.

Starving and cold, I looted a burned-out store for clothes, medicine, and bandages. I stuffed food, drugs, alcohol, and a set of knives into my backpack. While I filled a second pack with more food and bottled water, I flashed back to when I was a young child, and my adoptive auntie would take me to the local drugstore for candy and a soda. My birth mother didn't want me and the only memories I have of her are being left alone to fend for myself. I miss my aunt and her son to this day. When my aunt died, the couple I just buried took me in, but I always considered my aunt my real mother. A scuttling sound outside broke my musings and I noticed two teenaged brothers, Chip and Chaz, orphaned in the war, foraging through street rubble in what used to be New York City. I shared my haul from the store (minus the weapons, drugs, and alcohol) and the frightened boys willingly accepted me as their leader. When I was on my own, a quick catnap in the wrong place meant certain death if a mutant stumbled upon me in the dark. I organized grid searches to find other healthy survivors and safe shelter each night. Those we found the first weeks were either dead or dying and we had to abandon our hiding holes every few days because the mutants kept advancing. Food became harder to find and I sensed the boys beginning to lose faith in me. When I slept my dreams were haunted by the doll head's repeated accusatory question.

I planned for us to circle back and exhume my inheritance, so we could buy weapons and provisions from local dealers, but the mutants controlled the streets and kept pushing us farther away from home. We would bypass the roads on a moonless night and risk crossing Central Park—mutant territory—but as a drizzle settled on us, Chaz stepped in an animal trap and howled in pain a block into the park. By the time we freed him, the sound of marauder engines filled the street, approaching rapidly from the east. Panicked, the boys wanted to make a run for it into the trees, but I knew Chaz couldn't outrun them, so I held them back.

Whoops and laughter surrounded us, then the *clack clack clack* of hooves on the nearby street.

The sky opened, dropping an acid rain downpour on us.

The screamer engines cut off, I heard the *tick tick tick* sound of their engines around us as they cooled and then an eerie silence filled the park. The advance patrol appeared silently out of the mist, horse hooves yielding on the soft turf while they surrounded us. The riders sealed every exit and wielded machetes, crossbows, and lances.

A mutant with stringy long black hair approached first, flanked by others wielding automatic plasma weapons pointed directly at us. The mutants on horseback grinned at me; their tongues darted in and out of mouths filled with yellow, rotted teeth. Most had radiation burns on their faces and were missing hair. The leader barked orders to the riders,

"Take the boys to the quartermaster. See what use they can be. If they resist, put an arrow through the wounded one's eye." Four riders dismounted and the boys dropped their pitchfork and ax.

"Leave them be!" I called out. "We seek passage west is all. We mean you no harm," I said, freeing my hilt from its scabbard.

The black-haired mutant smiled and approached, he was tall and muscular, a raised white scar ran the length of his throat. He wore a bizarre amalgam of material, bits of armor mail, football shoulder pads, cowboy boots, a Nazi helmet, and camouflage sweat pant bottoms.

"Then why were you heading east? You've stumbled into a dangerous world, darling. You won't last the night without my help."

The rest of the riders dismounted and encircled me. "Thank you for the offer, but we'll take our chances on the open road." My sword sang as I unsheathed it.

His grin returned. "It wasn't an offer." Then, to his men: "Bring her to me. Alive. In one piece. Not too bruised." He pivoted to walk back to his horse.

The four men closed ranks, baring their teeth and hurling taunts about what they would soon be doing to me. One small wiry man charged me with a knife, wielding a trash can lid as a shield. I spun and swung my sword in a long, low arc, the blade sang and cleaved his left leg below the knee. He went down, howling in pain. The last things I remember as I fell backward to the pavement is the stab of searing pain in my right shoulder and the crooked smile of the bearded man who shot me with a crossbow.

The doll head revisited my dreams, tormenting me.

I woke up naked and feverish in what looked like a dungeon with my arms and legs chained to stone walls. I smelled mold, the air was thick with dampness, and the filthy mattress beneath me sticky with my own blood, the gaping wound high on my right shoulder oozed pus. In the hallway, doors opened and closed, allowing occasional shafts of sunlight in the prison, while occasional screams were interspersed with raucous male laughter. My lips cracked and swollen, my tongue thick in my throat, it hurt to swallow. I slipped in and out of consciousness and when I woke again it was nighttime. Candles guttered and reclaimed a tiny part of the darkness in the cold, gray stone hall. The whisper of soft soles on the gray marble preceded an overweight old woman carrying a pail. Wordlessly, she began the tasks of stripping away my torn, filthy clothes and washing me, taking great care to avoid eye contact.

"Where am I?" I whispered.

"It will go worse for a young lass like you if you speak or make trouble," she replied, under her breath.

She let out some slack in the chain suspending my injured arm. "Do not move. If you thrash about you will make my job harder and I could accidentally cause more damage." When I began to speak, she jammed a dowel of wood between my teeth and poured alcohol on my wound. The old nursemaid took forever as she stitched my shoulder without anesthetic. She observed calmly as my struggling and chest heaving at last slowed to near normal breathing. Then she cleaned and dressed my infected calf wound.

She leaned in close and whispered. "Good. You are tough. I give you this advice to live by only once: do not ask questions; do not talk; just obey; lay back and take it." She laid a fresher sheet on the mattress and fed me several spoonfuls of a murky broth that tasted like paste. She snapped a beige toga over me reminiscent of those used in hospitals two generations ago and read the look on my face. She brought her face to my ear as she completed dressing me. "It's far worse than the reports you've heard. Much worse for the pretty likes of you than an old crow like me." Up close, I noticed dark and fading bruises on her face and neck.

The wide, heavy door to the stone room swung open with a creak. She quickly gathered her rags, bowls, and salves. "Keep your mouth shut and you may live." She squeezed my arm and left in a hurry.

The old woman averted her eyes and gave the dark-haired man a wide berth as she left the dungeon.

The man, his long hair now washed and combed, wore a white shirt with bright blue epaulets and white sweatpants. He drank red wine from a flagon. His right eye secreted a milky discharge and when he looked at me it seemed he looked above and to the left of me. That's when I noticed the radiation burns.

He shook his head and made clucking noises with his tongue. "I told them not to bruise you too much, so they shot you." He shook his head and grinned. "You displayed bravery last night, but also stupidity. You made my most foolhardy man a cripple. I bear you no ill will, for he attacked you. It's hard to find good help these days." The remark set him off on a laughing jag and he took minutes to compose himself.

I turned away when he reached out to touch my face.

He frowned, then pressed his knuckles into my wound until I cried out in pain, seeing stars. He kept the pressure on until I passed out. The doll head returned in my dream and this time I remember what happened when the last bomb exploded. A man flew by while I clung to that tree. He screamed and reached out for me, a look of dread in his eyes, but I held fast to the trunk. The concussive blast sent him over the cliff to the rocks below. I was outside my adoptive family's compound seeing that man, an older man with whom I was having an affair. He was wealthy and everything Daniel wasn't. Guilt washed over me when I woke to find the dark-haired mutant inspecting my teeth, feeling my breasts, thighs, and ass like I was a prize hog at those obsolete county fairs forty years ago.

He unchained one of my arms. "Does it speak?" he asked.

In that moment I hated myself for cheating and not trying to save that man. Had I let him fall to his death intentionally? I was afraid.

Something else snapped in me. I decided to never be afraid again. "What the fuck kind of ugly-ass mutant are you with that drippy eye?"

The look of shock on his face didn't last long.

"It will answer direct questions with a simple 'yes' or 'no,' followed by 'my lord,'" he said. His powerful arms flipped me over, ripped the fresh toga from my body, his hands groped and pinched, and pushed me face down into the mattress. Forcing my legs apart, he raped me repeatedly. The pain was unbearable, all the while the milky secretions from his eye dripped onto my wounded shoulder. I cried into the mattress for him to stop, for someone to save me. I wish I'd been with my family when the plasma bomb killed everyone I loved. I hoped for the sweet release of death. I taunted this craven monster to kill me. I insulted him with every breath, with each of his thrusts. The more I struggled and threatened to kill him, the more it excited him.

Each endless night went like this. I spat at him. I vowed he would never break me; I told him one day I'd kill him and shit on his corpse.

The crow who patched me up each morning said I was now the property of Lord Gregori Razpudin, master of the castle and self-appointed ruler of New York City. My face spattered with fresh bruises, I spat on the floor and laughed. "No one owns me, crow."

Over the next months, Razpudin and his army withstood and turned back two attempts to overthrow the castle, during both violent firefights with other mutant armies I was certain death, or a new master lurked around the corner. If I would ever get free, I would murder him and as many of his men before they killed me. It mattered not which side won; I'd still be a prisoner, a plaything, an *it*. His men skewered the heads of the vanquished atop pikes outside the castle walls as warnings while refortifications commenced to strengthen the gates. Summer turned to fall and headed toward winter. I caught glimpses of leaves turning at the tops of trees and falling dead to the ground.

During lulls in battle, Razpudin forced me to wear black leather bondage gear and service his loyal friends. If I didn't satisfy them, he vowed to flay me alive. At times I was forced to please his enemies, which invariably resulted in their blood being splattered in my eyes when they fell forward on top of me and convulsed in their death throes. I never knew which was friend or foe, nor do I know how long this torture continued, long enough for me to forget my real name and erase all memory of my family. In feverish dreams I was Hester Payne, the conqueror and killer of men. I dimly remembered that the character in the old book committed some unforgivable sin and paid dearly for it while the men in her life suffered no immediate consequences. Hester Payne was far better than being an *it*. Whoever, whatever I used to be, no longer existed. With each passing night came the foulest of degradations … and Hester Payne grew angrier and more feral.

The oven timer dings so I put the book down and retrieve my meal while I consider the story line.

The unnamed heroine of *Bound* had birth parents who didn't want her. She was taken in by an adoptive aunt who had a son. When the aunt died, foster parents adopted her and now they're dead.

I skim over other parts while I snack, looking for possible insights into Blaze's personality that may have wormed their way into her writing. A dystopian thriller set in the year 2066, *Bound* starts near the end of World War Four, after ninety percent of the earth's population has been killed by world-wide drone strikes, plasma and radiation bombs. Many of the survivors have morphed into crazed mutants—their minds scarred by radiation bombs and their bodies burned by plasma bombs—who prowl the streets looking for victims while an unknown number of scattered survivors escaped physical harm from the bombs and hide under cover of darkness and the shadows. Unreliable news reports interrupt the final isolated sounds of war via ham radio wave operators scattered throughout the land. The puppet master behind the devastating worldwide launches that started World War Four is believed to be a thirteen-year-old Chinese computer hacker who intended to throw the planet into nuclear winter and is rumored to be living at an unknown location, deep in a fortified bunker. Her characters admit this could be the last urban legend while they spread the story by word of mouth. What used to be American society has collapsed into who can defend their fortress, who can access and control a dependable water and food supply, who has the greatest safety in numbers and the deadliest weapons. Survival of the fittest no longer exists. The mutants are marauders who pillage and kill the weak for at present they possess the most destructive weaponry; they kidnap, rape, and trade in women and weapons. The healthy US survivors are rumored to remain scattered in isolated pockets, lack sophisticated weaponry, and must forage for food and shelter; sporadic radio reports indicate at night they roam the vast wasteland of what used to be America, searching for other undamaged survivors to join their ranks, for weapons, for defendable shelter. The fortunate bands of survivors with shelter often exist inside abandoned but fortified churches or other large concrete edifices or institutions, such as libraries or government buildings constructed hundreds of years ago for stability or protection. Jewels and money can buy temporary safety and weapons from arms dealers, but only those willing to learn to fight and defend themselves will survive. If a man does not kill, he will be killed. If a woman does not kill, she will be raped, sold as property, raped again, and eventually killed.

Much of the middle section of *Bound* describes the arrivals and departures and the shattered lives of various female characters, who are all captured and forced to work either in the kitchens, stables, or as cleaners. Those who resist die horribly. More scenes of Razpudin cruelty fill the pages. A groom in the stable named Bloody Mary gradually assumes a more major role, given her physical strength and force of will demonstrated by refusing to be intimidated by the mutants and living to breathe another day. She relishes skinning and gutting freshly killed game and often enters scenes wearing a blood-soaked apron. Rumor has it she once threw a mutant from the castle roof to his death and as a result the mutants keep their distance.

With hot food in me, I put my feet up and return to the denouement scene of *Bound.*

One night, Razpudin said Commander Cooke had arrived and I was to service him. I'd been ordered to do this before. The Commander talked to himself and smelled like a fishing pier at low tide. Half of the hair on his head no longer grew due to damage from the plasma and radiation bombs, his neck and back scarred from the war, he was half-mad and often flew into rages on a whim. His huge hairy cock was so hard and spade-like I swear it could bore through concrete, for afterward I could barely walk for a day. That night, after having his way with me and living to talk about it, a drunken Cooke said he purchased me from Razpudin.

"You have a sweet honey pot. Not many can take in all of me. You have a talent, for which I paid a tidy sum. You will not be in chains inside my walls. I will be your lord and husband and as for you, consider yourself my wife and property. Continue to service me well and you will receive gifts in return. If any other man touches you, he will be boiled in oil."

The idea of being unbound and outside these four dank walls caused my heart to race.

The more Cooke drank the more his tongue wagged. He mentioned grandiose plans to rule the entire eastern seaboard. He leaned forward and said, "Play ball and you will have three hot meals a day, your own room with a bed and a closet filled with fancy clothes. What do you say, honey pot?"

The dream of partial freedom felt like a drug coursing through my veins. My inner predator came to attention when I fully grasped his initial words. "What do you need from me?"

He drunkenly whispered into my ear while he nibbled a lobe and caressed my thigh. Once in a great while he displayed a brief tender streak, unlike Razpudin. For a fleeting moment it felt as if we were equals. "Knowledge. Information that I'm sure you've been gathering since your first days as a prisoner. Like how many guards patrol at night and how much weaponry each carries? When do they change shifts and where is the wall vulnerable to a breach? I've studied the external castle layout, but you would know of any internal weaknesses. Is there an easier way inside, short of a full-frontal assault on the castle walls?"

"I might know something about that, but my life is worth more than a bed and clothes. Razpudin has spies everywhere; my crow could be one. If Razpudin found out, he'd flay me alive. In exchange for what you need, I want my freedom."

Cooke struck me so hard across the face I nearly passed out. The iron taste of blood filled my mouth.

"Stupid bitch, you should be thanking me. Have you not seen the new arrival?" A girl with raven hair, far younger and prettier than you, a recent capture from New York City. An advance patrol presented her to Razpudin the other day. I saw the look in his eyes when she entered his gates. Your days are numbered. In fact, you may have hours instead of days. That's why I negotiated to buy you, for a discount." His leer was vulpine. "You're about to be replaced. Even the likes of you should know by now that things which have outlived their usefulness in this world become worm food. He will use you as target practice for his guards and then feed you to his pigs." He fingers me and I shut my eyes. "Lucky for you, I like this honey pot. You now belong to the future ruler of the Eastern seaboard."

Paralyzed with fear, I knew there was no end in sight for me other than death. If I helped him overthrow Razpudin, I'd be a *thing* rather than an *it*.

Before he took his leave of me that night, I told him everything I knew about the patterns of the guards and the castle's lone vulnerable point. Before the war, the massive gray stone edifice had been a church for hundreds of years. A rectory, now long since abandoned, had been built alongside it with a connecting tunnel so the priests could come and go in inclement weather and engage in secret liaisons with local courtesans of both sexes. The tunnel door that led from the rectory to the church had merely been covered with drywall and could be easily breached once located. If Cooke and his men gained access to the tunnel, the only barrier between them and victory would be an ancient wooden door never guarded by Razpudin's men. He nodded, apparently satisfied by my answers. "Your crow has been ordered to prepare you for delivery to me tomorrow night at eight. That will allow my men to check your story, find the tunnel entrance, and launch the attack. After we kill Razpudin and his men, I will release you and the other women from your cells, but you will never be free. There no longer is such a thing as a free woman. If you try to escape from me, you will find yourself strapped upside down to a spiked wooden cross, your blood will be let and my hounds will tear at your flesh, fighting one another for your tender parts. Then I'd coat your leg in tar, set it on fire and wrap your wounds with bags of salt to keep you alive to endure more pain. The last honey pot who tried to escape experienced the punishment and went mad for six months before she died. Keep me happy and you keep air in your lungs and everything I promised; all else gets you the punishment and I will keep drilling that honey pot for as long as my old crow healers can keep your carcass alive."

    I didn't believe a word Cooke said. If he succeeded in killing Razpudin and took command of the castle tomorrow, he would also claim the young raven-haired beauty as his personal plaything. Why keep me? a proven traitor to my current master. That night I spread muffled words through the walls and bars of our cells to be ready, while Razpudin's sentries carried on as if tonight were just another night.

In the morning, I helped the crows with the laundry, food preparation, and cleaning. A pecking order existed among the women: I was at the top of their rank; followed by other young handmaids who mostly worked as food preparers, servers, barmaids, or in the fields and makeshift stables grooming the horses and maintaining the tack; then came the crows, some young but mostly old, with a semblance of medical knowledge or familiarity; and lastly came the old, often broken-down crows whose looks had long deserted them and lacked useful talents, used for menial tasks such as cleaning and laundry. If I read their looks correctly, they were ready, just in case.

The next night, my old crow drew me a soapy warm water bath, combed knots from my blonde hair, and administered salves to my cuts and bruises. My dinner bowl contained meat, beans, and stale bread, a welcome deviation from the pasty gruel.

Cooke and his men entered exactly as planned, a raging thunderstorm muffled the sounds of breaking through the tunnel door. All would have gone smoothly for them had I not warned Razpudin and his men. The two forces clashed in what used to be the nave of the former church; the element of surprise benefitted Cooke's army, but Razpudin's stronger firepower proved the equalizer. All the crows watched intently for hours while the battles raged; severe casualties decimated both sides. Those still breathing lay wounded on the marble floors, scattered behind columns and furniture.

    I led the handmaids, fieldhands, and crows into the nave once the sounds of battle and movement on both sides nearly ceased. I came upon Cooke first. He crawled away slowly, weaponless, his shattered legs useless and trailing blood. I turned to Bloody Mary and held out my hand. She passed me a farrier's knife from the stable where she worked while three crows flipped him over and held him down. He begged for mercy. Silently, I removed his pants and then his manhood. To silence his screams, I stuffed his member into his mouth and watched him bleed out. I nodded to the others, saying, "Kill the rest, but leave me Razpudin." Soon the thud of a hammer cracked open a skull and knives slit throats followed by gasping, choking, and gurgling sounds. Bloody Mary, all six feet and two hundred pounds of her, happened upon Razpudin's second-in-command who was getting to his feet with a katana sword. She kicked it from his hands and beheaded him with it. Chip and Chaz were not among the dead or wounded. The crows killed the other wounded, but I saw no sign of Razpudin until one of the crows that worked in the kitchen fell forward, an arrow in her back. He stood behind the fallen crow, grinning with me in the sights of his crossbow. The crows raced toward him but could not prevent his shot. A blur of movement flashed before me as the arrow sunk into flesh, but I felt no pain. I staggered from the force of Bloody Mary hurling herself in front of me. She went to one knee and grunted, "Get that fucker!" We chased him through the nave, but he escaped into the night through the front doors of the old church that had been blown outward by plasma grenades during the firefight. Bloody Mary's face had turned white when we returned, for she'd already pulled the arrow from her stomach. Her shirt soaked in blood; my old crow immediately tended to her.

The survivors in the nave numbered twenty-three women and I sent a crow to the dungeon below to free eleven more held captive in cells, including the young raven-haired beauty who was fifteen years old and in shock from Razpudin raping her that first night. The others freed were sex slaves for Razpudin's underlings. I never knew they existed until now.

The women turned my way, even supine Bloody Mary, whose abdomen was being stitched, raised herself on one elbow and looked to me.

"Listen up, women! You are no longer slaves! You are no longer handmaids, or field hands or crows! As of now, those words no longer apply to women. As of tonight, we are all free! Time is crucial. Razpudin got away. He may have a night patrol out there he's hooking up with as I speak, and with the castle doors destroyed we're vulnerable to attack, and at their mercy if they have more plasma weapons. I want the women who worked in the stables to search the castle for every working weapon. Those who labored in the kitchens, organize and pack as much non-perishable food and liquid as the horse carts can hold. I want the healers to gather every medicine, bandage, and ointment they can carry."

I turned to the raven-haired beauty. "What's your name, love?

She stood up tall and managed a confident smile. "Jet, for my hair."

"You know how to drive, Jet?"

"I had three older brothers. Hell, yes. Anything damn thing with wheels."

"Good. Come with me."

At the castle entrance I mounted Cooke's severed head on a spike and instructed the kitchen women to feed the rest of him to the pigs. I scribbled a simple message for

Razpudin which I nailed to the fallen castle door: *you're next*.

I turned to the women while they busied themselves with their assigned tasks. "God has abandoned this world. There must be something better beyond these walls. We will no longer exist in shame and degradation and pain. We will gain our freedom and fight for our rightful place in this world!"

A chorus of "Hester! Hester! Hester!" slowly built to a crescendo in the nave. As Bloody Mary raised herself from the floor to join in agreement with the others, a flaming arrow buried itself in the ruined castle door. I rushed outside but there was only darkness and a cold, stinging rain.

The odd shape of the shaft drew my attention and I pulled it from the wood. I unfolded a note wrapped around it which contained the words: *Try to leave and my army will take pliers and slowly rip every one of you apart; their blood will be on your hands.*

"Double time it, ladies. We need to leave in fifteen minutes!"

Bound ends this way, like an old dime novel, leaving the reader to wonder whether the newly freed women will escape the castle. The back pages remind the reader to buy book two in the series, Out?!?, to learn what happens next.

I understand why the English teacher voiced her concerns over the incessant violence, but I'm more interested in the parallels between fiction and life. Blaze's terrifying history of captivity at nineteen could have caused a schism in her personality, much like her unnamed female antagonist, and DID research confirms this often occurs in mid to late adolescence. Blaze's early history, even her real identity, remains shrouded to this day. Naming her protagonist a spinoff of Hawthorne's Hester Prynne intrigues me—the scarlet *A* Hester is forced to wear while the males suffer no such (immediate) consequences. Themes in *The Scarlet Letter* are shaming and social stigmatization, which don't seem to jibe with *Bound* so far, but are key issues that impact today's disaffected youth. Tapping the right vein, as Blaze put it. Hester Payne brutally kills her soon-to-be husband (of sorts) after protracted abuse and torture and now Blaze claims to have murdered her husband Sam.

My mind numb from page after page of violence and too much gin, I close the book and drift off to sleep in my recliner. My cell rings. It's Baker. "Blaze gonna enter her plea tomorrow and the judge will rule on the defense request for bail. What's it gonna be, Breezy … a surprise or a clusterfuck?"

I wipe the sleep from my eyes. "Prepare for both."

He lowers his voice. "Any word from Miranda?"

"'Night, JoJo."

OUT?!?

On my way inside the building that houses the 22nd judicial court for the state of Missouri, a phalanx of busy cops explains to the mob of fans eager to attend Blaze's arraignment that there aren't enough seats to accommodate everyone. Those denied entrance picket in a circle across the street, wave banners, and chant for Blaze's release. The costumed fans aren't allowed inside. I take a seat in the back row while her fans pack both sides of the courtroom, interspersed with heightened police presence among their ranks, in case anyone gets out of line.

Blaze enters the courtroom in shackles and prison oranges on her third day of confinement, accompanied by four bailiffs and six other prisoners to be arraigned. Her hair a touch grayer, she stands tall and erect in what I assume is meant to be a show of strength for her fans before she takes a seat on a bench with the others in chains.

Third in the queue, Blaze waives her right to have the bailiff read the charges against her. When the judge asks how she pleads she stands and answers a defiant not guilty, which creates a buzz in the courtroom, a brief flurry of contained claps and woops that the judge silences with a threat to clear the courtroom. My focus remains on Blaze, who calmly yanks out a thick hank of hair, stuffs it in her mouth, chews, and swallows it. She grins up at the judge and curtsies while a trickle of blood weaves its way down her forehead.

The judge looks to counsel.

The prosecuting attorney confers briefly with his cohort, stands, and says, "Your Honor, in light of this and other behaviors observed at the jail, we request a psychiatric evaluation of the prisoner before this case moves forward."

The judge motions for a bailiff and turns to the defense team. "May the bailiff approach the prisoner and offer her tissues?"

Two members of her team are already at her side with handkerchiefs. Blaze offers no resistance.

The judge turns back to the prosecution. "What are these *other behaviors* you alluded to, Counselor?"

The prosecutor refers to a note pad. "Observations from guards of the prisoner: talking to people not present; animated conversations with herself; slapping herself in the face; and a consensus layperson's belief that the prisoner may have a multiple personality disorder. I have a witness standing by outside the courtroom, if need be, Your Honor."

Blaze reaches up for another hank of hair, but a member of her team bats her hand away.

The judge yells, "Stop that, young lady!"

The bailiff reappears with gauze and bandages, handing them to her nearest attorney. He quits applying pressure and affixes the gauze with the bandages. Again, Blaze offers no resistance, smiling. She rocks slowly back and forth, seemingly lost in her own world.

He turns his attention to the prosecutor. "Do you have someone in mind, Counselor?"

"Dr. Mitchell Adams."

I groan and shut my eyes. Part of me wants to add to the perplexing scene and object from the back of the courtroom, but I don't. This places me in an ethical dilemma, and I begin to feel pulled apart. Since my personal run-in years ago with City Homicide, the prosecutor's office had benefitted from my Certification in Forensic Services skills and obtained several convictions. Now I wish they weren't so pleased with my work. I have an allegiance to Blaze but also want to know the truth.

"So granted, Counselor," the judge says. "I want to keep this line moving. What's your next order of business?"

The two attorneys guide Blaze back to her spot on the bench.

The prosecutor stands. "Your Honor, I'd like to remind the court that Blaze Stark confessed to the premeditated murder of her husband and has no ties or residence in the community. Given these facts and the severity of the crime, we believe she poses a flight risk, that her passport should be confiscated, and bail be denied."

The judge looks to the other side.

Her dream team of nationally known lawyers calmly and quickly ask for the moon. The lead attorney stands. "Your Honor, we request that Blaze Stark be released on her own recognizance pending the court date since she has no prior history of arrest and poses no flight risk or danger to the community. Her confession was coerced after ten hours of interrogation and sleep deprivation, without the presence of legal counsel, all while in a state of shock and grief immediately following her husband's fatal and unexpected heart attack. Since she is a well-known and respected member of the community, Ms. Stark should be released to resume her schedule of cross-country book tours vital to her livelihood."

The judge asks a few brief questions regarding her current living situation and weighs the evidence. Before he announces his decisions, both sides huddle and consult among themselves.

The judge pounds his gavel. "I will grant temporary release from custody for Ms. Stark pending her court date only if she agrees to and completes all of the following stipulations, that she: post a three-million-dollar bail; surrender her passport prior to release; and wear an electronic ankle bracelet from now until the trial. Her travel shall be restricted solely to round-trips from her hotel to the offices of the forensic examiners until the evaluations are completed."

Her legal team counters that bail be reduced and she be allowed to continue her book tour.

The gavel sounds again. "Bail is reduced to two million, but the signing tour is denied. It would make house arrest meaningless and create a logistical enforcement nightmare." He glances down to the row of prisoners, frowning. "It also does not appear to be in the current best interests of Miss Stark. I have a schedule to keep. Next case."

Most arraignments happen quickly, like ripping off a Band-Aid, but hers lasted almost thirty minutes. Once the judge rules on Blaze, her fans rise to leave and the judge calls for a swift, silent, and orderly exit.

When the crowd thins, Debbie Macklin, sans cameraman, approaches from the other side of the aisle. I acknowledge her with a nod and she says, "I apologize for my behavior outside the library that night. I know better than to treat an old friend of the station that way, especially after what you just went through."

I let the *friend of the station* remark slide while we exit the courtroom in the wake of Blaze's fans.

She turns to me as we walk. "You looked shocked when your name was mentioned. Were you?"

I look straight ahead. "No comment."

"Fair enough. You know what this means, don't you? She could be freed as early as tonight."

I nod. "I'm certain one of her attorneys has already started the ball rolling with a bonding company to put up a property bail for the two mil. She probably has already been counselled to surrender her passport and consent to the ankle bracelet."

When we exit the building, a cheer rises from across the street once word spreads of Blaze's pending release. Signs wave, horns honk, and the chant I first heard that night outside the library resumes: *A new day has come, we have risen; you cannot stop us, you cannot silence us.*

The same burly cameraman films the crowd across the street, then spots me, and walks toward us. Debbie motions for the cameraman to stay put and turns to me. "Off the record, rumor has it you've been Blaze's therapist for some time now and that she requested you."

"If you say that's the rumor, then that's the rumor. I doubt her team chose me based on the whims of their client."

"Based on what we saw in there, do you think that her plea will switch to NGRI?"

Not guilty by reason of insanity. "You're jumping way ahead. Ask her legal team. Better yet, consult a crystal ball or read tea leaves."

"C'mon, Mitch. Throw me a bone, for old time's sake."

I smile. "You want the next scoop? Post a crew here overnight to film her leaving jail. Follow the fans. The rabid ones will camp out nearby for a glimpse of her, however brief. They'll spot her first and cheer."

"Good idea." She stops walking, touches the sleeve of my coat, and moves closer. "Can I buy you a drink? For old time's sake."

I recall what happened years ago, when she was three sheets to the wind and her inhibitions were reduced. She didn't handle rejection well then. "That's not a good idea and I have work to do." I turn and walk to my car.

She calls after me. "Keep me in the loop!"

∞ ∞ ∞

Hoping to track down a ghost, I drive to the pauper's cemetery near the airport and park in the empty visitor lot. I feel time running out to solve the twin mysteries of Sam Golding's death and whether Blaze penned the three most commercially successful books ever written. I follow Gianelli's directions to the lot and plot number for Karen Jackson's grave. The marble offerings are stark: name and years of birth and death. I place a bouquet of yellow mums in a marble vase next to the headstone and take in the scene. The freshly mown and watered grass stands out from the other neglected plots over-ridden by weeds. A large assortment of brown, shriveled flowers lay scattered across the grave, I assume the remnants from Blaze's recent visit. I scan the family names of those interred around me and look on the opposite side of Karen's headstone. There, chiseled in weathered marble, I read: Dwight Jackson, 1949-2016, and Tiara Washington, 1953—. Gianelli must not have bothered with the other side of Karen's tombstone.

On my walk to the open cemetery office, I adopt a different approach than Gianelli's. The lady behind the front desk is a young, full-figured African American wearing a bright dashiki dress and a warm smile. The wooden nameplate on the front of her desk indicates her name is Shondra Jones. She looks up at me and says, "May I help you, sir?"

I return her smile. "I hope so, Miss Jones. I visited and left flowers at Karen Jackson's grave in Lot B, plot 263.

I'd like to make arrangements for the long-term upkeep of the plot."

Her smile blooms. "What a thoughtful gift! I wish we could maintain all our grounds, but we don't have the money or staff. Please give me a minute to pull up that plot." She turns to her computer and clacks the keyboard. In a few moments I see the startle reaction and when she addresses me again, something colder replaces the bloom—wariness? Suspicion?

"I'm sorry, sir, but maintenance for that plot has already been taken care of by another party. Were you a friend of the deceased?"

"No, but I work with the *other party* you speak of and have it under good authority that she may be … indisposed for a significant length of time."

Shondra hits me with a steely-eyed stare before she consults her computer. "The arrangements have been made in perpetuity. What is your name, sir?"

"Dr. Mitchell Adams."

Another glance at the screen. "You're not on the list."

I take a shot in the dark. "Like the *other party*, Alonzo Jefferson is an associate of mine and I understand his mother Tiara is not well. I recently arrived in town and would like to pay my respects to her."

My name-dropping seems to ease her mind some, for after a final glance at her screen the radiant smile returns. "I wish I could help, but you should speak with the other party or Mr. Jefferson directly. Have a nice day, sir."

It seems my shot in the dark struck something. On the walk to my Solstice, I imagine possible scenarios of the histories that Blaze and Alonzo share. They may not be lovers, but I think he's protecting more than her body.

∞ ∞ ∞

On my drive to the market for something to grill, I try to make sense of it all. Blaze is cunning and mixes truth with lies. I recall what she said after her mother died about a neighbor lady and her son. Is Karen Jackson merely a dead person who shared Blaze's birthdate, making her a convenient target for a forger to steal her identity, or is there more to her than meets the eye?

If Golding threatened to tell the world he penned the *Boundless* trilogy, that could be enough motive for Blaze. If true, he could certainly prove it, but why would he willingly relinquish his entire oeuvre to Blaze in the first place? Did she threaten to out him as a kidnapper and spousal abuser in exchange for his trilogy? Today's cancel culture would vilify him. Was it simple revenge for years of chronic abuse or for the money—to inherit billions on top of her millions? If Blaze was innocent and the cause of death was an overdose of potassium, then who injected Golding and why? Does Lamping's murder fit in somehow or was it a burglar who panicked and killed to avoid detection? The suppositions all seem possible, but instinct tells me I'm missing a bigger picture.

Late afternoon proves warmer than all of last week, the sunset a glimmering display of brilliant reds and oranges, magnificent lavenders and deep indigos. I eat a healthy dinner out on the deck—wild caught Pacific salmon with grilled veggies and a salad—and wash it down with water and a slice of orange. A mama deer guides her two fauns out of the woods to graze in the common ground. She watches me watch them.

No word from Miranda.

At ten, Channel Four runs exclusive video of Alonso driving Blaze from jail under the cloak of darkness. A contingent of fans camping out runs toward the limo and cheers. A back window powers down and Blaze, martini glass in hand, waves and blows kisses to her fans before the car leaves them in its wake. Brief, random interviews of those on the street proclaim her innocence, some accuse the police of strong-arm tactics, and a voice behind the person being interviewed labels Sam Golding a sexual predator who got what he deserved. The screen shifts to an earlier interview Debbie taped with a criminology expert from a local chapter of the ACLU who admits that while he has no firsthand knowledge of Blaze's case, his study of recent research reveals that as many as a quarter of suspects who confess to crimes are later found to be innocent for various reasons. A lot of supposition and nothing concrete. Fodder for social media.

The fall chill quickly returns to the night air once the sun sets, so I soak the dirty plates in the sink and wrap the leftovers. I put my feet up and crack open Blaze's second book, *Out?!?*, which picks up where the first ended. The glowing dedication, identical to the one in *Bound*, reads: *To my beloved Sam, through which all things are possible.*

My last instructions before our caravan exited the castle grounds were for Bloody Mary and Jet to ready the torches. While the teams of women hurried about to complete their assigned tasks, I poured what gasoline I thought we could spare throughout key rooms of the castle, specifically rooms that contained extra provisions, clothing, and weapons we had to leave behind. I tore apart Razpudin's personal quarters, looking for his gold, jewelry, and money to barter for what my army of women would need along our journey. Hidden behind a false wall I found a safe but no key and called for Bloody Mary and two others to carry it to the screamers.

Jet appeared at the front of the castle driving a screamer engine, followed by a second driven by another previous sex slave named Bones.

"How many screamers are out back?" I asked Jet.

She frowned. "Just these two. And a fresh trail of blood in the garage where the others should've been."

Damn, that means Razpudin escaped with a confederate and the other two transports. There'd been rumors that Razpudin's castle was impenetrable to siege in part because he kept another army bivouacked in the forest nearby, but we destroyed it from within in less than a night. If tales about the backup army were true, we had to leave now, put distance between us, and find and establish a defensible perimeter somewhere.

The crews filled the front trailer compartments towed by Jet's screamer with food, water, weapons, blankets, clothes, tents, and tools. The second last was filled with armed women acting as guards while the last trailer was reserved for chickens and pigs. Each screamer cab could hold up to eight women, ten in a pinch.

I took the torch from Jet and set fire to the inner rooms before we threw the other torches into the main room. Razpudin may be alive, but he won't have his castle to fall back on.

"Let's roll!" I shouted, as I climbed into the front passenger seat of the lead screamer, with the hulking Bloody Mary by my side, behind the wheel. On a side pocket of the screamer door, I found old maps of New York, the eastern seaboard, and what used to be the United States. I heard static nearby that seemed to come from the dashboard, followed by Jet's voice. Clipped to the dash was a radio. I put the headset on and said, "Jet, can you read me?"

"Loud and clear, Boss!"

Boss. I liked the sound of that.

A distant memory tugged at me. "Follow us. First stop is east."

"Come again. I thought the plan was to go west and put this hellhole behind us. Over!" Jet said.

"East first. We need travel insurance and I know where some is buried."

"What about Razpudin's safe?" Bloody Mary asked.

"There could be nothing in it," I said and pointed to the route on the map we needed to take. As our caravan of freed women set out, massive explosions rattled the very foundations of the castle and merlons fell from the top of the wall, imbedding themselves with loud *thwumps* in the soft ground. We all turned in silence to watch the destruction of our old world.

All but one.

Bloody Mary.

Bloody Mary rises above the fray and uncertainty. In a hoarse, off-key voice, she sings, "A new day has come, we have risen; you cannot stop us, you cannot silence us." One by one, Jet, my old crow, and the rest of my female warriors take up the chant; their voices grow in strength and unison in the screamer and over the radio until my ears ring.

We created and left behind those sounds of destruction. Unchained from that hellish part of my life; I face forward to the future and grin. It never felt so fucking great to be alive before now. I've been reborn from the muck, from the ooze, reincarnated as a queen, a leader of my people.

A lean female lion, most likely freed from its zoo cage when the plasma bombs rained down for the last time, followed us for miles until deciding we—and the chickens and pigs in the last compartment—weren't food she could run down. I looked at her when she gave up the chase and smiled, beating my chest. I grabbed the microphone and spoke to the women in both screamers who may have felt fear while the lion stalked us, "There's proof positive, warriors. *We* are the queens of beasts—not female lions and certainly not men!"

Chants soon filled the screamer: Hester! Hester! Hester!

The going soon became slow upon re-entering the city, given the damage the roads suffered during the bombings and the glut of disabled vehicles. Our appearance failed to interrupt the crows and ravens as they feasted on carrion in the gray light of dawn.

By the time we arrived at the site where my father had buried our valuables and life savings, the sun loomed high in the sky but remained obfuscated by the seemingly perpetual fallout from plasma bombs and detritus from other weapons of war that swirled about the atmosphere.

I grabbed a shovel from the caravan Jet drove. "Jet, you're in charge. Send our best soldiers to defend our perimeter. Give orders to kill anyone else that approaches unless it waves a white flag. I won't be long. Bloody Mary, come with me and bring your new friend."

Bloody Mary followed close behind, an ancient Prussian helmet protecting her head and a plasma machine gun clutched close to her chest. A bandolier that crisscrossed her chest held extra plasma shells for her new toy she named *Burnie*.

I turned my head slightly but did not slow the pace when we passed the crater. Images flashed back in my mind until I pieced together their meaning. The remains of people I used to know were in that hole, but that part of my life was, like my time as a sex slave in Razpudin's castle dungeon, over and buried. If I was to survive and lead these women to some sort of meaningful new life, I had to repress everything in the past and become a new person. Hester Payne was as good a name as any.

Instinct took over. A vague memory of a swing set ahead formed in my mind. A metal swing set, its red seats fused by a plasma bomb, creaked in the breeze. Like an animal following a scent, I began to dig beneath the blood red seats. Nothing.

The sound of running feet approached us from behind.

Bloody Mary raised her plasma gun, ready to fire.

Bones appeared, breathing heavy, as Mary lowered her weapon. "Hester! Jet sent me. Razpudin's on the radio! He found our frequency! He wants to talk to you!"

"Okay, go back. Tell Jet to stay on high alert and prepare the caravan to leave as soon as we return."

Bones ran back and I dug more frantically. Mary knelt and scooped up great hunks of dirt with her bare hands, apparently oblivious to the pain from her wound. At last, the shovel struck metal. I dug around the box until Mary could use her immense strength to pry it from the loosened ground. When Jet saw us sprinting, she fired up her blue screamer while Bones did the same to our white one.

"Mary, I want you and Burnie in that open car with the other fighters in case we come across Razpudin and his men. Be ready for a fire fight."

Once I climbed in front and showed Bones our route on the map, she handed me the two-way radio.

I clicked talk. "Razpudin, you back for more punishment?"

Silence on the other end, then a faint voice that cut in and out: "You stole my life's work. Return the safe unopened and intact to the castle entrance by dawn, and I let you cunts walk."

Static filled the cabin. I improvised. "That's not going to happen. Besides, there was nothing in that safe. If there ever was anything of value inside, one of your men stole it. You have a rat in your midst."

More static, and after minutes passed his voice sounded clearer, stronger. Almost in the cabin with us. "Return the safe now."

An icy hand crawled up my spine and settled there. "Go fuck yourself."

"When we find you, I will force you to watch your friends die one at a time, in unspeakable ways. Ways you can't imagine. I will force *you* to torture them. With you, I will—"

I ended the transmission and sent a question for Jet to relay to military-savvy Bloody Mary about these walkie-talkies.

Five minutes later, a sober Bloody Mary responds, "The latest walkie-talkies of the pre-war 2050's possess a wide range, over a thousand miles, but these screamers are dinosaurs compared to modern armored troop transports. Not knowing exactly when this model was built, I'd say the range of these babies could be anywhere from two to twenty-five miles, tops."

I cursed. Razpudin and his army were much closer than I hoped. We had no clue as to the size and weaponry of the second army that he kept in the woods near the castle. "That's why the signal grew stronger the more we spoke?"

"You got it, boss. He altered course to track us based on signal strength. What about any GPS tracking systems on the screamers?"

"Way ahead of you. I yanked them both out before we left the castle."

"Thanks, Mary. You're worth your weight in gold. How's your wound?"

Her laughter filled my ear. "Wound? I don't have any fucking wound!"

"Radio silence for now, everyone. Only break it if attack is imminent or you spot hostiles. Jet, follow us. No questions asked. Trust me, over!"

"Roger that. We follow you to the end!"

The radios off, I charted a course for Bones to guide us due south rather than west, the direction Razpudin expects us to head. North would have been the most unexpected but also riskiest, as there'd been rumors of nuclear winter fallout spreading south down from the 45th North American parallel. I estimated the screamers had at least another three hundred miles of gas in their tanks before we'd have to refill them. Hopefully, we'll find safe lodging before then for the night—to refuel, eat, and gain much needed sleep.

The adrenaline spent surviving the bloody battle and our hasty escape began to catch up with me. "Bones, tell me when you need a break from driving. Gonna shut my eyes for a moment."

I drifted off to an uneven, restless sleep and Razpudin's face loomed before me. His words echoed in my mind: *You stole my life's work.* In my mind I saw his army trap us between a vast, flat expanse of open plains and a massive wall I'd never seen before. They obliterated us before we could scale the wall (in the dream I had a vague sense that freedom lay on the other side), but at least we died fighting. Razpudin ran me through with a sword and grinned while the light left my eyes. The overriding feeling in the dream was dread: who am I kidding? I bought us a day of freedom, maybe two at most. What horrors am I leading my sisters into?

Back date the tale from 2057 to current time, replace Hester Prynne with Blaze and Razpudin with Sam. Sam kidnaps, tortures, then makes Blaze his property via marriage. Blaze admits to disassociation (creating multiple personalities in her head) as a primitive way to cope with Sam's abuse. Blaze eventually escapes from Sam's control and absconds with his fortune (an oblique reference to stealing his life's work). Sam vows to regain his fortune and kill Blaze. Blaze responds with similar fury.

The subject matter and protagonists point to the true author more likely being female, but I have no proof this is true. Ted Lamping himself suspected his friend Sam may have penned the trilogy, but his spastic little fixer Gianelli is drawing a blank on finding proof of that, too.

My mind wanders to the ghost that is Karen Jackson and how Alonso Jefferson, his mother Tiara Washington, Dwight Jackson, and Blaze fit into the puzzle.

It takes hours of digging, computer searches, and calling in a favor from a friend, but I discover a past link between Dwight Jackson and Tiara Washington. From there I think I can sort out some of the name confusion.

∞ ∞ ∞

I wake to incessant barking, Blaze's book face-down and open on my stomach, and I reach for the cell. Midnight. A three-hour nap. Since Miranda and Barney left, sleep's been sporadic.

Miranda on caller ID.

I fumble for the phone and say: *Hi*. I rub sleep from my eyes, instantly awake.

"Hi. Did I wake you?"

"No. Not at all."

"You sound sleepy. I think I did. I'm sorry." Her voice tentative, she adds, "Can I come over?"

I stand and start to tidy up the messy living room. "Sure."

"Thanks." Her voice sounds shaky or slightly out of breath. "I'll be there in fifteen."

She hangs up before I can ask what's wrong. Our stunted calls continue to be maddening.

I tuck my shirt in and put the plates and silverware in the dishwasher when the front bell rings.

Miranda stands at the door in running gear and our eyes meet. There's no Barney, no Prius. She stands awkwardly in the foyer, hands crossed in front of her as if she doesn't know what to do with them.

I invite her in. "Did you run here?"

She nods. Her eyes red from crying, she says, "Timmy died today."

"Miranda, I'm so sorry." I take a step toward her, and she walks to the sofa and sits. She grabs tissues from the table and blows her red nose.

I slide the tissue box closer to her and sit on the other end of the sofa. "I know you cared a lot for Tim and his family. It takes a special type of person to do a tough job as well as you do." I ask my standard question on past occasions after a client dies on her watch. "You want to talk about it?"

She bites her lower lip, a nervous habit. "That's not why I'm here." She looks at the tissues in her hand before she looks to me. A big exhale. "Boy, this is tough. I can't deal with this anymore. The rape in college. My kidnapping last year. The flashbacks. Before we met, a client almost killed you and a year later that politician's bodyguard shot you. Excluding the rape, the other incidents are all related to your job and now there's Blaze. She's been released and you're going to perform a psych eval on her. It's starting all over again. I feel it in my bones."

"This is what I do—"

"I know, I know." More tears. "I don't expect you to quit your job and I'm not asking you to. I've been slowly falling apart since the rape and later the kidnapping, the flashbacks, lack of sleep, and the anxiety. I still see the faces of the rapists in that van at night. Other nights, it's Danny I see."

We've talked about this before. "What are you not telling me, Miranda?"

Another look to her lap, a dab at her eyes. "I love you, but I can't be with you anymore. I started seeing someone else. I wasn't looking, it just happened. We met by accident. He's an accountant, works a safe 9-to-5 job. Please don't hate me. The flashbacks aren't as bad when I'm with him."

More nose blowing. "Before you ask, I have an appointment with a new female therapist tomorrow." She stands and paces. "My heart is breaking. Please say something."

I stand, the length of the sofa between us feels like a football field. The news of another man comes from out of the blue and slaps me in the face. I feel flushed and my mouth dries up. I wonder when she began seeing him and I have a hundred other questions that seem pointless to ask now. "We agreed to be exclusive last year. You made this decision—"

"Out of self-preservation, which makes me feel even more selfish."

I swallow my pride and feel a lump form in my throat. I know she's under a ton of stress, but I still feel betrayed. "But you made the decision to sleep with someone else without telling me."

She averts her eyes to the door then back to me.

"I wish I could undo all that's happened, Miranda, but no one can." Every fiber of my body wants to go to her, but I stay put and say, "I know it's not enough, but for what it's worth, I love you, too. I'm going to miss you like hell."

She opens the door and turns to face me. Pausing, she takes a tentative step forward, then stops. "Just so you know, I met him after we were last together. I'm sorry I …"

With that, she turns and runs down the sidewalk, leaving the front door open. I go to close it and watch her run down the cul-de-sac and turn onto the main street in the small, unincorporated subdivision. The last thing I see of Miranda is her blond ponytail bounce left to right from the back of her ballcap while she passes beneath a streetlight. The next instant the night swallows her and she's gone.

I feel hollow inside.

This is uncharted territory for me—in college, through Ph.D. school, and for the years spent building and nourishing my private practice—I'd always been the ender of relationships when a woman broached commitment. I'd never fallen in love before I met Kristin about four years ago, and the circumstances around her murder threatened not only to derail me but kill me. Miranda, the second love of my life, followed a year or so later and now she's gone.

One love dead.

One love ran off with another man and I already miss her and her dog.

The woman who wants to see me is fresh out of jail and may be a crazy murderess.

My life, now a country song.

A FIGHT AND INK BLOTS

An hour before her court-ordered appointment, the construction crew removes the last of their power tools and tarps from the H-shaped suite of rooms in my private practice, then cleans and vacuums up every trace of their presence. The specialists did a superb job, the foreman walks me through the features; the area behind my desk appears no different from before. I sign off on the hefty final invoice for the work. In debt for the first time in years, this will take sixty months to pay off.

For today, I hire a temporary secretary who I know is reliable and position her at the front desk. I give Emily one very specific instruction in addition to answering the phone.

From my slightly ajar office door, I watch Blaze, dressed in the same shades, scarf, and coat from the first night we met, enter the front office on time. She appears surprised to see Emily behind the desk near the front door and initiates a conversation I can't hear from my vantage point. Emily excuses herself with a smile and buzzes me to say my appointment is here.

I greet Blaze. "Welcome back. How does it feel to be released?"

Her face lights up and maybe for the first time, the true physical beauty of her shines through. "Wonderful. I missed the little things: a hand mirror; a hair dryer; my morning espresso; and of course, my freedom."

"Quite different from the last time we met," I say.

She nods. "That tiny room smelled of mold and desperation, but it was good to see you."

No mention of the attack. "Did Alonso drive you here today?"

A nod. "He's in the waiting room, reading a football magazine, and will return me directly to my suite when we're done. I will comply fully with the court order."

"Good to know," I say and escort her to a larger office usually reserved for staff or family meetings. She removes her shades, sable coat, and scarf, revealing a black cashmere sweater and designer jeans. She hikes up one leg of her jeans to reveal the black GPS monitoring system strapped to her ankle. I notice the flesh-colored square bandage near the natural part in her hair.

I offer her a seat facing the floor-to-ceiling windows with a view of downtown Clayton and say, "Before we get started, you need to know and remember this important reality. The people who want to put you away for murder, the prosecution, have requested me to perform an evaluation of your mental state and personality. This alters our prior arrangement of client/doctor confidentiality as of now. Until the evaluation is complete, I am duty bound to report your behaviors and any relevant words you say about the events leading up to and including Sam's death in my assessment to the prosecution."

Blaze folds her hands in her lap. "I understand."

"I heard from Detective Baker, his boss, and others at the jail that they observed your other personalities, but that you would speak only with me—"

"I never said that," she says, looking stunned. "Cops lie."

"Do you remember what you did in court?"

"I stood up and told the truth. I'm innocent."

I point to her head. "You don't remember ripping a hunk of your hair out and eating it in front of the judge? You curtsied and smiled at him."

She looks aghast. "I most certainly did not! I don't know where you get your information, but it's wrong. A female guard was jealous of me and pulled it out, the cow!"

She notices the two pencils and bottle of water on the table.

I remain standing, an MMPI-2 booklet in hand. "Today, I have a series of questions I want you to answer either true or false, as each question applies to you. There are 567 true/false statements; please make certain to answer every question. This will take between 60-90 minutes. When you complete the questions, please notify Emily at the front desk and I will return."

"I thought we were going to sit down and talk, like we usually do." Her eyes narrow when she looks up at me. "You're trying to get inside my head with all these questions, to see if I'm nuts, aren't you?"

"There are no right or wrong answers. As I said, answer each one as it applies to you, either true or false. I'm currently talking with Blaze, right? Not Sarah, Desiree, Boo, or Midnight Man."

She frowns. "This is me, Blaze. Please close the door when you leave. I can't have other patients see me here."

There's a reason I positioned Emily facing the group room Blaze occupies.

"That won't be necessary. No other clients are scheduled during our time today."

"What about drop-ins? I was one, once. Or emergencies? What if your secretary tells all her friends I'm here?"

"None of that will happen. The outer door is locked so there will be no interruptions. Take your time on the questions and answer truthfully."

She turns and briefly frowns at Emily who smiles reassuringly at her before she reluctantly opens the booklet and grabs a pencil.

I walk toward my office in the H-shape group of rooms but pass it for the waiting room. I remind Emily to text "!" in my phone when Blaze completes the questions or makes a move for the waiting room.

∞   ∞   ∞

Alonso looks surprised to see me sit across from him in the waiting room and places the magazine on the seat next to him.

I take a deep breath and let it out. This plan could blow up in my face. I lean forward and make eye contact with him. "Blaze just began a written test that will take about an hour. I know you care about her. I know you want what is best for her. I also know you two have a history together …" I lower my voice. "Beyond that of bodyguard and employer."

His weight shifts in the tiny chair; he leans back and his hands ball into fists. For an instant I think he's about to hit me. "What are you insinuating?"

I stand and remove my sport coat and hang it across a chair back. "Remember when I said I'd fight you for my Dictaphone?"

The look on his face tells me he's growing more perturbed. "Sure do. I believe I asked if you had a death wish."

"Stand up, Big Man," I tell him, adding a healthy dose of derision and cockiness to my voice. "You had a cup of coffee in the NFL until you blew out your knee, right? You outweigh me by at least sixty pounds, right?"

He stands, towering over me, and removes his suit coat. "Yeah, so what?"

"If I beat you, you answer my questions truthfully, most of which will only confirm what I already know about you and Blaze. Agree?"

He chuckles but I sense a trace of uncertainty in his laugh. "That won't happen. What do I get when I beat you?"

I smile up at him. "What do you want, Big Man? Name your price."

He returns my smile with a broader one of his own. "You must have a death wish." He thinks for a moment. "Okay, I don't need money, but I like your ride. When I beat you, you sign the title of your car over to me."

"Agreed." We shake on it.

His smile becomes a grin from ear to ear. "Man, this is the easiest bet I've ever won. You can throw the first punch."

He walks up close to me. I grab his hands in mine, force his hands close together, lower my center of gravity, and start to push him back toward the wall behind him. The element of surprise with me, I say, "First one to push the other against the wall behind them wins."

I go even lower and push him backward. His anger and height advantage work against him and I continue my forward momentum. As we near his wall, his immense strength stops me as he struggles to go lower than my center of gravity, but I don't allow it, nor do I let him spread his hands and overpower me with his massive upper body strength. We're both grunting, my hands start to feel crushed by his larger, stronger ones and I know that the longer this goes on he will win, so I go even lower and pump my legs like pistons, pushing with all my might until his back touches the wall.

I let go. My hands aching, my shirt soaked through.

"You tricked me!"

It takes a moment before I can talk, my breathing is that labored. I put an arm around his shoulder in a show of friendship, but also to support myself. "I had to. If we traded punches, I'd be laid out on the carpet in three seconds. Alonso, you are some kind of strong, but a deal's a deal."

I reach over the back of a chair and toss him a towel and bottle of water, then take one of each for myself.

He grins. "I wondered what those were doing in an empty waiting room."

Grateful I still own my car; I wipe my forehead with a towel and take a sip of water before I sit across from him again. "I know you and Blaze go way, way back, and I also know you're not lovers. I made the false insinuation to throw you off your game."

He tucks in his white dress shirt. "It worked."

"You and Blaze do share a love … more like that of brother and sister or, more accurately, of brother and adopted neighbor taken in by your kind mother Tiara after Blaze's mother overdosed. How old were the two of you when Blaze's mother died?"

His eyes goggle. "How do you know—did Blaze tell you this?"

"She told me bits and pieces. The rest I will share after you answer my questions."

He rubs a broad hand across his face and thinks a moment. "I was probably fourteen. She was eleven, maybe twelve."

"Blaze said her birth mother was a prostitute and her father one of her johns, is that true?"

He nods.

"And that her mother was a difficult person to live with, wasn't she?"

A scowl appears and he shifts his weight in the chair. "More like a walking timebomb. She once tried to seduce me when I was maybe twelve. I never told Tiara, never breathed it to a soul until I told Blaze one night, years after her mom was in the ground."

Here's where I take a clinical leap of faith.

"How long did her mom offer Blaze to select johns?"

His eyes grow large as saucers until sadness replaces the shock. "The last year before her mom died. We didn't learn this until years later. Tiara told Blaze she could stay with us whenever Sonya—Blaze's birth mother—was high or *entertaining*, as she put it. Tiara tried to help Sonya get clean for years, but she'd always return to the lifestyle. Sonya Sparrow had no interest in an honest day's work for an honest day's pay. It was all about fast, easy money, with her. No matter what effect it had on her or Blaze. Sonya would talk to people that weren't there. One moment she'd fly off into a rage, then talk like a little girl. I saw her cut her wrist and arms a few times. Didn't draw much blood, but it felt spooky to watch an adult do that to themselves when you're a little kid."

"That's in part why you're so protective of and concerned for Blaze, isn't it? You two are like brother and sister, and you worry now that she's showing the same symptoms as her mom."

Another head nod and we lapse into a moment of silence.

"Sonya Sparrow?"

Alonso nods again. "She told us it was her stage name, though I don't think she ever acted anywhere, unless it was for her johns. She always went by it. We never knew her real name, even after she died."

"The acting may have been a coping mechanism in response to hooking." I glance at my phone on the nearby seat. Nothing. *Time for another leap of faith.*

"I know about the pauper's graveyard near the airport. I left flowers at the same headstone Blaze did when you both flew into town. It certainly stands out from the others." I pause for a beat. "I also saw the names on the opposite side of the marker."

I notice him tense ever so slightly. He says nothing.

"Records show Dwight was Karen Jackson's father from a prior union, and years later he married your mother Tiara, but they were together only a few years until he died. Tiara gave birth to you when she was quite young."

Alonso stiffens. "Never knew him. Mama T raised me as a single parent, worked two jobs, and made me walk the straight and narrow. She's the strongest, kindest person I know."

"I assume it's why she and you retain her maiden name."

He nods a third time.

"Blaze pays for the upkeep of Karen Jackson's grave, but not Dwight's. Blaze admits she went to great lengths to assume Karen's identity. She tells me for all intents and purposes, she *is* Karen Jackson, Blaze Stark is her nom de plume, and that no one will ever know her real identity. Blaze didn't ghost her identity for the usual reasons—the real Karen Jackson had no Social Security or Medicare pension to cash, no property to acquire. The real Karen Jackson didn't work and never filed a tax return, so for all practical purposes the government doesn't know the dead Karen Jackson ever existed."

I never thought it possible, but Alonso's great bulk shrinks in the chair and a look of dread crosses his face. He knows I know.

My hunch was right, so I continue. "Blaze went to all this trouble for a reason. The Karen Jackson lying in that pauper's graveyard was the real author of the *Boundless* trilogy."

I stare and wait him out, hoping he talks.

He leans back, seemingly lost in thought. "Karen had a brilliant mind, but she developed severe agoraphobia and social anxiety disorder. She barely graduated high school and *never* ventured outside afterwards. I give Dwight some credit, even though he was an alcoholic at the time—he owned a run-down duplex in the worst section of the near North City, let her live in one half, brought her groceries, and checked in on her semi-regularly. Karen never watched television. She read every kind of book Dwight could get his hands on—non-fiction; memoirs; adventure stories; suspense; mystery; westerns; romance; young adult; religious; cheesy dime novels; even comic books. Name a genre, she read it.

"She never saw a doctor, being a shut-in and all, and by the time Dwight learned she was sick, it was too late. The funeral service took place in Mama T's church, and their situation touched her so deeply that she took Dwight under her wing, cleaned him up, and he accompanied her to church every Sunday. After six months or so, they began dating."

"Karen did more than read books. She put pen to paper."

He wrings his hands and hesitates. "When Mama T offered to help clean out Karen's side of the duplex, I accompanied her. Dwight organized a yard sale for Karen's clothes, all her books, and other personal items. He sold her bed and dresser. All the money went to the funeral home to offset the cost of her burial and Mama T started a Go Fund Me account in Karen's name." He pauses to laugh. "I remember seeing stacks of milk crate boxes stuffed with papers and folders and composition books on the front lawn. It was beginning to rain when somebody offered to buy the milk crates for a dollar if we'd throw away the papers, but we ran out of trash bags, so the deal was off. The milk crates and the papers were the only items that didn't sell. A tired Mama T grumbled about the lost dollar while I loaded the boxes in her station wagon. She told me to throw the crates in the Dumpster when we got home, but I thought I could use them in my room. I was saving money to buy a stereo and planned to use the crates as shelving—"

"And Blaze was living with you at the time."

Another nod. "She bought Karen's books on writing for a nickel each at the yard sale and helped carry the milk crates up to my room. One night I found her engrossed in her room with the papers, the files from the boxes scattered all over the floor, the bed, everywhere. She did this for weeks and when I asked what she seemed so excited about she always said: *nothing*. I have no idea whether Blaze altered the words on those pages. It was years later when I realized that anyone could have purchased the future best-selling trilogy of all-time at a yard sale on the near North side of the city for a buck. Talk about your return on investment."

"How old were you and Blaze when Karen died?"

He looks at the ceiling, thinking. "I was nineteen and Blaze was probably seventeen, maybe eighteen."

The real author was quite young and died before she had a chance to reap the rewards of her efforts. "When did Blaze leave Mama T's home?"

"At nineteen. She became consumed with writing after she bought those books from the yard sale for Karen. She announced she was going to be a famous writer. I didn't believe her, but Mama T encouraged her interest. She saved her money and, on her birthday flew to a writer's workshop in New York. We never heard from her until years later, about a week after she married Sam Golding. On her first trip back home, she hired me as her personal driver and made peace with Mama T for being gone all that time without a word." He chuckles. "*That* last part took some doing!"

"Did she mention where she'd been living all that time? Who she was with?"

He shakes his head. "She was tight-lipped about it, even with Mama T. She told us she was deliriously happy because she signed a three-book deal with a major publisher and met, fell in love with, and married this wealthy man. I had no idea until later exactly how rich this older man was. Mama T. pressed her hard for more info, but she held fast. I thought: she'll tell me what she did all those years once we were alone, but she never did."

He wrings his hands. "Will you go to the police about the identity theft? Will you tell the world about *Boundless*? She'll be devastated."

"She's on trial for murder, that's her most pressing hurdle. My job is to determine whether she's competent to stand trial and assess her mental health—"

"I think she's schizophrenic—"

The public often conflates schizophrenia with DID. "I've observed the symptoms, but it's not schizophrenia. When did you first notice her behaving this way?"

He pauses to think. "A month or two before she started this book tour."

"Never before?"

He shakes his head.

My phone dings. "*!*" appears on my screen and a light bulb turns on in my head

"Thanks, Alonso. This helps."

I stand and walk to the office door. "I know you care. I can't prevent you from telling Blaze we spoke, but in my opinion it's in her best clinical interests if you don't."

∞ ∞ ∞

I return to the office via the client privacy exit door, so it appears like I'm joining them in the front room from the direction of my office. Blaze stands at Emily's desk, clearly agitated, while Emily, a veteran of similar standoffs, displays the epitome of restraint.

Blaze doesn't hear me approach from behind while she dresses down Emily. "I completed his stupid test. Where is he? Is he here? I demand to see him now!"

"Here I am, Blaze. Will you follow me, please?" I turn to Emily and thank her.

"Where were you?"

"Working. I didn't need to stare at you while you complete a written test."

"So many repetitive questions, weird ones too. I have no idea what you expect to get from that waste of time."

You'd be surprised.

I offer her a seat across from my desk. "Next I'm going to show you some pictures. A series of ten inkblots."

"I've heard of those! The Rorschach test, right?"

"That's correct. One picture at a time, I want you to tell me what you see." I show her Inkblot One.

She studies it, then turns it ninety degrees and frowns, before she rights it. "This first way, I see an angel with outstretched wings, but on its side, it looks like a military ship cutting through the water. I don't like it from that angle."

Most responders to this projective test think the first blot is easy. They often see a bat, a butterfly, or a moth, possibly a mask or a hollowed pumpkin with a light on inside.

Most people see the second blot as two humans or two four-legged animals—often dogs, elephants, or bears. When she considers this, she says, "The two main figures are bears fighting and there's blood everywhere."

I ask her to point to the bears, which she does.

"Do you see anything else?"

"Sure. It's obvious, there's a vagina between them. That's where all the blood is coming from."

In the third blot, most people see two human figures engaged in an activity. Blaze reports she sees: *Two women fighting over a basket while a butterfly floats between them.*

"Do you see anything else in the blot?"

"The women could be chickens … now their breasts look like wings, but they're still fighting over the basket. They might also have penises." She points to where she sees them.

Most people see an animal hide, a giant, a gorilla, or a man in a big coat in the fourth image. Some see a dragon with big feet coming towards them. Blaze says, "I see a horned dragon with big feet and a huge penis. The penis has teeth on its end." She points out the areas to me. This fourth card is the "father card."

The fifth blot is by far the easiest for people to interpret. Most see a bat, a swallow, or a butterfly. Blaze studies it, turns in her hands several times and says, "I see two animals—rams—butting their heads together in a fight to the death."

"Do you see anything else?"

She grins and locks eyes with me. "I'm not sure, but I think this one is male, and the other is female. The female is winning." She winks.

The sixth image garners the most sexual responses from people and elicits a variety of responses from Blaze. "Right side up, it's obviously female genitalia, there's the labia, the clitoris, and hair, with a penis about to enter it from above." She rotates it ninety degrees and says, "Here, it's a

U-boat on calm water with its mirror image below." Rotating the blot another ninety degrees, she says, "Now it's an animal hide hanging from a wall."

Blaze studies the next card and says, "Two skinny women, worlds apart, locked in a fight to the death." She rotates it and adds, "That's it, that's all I see." Blot seven is the "mother card."

Most viewers see a pair of four-legged animals on the sides of the eighth blot and some see a dragon or butterfly in the middle of the design. Blaze says, "I see a fire-breathing dragon flying over twin peaks, coming for me." She turns the card 90 degrees. "Now I see a hyena standing on a rock, her image reflected in a pool there." Then she turns it 180 degrees and adds, "Now, it's a grinning Jack-o-lantern with teeth."

In the ninth card, Blaze points to the middle and lower sections and says, "That's a rocket blasting off with the flames below."

"Do you see anything else?"

She pauses and points to the top of the blot. "Those are two men fighting, or maybe they're monsters about to lock horns." She doesn't turn this card.

In the final card, Blaze mentions and points to all the depicted images of creatures such as blue crabs, gray crabs and shrimp, orange caterpillars, red sea cucumbers, and brown mice.

"Do all those creatures together mean anything to you?"

She pauses to consider the question. "Nope. They're just there; living their short little lives until they die. Are we done here?"

"With the ink blots, yes.

"So, do they tell you I'm crazy as a loon or sober as a preacher?"

"I interpret them later. Thanks for your answers.

"Remembering that I must include in my report to the prosecution anything you tell me about your actions and the events leading up to, during, and after Sam's death, how do you reconcile telling me that night in your suite that you killed Sam by lacing his drinks with anti-freeze?"

She looks puzzled. "I never said that."

I refer briefly to my notes. "That was Sarah, the nineteen-year-old in you."

"She's mistaken. The only thing I ever put in Sam's drinks was ice."

"Do you communicate with Sarah and Boo often?"

"There's no pattern to it as I can tell. I think things happen and time goes by while the three of us aren't present.

I don't know if that's when Midnight Man takes control or not. As I said, there can be lengthy periods when I—we—black out. Sometimes for days at a time. I blacked out when Judith was killed, when I came to, it was just the five of us; the same thing happened with Laurie, I came to, and we were down to four."

My phone vibrates but I ignore it.

Her head drops to her chest. When she raises it, the sultry grin takes me in.

"Hello, handsome."

"Hi, Desiree. How are you?"

Her eyes widen. "You've been talking to the others. Who blabbed my name? It was Sarah, wasn't it? She never could keep her trap shut."

"How long have you known Blaze, Sarah, Boo, and Midnight Man?"

She absentmindedly twirls an end of her hair and takes in the office as if for the first time. "Must we always talk shop? How about a compliment from you today on how I look?"

"How long, Desiree?"

She rolls her eyes. "It seems like forever. Since I was eleven, twelve maybe."

"What happened when you were that age?"

She grimaces and shifts in the chair. "I don't want to talk about it."

I try to draw her out with other questions, but she dodges answering them. Then her head lowers and Blaze returns. She reports the same rough time frame for the emergence of the other personalities and refuses to talk about what triggered them. She shuts down and I notice her anxiety level rise.

"We've completed the tests for today. The only other question I have for you today is when did you last see your publisher Ted Lamping?"

She looks away briefly then back at me. "At the signing. When he refused to give me Sam's phone. That was rude. It still hasn't been returned to me."

"Are you aware someone murdered Ted the day after your husband died?"

The cell phone in my pocket vibrates a second and third time. I ignore it.

She huffs. "You suspect me? The killer is probably an angry husband or boyfriend of one of the female writers he coerced to sleep with him in exchange for the promise of a book contract. Your friend, that mountain of a detective, should start his search there."

"Where were you the morning Ted was killed?"

Her eyes narrow. "In bed at my suite, asleep, and no one else was with me. I usually don't rise before noon and that morning was no different."

Is there anything else you want to discuss before we end for the day?"

She folds her arms across her chest. "Only that I'm innocent. I confessed to stop the interrogation and use the ladies' room. They wanted to know how I killed him, and the first thing that came to mind was anti-freeze. I'd do it again to get out of that room after being stuck there half a day."

I walk Blaze to the waiting room and make brief eye contact with Alonso. He nods and they leave together.

I listen to my messages, all from Baker.

"Where you at?" Sounding frustrated.

"Damn it, Breezy. Answer your damn phone!" Pissed off.

"Big news. Get your ass to interrogation room one ASAP. I'll tell the desk sergeant to let you through." Calmer, resigned. Dead serious.

REVELATIONS AND STORIES

On the drive east, I return his calls and get voice mail. "I'm on my way."

At least the protestors have dispersed and downtown seems much quieter than normal, almost tranquil.

My visitor badge around my neck, I meet Baker and his boss in the adjacent room next to interrogation room one, where a small, slender black man squirms nervously on a chair in the tiny room. He looks fiftyish, maybe a hundred and thirty pounds, with a closely cropped afro and prominent vitiligo on his face and neck. Coughing into the sleeve of his sweatshirt frequently, his eyes shift about the room, but he purposely avoids the one-way mirror, behind which we stand watching. He's alone, the thermostat purposely set in the small interview room at 82 degrees, for him to stew in his own juices.

Lt. Harris takes the lead. "You're looking at Jamal Jones, 59. A few minor priors for minor peace disturbance, writing bad checks, selling small amounts of marijuana, driving with a suspended license, and some parking tickets. Did a few overnight stays. No known history of violence. Detective Baker has been working the case almost non-stop, interviewing hotel staff and visitors, studying CCTV tape to eliminate potential suspects one-by-one. His initial process of elimination could not rule out Mr. Jones. In fact, it later implicated him once physical evidence was gathered at the scene. Detective Baker's initial interview of the suspect led to probable cause to obtain a search warrant of Mr. Jones' house, which led to his confession not only to the murder of Ted Lamping but also his involvement in the death of Sam Golding. The detective suggested your presence here during the interrogation. For a different set of experienced eyes."

There's no need to hide the surprise on my face and I turn to Baker. "I can't wait to hear this."

"Take it from here, Detective," Harris says.

The toothpick shifts in Baker's mouth before he begins. "Mr. Jamal Jones, or JJ as he's known on the streets, ironically lives on Hebert Street, about five doors down from Lakeesha Washington. I know that name rings a bell for you."

A flood of memories rushes back. Her son Lonnie was imprisoned for his role in counterfeiting 25 million dollars. What he did with his share of the perfect reproductions of hundred-dollar bills has probably never been done in the annals of criminal history. A brilliant, talented, and sensitive man with a severe club foot, Lonnie was murdered in prison. To this day, some of his artwork hangs in my townhouse. I'll never forget him.

"It does."

Baker continues. "CCTV shows Mr. Jones in the lobby the morning Lamping was murdered. He appears in a heightened state of activity. He doesn't work in the hotel, nor is he a guest. The tape shows Ted Lamping enter the lobby from the street and walk to the elevators at 8:02 in the morning. Jamal notices him and ten minutes later, when his concierge friend has his back turned helping guests, grabs a brown package off the desk and walks to the same bank of elevators. CCTV shows Jamal exit the elevator on Mr. Lamping's floor and walk in the direction of his suite. Forty-five minutes later, Jamal re-appears in the lobby. He's acting calm, no one remembers seeing blood on his clothes or any unusual behavior. While the lab crew gathers crime scene evidence for analysis, I review prior tapes of the lobby the previous week for patterns—Jamal appears in every morning tape when his concierge friend works, and they chat when the concierge has free time. In my opinion Mr. Jones seems to be casing the guests. I discussed this with hotel security, and they understood my concern. They spoke with the concierge, a long-time employee with a spotless work history and clean record, who vouched for his friend.

"Then the lab results come in, and I paid a visit to Jamal's house with a patrolman. The little dude was as nervous as he is now but invited us in and cooperated fully after I gave him the search warrant. He remained seated with the officer in the kitchen, coughing up a storm like he is now, while I conducted the search." He turns toward the mirror. "He looks ready. I'm going in."

Jamal's head instantly swivels to Baker's looming presence when he enters. A knee bounces faster under the table while Baker sits across from him at the table. His eyes never leave Baker.

"Jamal Jones, you've been read your rights already, but I'll repeat them. You have the right to remain silent. Anything you say can and will be used against you in a court of law. You have the right to an attorney. If you cannot afford an attorney, one will be provided for you. Do you understand this, Mr. Jones?"

He nods and is wracked by another coughing jag that rattles deep in his lungs. He wipes his mouth on a sleeve. "Sure. I watch television. I know the drill. I don't need one. Won't do any good."

The toothpick dances again to the other side of Baker's mouth. He places an evidence bag on the table between them. "When I searched your house earlier today, I found this wallet hidden beneath your underwear in a dresser. It belongs to a Theodore Lamping, now deceased, a recent visitor to our fair city. Inside are his ID, credit cards, but no cash. Your fingerprints are all over it. How did you come to be in possession of this wallet, Mr. Jones?"

A coughing fit doubles him over and this time I notice a trace of blood on his sleeve after he wipes his mouth.

"Simple. I robbed him inside his room at the Chase."

Baker's eyebrows rise briefly, and he glances at the mirror. "What day did you rob Mr. Lamping and was it in the morning, afternoon, or evening?"

Jamal rattles off the correct date and says, "About mid-morning."

"How did you choose Mr. Lamping and enter his hotel suite?"

Another coughing fit almost lifts him from the chair. "I spend time in the lobby and noticed the expensive clothes and the limo. He was big, but out of shape and slow-moving. He waddled when he walked, so I thought he'd be an easy fish. He was always alone when he came and went."

"How did you gain entrance to Mr. Lamping's suite, Mr. Jones?"

He puts a fist to his mouth as if he's about to be sick until he regains control. "I knocked on the door. Said a package had come for him."

"Do you know anything about a platinum Rolex Mr. Lamping may have had?"

"I pawned it and drove to the boat. I lost that money and all the cash in the wallet." The *boat* is local shorthand for casino, since the first area ones technically had to be on a body of water. He provides the name of the pawn shop before he succumbs to another coughing jag.

He turns away from Baker, toward the mirror and it looks like he may vomit but doesn't.

"So, you cased potential victims from the lobby?"

He shrugs and says, matter-of-factly, "I guess so, if you want to call it that."

Baker points to the evidence bag. "That wallet also contains something else on it besides your prints, blood. How do you explain the blood on the wallet, Mr. Jones?"

More coughing. His face contorts in pain, and he places a hand on his stomach.

He looks to the ceiling. "I have a gambling addiction. I need money. I saw the wallet on a table by the door and took it. We struggled and hit each other. He didn't want me to escape, so he pulled me into the kitchen, and started to call hotel security. He was stronger than he looked, but I had to stop him. I grabbed a knife on the kitchen counter and told him to put the phone down, but he didn't." He pauses and appears ready to break into tears. "He wasn't going to let me go. I attacked and cut him. He resisted. I had to keep stabbing him to get away."

"Approximately how many times did you stab Mr. Lamping and where were his wounds?"

More coughing. Now he's crying. "Enough for my arm to get tired."

"Where were his wounds, Mr. Jones?"

He wipes tears onto the bloody sleeve. "His hands and arms. He lost his balance but kept coming for me. I cut his hamstrings to disable him. He kept calling me a dickless nigger and I flew into a rage. I'm not proud of it, but I stabbed him in the dick." He pauses, as if reliving the scene. "There was so much blood."

Baker makes a face while Jamal hacks mucus from his lungs. "We also found a meat cleaver in your kitchen. The same brand the hotel provides in all the suites. A cleaver was missing from Mr. Lamping's suite. The one in your kitchen sat in the drying tray next to your sink. There were trace amounts of blood on it. When the lab work comes back, are we going to find that the blood on the wallet and knife matches Mr. Lamping's?"

Jamal bows his head and looks exhausted, defeated. "Yes, sir."

Baker's face void of emotion, he takes a longer look at the mirror. "Where do you work, Mr. Jones?"

"Without looking up, he says through his tears, "I don't have a job."

Baker appears briefly taken aback. "Where were you most recently employed?"

"The city library. Part-time custodian."

Baker rattles off the date of Blaze's book signing. "Did you work that day and if so, what were your hours?"

He nods.

"I need a verbal response, Mr. Jones."

His eyes still staring at the floor, he says, "I was scheduled to work afternoon shift that day. From three to eleven."

That would have placed him at the scene before and after Sam fell to the floor.

"Did you work the entire shift?"

He shakes his head slowly.

"Mr. Jones?"

He straightens up, then his eyes find the floor again. In a soft voice, he says, "No, sir. My timecard will show I'm telling the truth."

"Why did you leave work early?"

In a barely audible voice, he says, "Something happened. In the john."

Baker glances at the mirror again. "What happened there?"

"Don't make me say it!"

Baker moves closer and sits on the edge of the desk. He removes the toothpick and breaks it in half. He pockets the pieces before inserting a fresh one. "You've come this far, Mr. Jones. It'll feel good to get it off your chest once and for all."

He seems to cringe at Baker's choice of words and looks up as the detective looms over him. He pauses to take several shallow breaths and look at the floor. "Maybe you're right. I went in there … to kill myself. I studied ways to do it. I will never tell you my source for the drugs, but I obtained large doses of potassium chloride—"

"You're saying you planned to kill yourself in the men's room at the city library. Why in holy hell would you do it there?"

He shifts his weight. "I live alone. It'd be days before anybody would find me. I didn't want that."

"Did you leave a suicide note?"

He frowns. "No, sir. My life isn't worth nothing."

"Then what happened?"

"As I was about to inject, a man enters the john. He sees the syringe and orders me to stop. He gets in my face. Here I am, sitting on the toilet, and I don't even have the privacy to kill myself, so I tell the man to leave. We struggle over the syringe, and when he pulls it away from me, he's stabbed in the chest. I guess my hand was on the plunger. I pulled it back and saw liquid fly in the space between us. I didn't think it was a lethal dose, but I read later the police believe that may be how the man died."

"How many times did you stab him with the needle?"

His temper flares. "I didn't stab the man. We fought over it. It was a reflex, I guess. He stabbed himself with it when he wrenched it from me."

"How many times, Mr. Jones?"

He seems confused by the question. "I don't know. I thought it was just once, but it may have been more. It was hectic in there and everything happened so fast. We both struggled for the syringe."

Baker stares at the mirror before he returns his attention to the suspect. "We found a syringe in a trash bag outside your house. That syringe is being analyzed. The bag also contained discarded mail addressed to you. Is that the syringe you brought into the men's room at the city library?"

At last, he looks up to meet Baker's eyes. The anger leaves his body, and he appears to steel himself. "Yes, sir, but I meant to kill me, not him. I should have told him what was in the syringe, but I hoped most of it ended up on his shirt. I panicked and told the boss I was sick and had to leave. He fired me for too many absences."

"Mr. Jones, are you admitting you accidentally injected a lethal dose of potassium chloride into the stomach of Mr. Sam Golding and left the scene?"

"I guess I am."

"There's no guessing here. Do you admit doing so?"

"Yes, sir."

Baker works the new toothpick to the other side of his mouth. "Are you aware that Mr. Golding was a close friend of Mr. Lamping?"

A look of surprise crosses his face, followed by what appears to be one of understanding. He seems to ponder the question for some time. "I'll be damned. I didn't know that."

"Are you willing to put down in writing everything you've just told me?"

Another coughing fit. "Yes, sir."

"That's some nasty cough, Mr. Jones. Is there anything we should know about your health?"

He cracks a sardonic grin. "No, sir."

"I'll have a doctor examine you. Hang tight here."

Baker exits the room and rejoins us. The brows raise again. "Thoughts?"

They both look to me and it's clear they wanted me here for a reason.

I recall something we talked about earlier. "Does Jamal have a history of confessing to crimes he didn't commit?"

"He doesn't show up in the data base as one," Harris says.

"Has he lived in St. Louis all his life?"

"Since birth," Harris says.

I turn to Baker. "You said Jamal cooperated fully when you arrived at his house. Did he ask what the search was about?"

Baker removes the toothpick and pockets it. "He did not."

"Isn't that unusual?"

"Yes, but I've seen the reaction before when I serve warrants."

"Then what?"

Baker clears his throat. "Jones proceeded to hold open the screen door. Like he was resigned to it. Some perps feel guilty and show relief the moments before capture. Their emotions go flat."

"Coincidences don't sit well with me. What are the odds that Jamal encounters and kills Golding one day and Lamping the next?"

"Long but not impossible. He worked at the library that day and admits to casing the hotel for an easy mark. That speaks to opportunity and motive," Baker replies.

"For Lamping, not Golding. Robbery's a big leap from writing bad checks and minor peace disturbance."

"It happens, Breezy."

"You found almost every missing piece of evidence on his property, hidden in plain sight, except the syringe and Rolex."

"Most perps aren't geniuses."

With that, my thoughts drift to Lonnie Washington. "Ask if he ever tried to kill himself before; what's the severity of his pulmonary condition; and who's important in his life. I bet he denies prior attempts, remains vague about his health, and claims he has no one, but I think he'll be lying about the last part. To catch him in this lie, it may take extra departmental legwork and hours. If I'm right, it will lend credence to what I think may going on."

Harris and Baker do their best to draw out my theory, but I keep it to myself. Too often detectives find what they want to find. I want to hear more from Jamal.

Baker re-enters the interrogation room and Jamal denies prior suicide attempts, speaks in circles about his health other than to say he's not contagious, and insists he has no family or friends. He tells Baker he never married, had one child (whereabouts unknown) and that he's had no contact with his twenty-five-year-old daughter since she was born.

When Baker returns, I say, "How quickly can you get some men in blue to ask around the neighborhood to confirm Jamal's story?"

He defers to Harris, who says, "We have a subject in custody who admits to killing two people and agrees to sign a confession. Word about this will leak and be tomorrow's headline. If the physical evidence backs up his statement, I will not authorize any more man hours on these cases without a sound reason."

I turn back to Baker. "Didn't Lamping have other visitors to his suite? He flew into St. Louis with a group. There's Blaze and her entourage: her chauffeur/bodyguard Alonso Washington; her publicist Miles Hawking; and her agent Harry Firestone. They were planning a nation-wide publicity tour together."

"They're all on CCTV as visitors, even Golding, but only the morning of the book signing. They arrived and departed with Lamping down the hallway as a group to the elevators for the library, according to the tapes. No one in the party other than Lamping returned the night Golding died, according to CCTV. The techs lifted numerous prints of them all in the suite. We're waiting on DNA results."

"Is there a preponderance of prints in the suite from anyone in the entourage?"

"Your client."

Lt. Harris steps forward. "None of that matters now that we have Jamal Jones."

∞ ∞ ∞

On the drive home, I purchase a copy of the third book in Blaze's trilogy, *Boundless*, since I'd left the one I already paid for in the city library during the melee once Sam collapsed.

Having nothing better to do, I order a pizza and make a Tanq and tonic before I sit down in front of the gas fireplace.

The dedication reads: *To my readers, male and female, never underestimate or underappreciate the power of women.*

The last installment begins with frenetic chase scenes at night during which Hester and her army of women narrowly escape capture while they arduously make their way west. When the sun rises, they pull off the roads and seek cover to avoid detection. During the day Hester dispatches small bands of hunters on foot to seek food and fuel. Their numbers double along the way and they purchase two old screamers from black marketeers to accommodate the additional free women, but the more mouths to feed force them to kill the last of their livestock. Starving and exhausted, both factions lose minor characters during brutal skirmishes.

I never read a book so bloated with adverbs until this trilogy. The violence in this book is so over the top and around every corner, it dwarfs the carnage in the first two. I develop a blasé attitude to the gore and cruelty like the indifference one develops watching a recent zombie television show that somehow managed to survive ten brain-splattered seasons.

Razpudin *did* have a second army that merged with his original band as they pursue Hester through the Ohio

Valley and past the bombed wasteland of St. Louis. Hester sells her family fortune and the jewels and cash from Razpudin's stolen safe to purchase more firepower, fuel, and free women held in captivity along the way. Some arms traders willingly barter for cash and jewels in the hope that one day society will return close to the old normal and make them wealthy as kings. On the black market, weapons and fuel carry a higher price tag than most female slaves. Her forces grow in number to nearly rival those of her tormentor. Hester and her all-woman army occasionally battle hostile takeovers with arms dealers and come out on top.

The doorbell rings and it's the delivery girl with my pepperoni pizza. She reminds me of a younger version of Miranda and her tip equals the cost of the pie.

With the approach of midnight, only edges of crust remain (Barney loved pizza crust) and the gin is gone. The book marches toward its inevitable climax when I resume reading.

I regret changing from a westerly to a southern course after the latest battle, but it was the safer judgment call and I had precious little time to make it. Rumors about the west claim it contains a huge gathering place where the remaining healthy survivors travel to organize and fight the mutants. Word among the new arrivals has it that the west has established their own protected communities, even an upstart government. If we can ever shake Razpudin's armies, we still can resume a westerly course, but that's where he expects us to flee. Mexico poses a riskier proposition and less is known about the events that occur on the other side of the wall. We lost two good soldiers and my old crow in the firefight. Our new recruits, capable but green warriors, helped us survive the night fighting. I'd hoped changing course would throw Razpudin off the trail, but his backup army chose the same less traveled fork we did and must have radioed their leader to head due south once he knew he'd guessed right.

I stare off into the blackness of the road on a moonless night and ruminate. That makes twelve women or girls dead on my watch. Had I made the wrong decision? Have I condemned every woman here and myself to a similar violent end?

From the driver's seat, Mary reads the look on my face and says, "Your old crow loved you in her own way. She'd follow you anywhere. The newbies jumped at the chance to join our ranks. They died free women with the sun and wind on their faces, weapons in their hands, and a sense of purpose. They were no longer slaves or crows to be beaten, raped, sold, or used for target practice. They were grateful for each day of freedom as opposed to a lifetime of torture and abuse. You gave them hope. The rest of us are free now because of you. We'd follow you into hell if need be. So what if we didn't make it to the west; we're one step closer to the wall and Mexico. Jet said it's the new land of milk and honey for remaining neutral during the war and those who make it over the wall that are willing to work for a living earn immunity and citizenship with no questions asked. They're given own piece of land to farm or raise livestock."

Exhausted, I force myself to meet her gaze and smile. "We'll see, Mary. I don't believe in a real-life Shangri-La, but I hope she's right."

"You saved us. I wouldn't trade a second of this for a lifetime in Razpudin's castle."

The radio sparked to life and I recognized the voice on it, though it sounded older and far more angry than when I last heard it. "You may as give up now, Hester. It's only a matter of time before we run your screamers down. Surrender now and he promises you a quick, painless death," Chaz said, the radio lending a hollow, robotic tone to his voice.

"What about my sisters, the brave warriors with me?"

There's a delay before he speaks again. Is he asking Razpudin for the answer?

"They will be offered a one-time only deal. Return to their past stations in life and all will be forgiven. They will be considered as pawns used by you in your attempt to obtain power and change society. No deaths, no beatings."

"But they return to being slaves," I say.

"They return to their former roles, no questions asked."

"I'm supposed to believe Razpudin after all that's happened? No way. Why would any of us want to return to that?"

"Hey, it beats having your head cut off. Just stop along the road you're on and we will be there soon."

If I could believe a word of this, I might be inclined to end the carnage, but Razpudin is lying. If he catches us, we will all be tortured and eventually killed. My sisters near enough to hear the exchange grumble and plead with me not to listen to him.

"I guess you fail to remember when I found you and Chip wandering the wasteland of New York alone and terrified. You would have been killed had I not led and taught you both how to survive before Razpudin captured us. Why should our sex determine our status in life?"

Laughter on the other end. "It's the new world order, babe. Might makes right."

I can't resist to laugh back at him. "Tell that to all the men we've killed. Our blades and weapons are ready for more notches, if you insist. My suggestion to Razpudin is turn around and cut your losses. Start over and rebuild your shitty male-dominated empire. Leave us be and we will let you be. The world is big enough for both of us."

More silence on the other end. Then: "Chip and I are going to fuck and kill you ourselves. Razpudin will sever your head and place it on his screamer for the world to see. Your followers will suffer unimaginable pain and suffering for the rest of their days."

I turn off the radio.

Once we pass the broken highway sign that indicated the city of San Antonio lay ten miles south, the ground begins to shake and the trees near the road burst into flames. I felt the heat and the black sky lights up in angry reds and oranges. "Plasma bombs! Evasive maneuvers! There's an off ramp ahead. Take it!" I raise Jet on the radio. "Follow our lead! We're going off road! How close are they? Have your rear guard engage if you spot targets!"

"Will do, boss. Over."

As we neared the off-ramp, two screamers approached us going the wrong way on the highway. Razpudin's other army had driven around our flank and come up from the south. Our lead screamer took sporadic gunfire rounds but nothing more serious.

My tormentor found our channel, for his guttural voice fills the cab. "The only reason you're not barbecue right now is I couldn't risk friendly fire from my other army. You have nowhere to go. Surrender now and death will be quick. Fail to do so and all bets are off."

As the screamers rapidly closed the distance between us from the south, their lead screamer increased to breakneck speed. It had an old iron cowcatcher attached to its front grille and intended to destroy my screamer.

"Mary, floor it! On my mark, make a hard right onto the off ramp. You can do this but wait for my signal! Jet, pull back your throttle! You're going to need maneuvering room to make the ramp. Those of you in the lead screamer, sit as far to the left as you can. Now! That's an order! Then to Jet: If we don't make it, take the ramp and head due south without us!"

Mary looked from the road to me and back again several times in quick succession. "Now, boss?" she kept asking, her voice growing more urgent.

The cowcatcher loomed so close in front of us I saw the wild grin and rage on Razpudin's face as the two screamers were seconds from a head-on collision. Our screamer would be cut in half upon impact. Chaz and Chip flanked Razpudin. They also smiled. I hope I didn't wait too long.

"Now, Mary!" I yelled.

Mary cut the wheel hard right and the left-side tires went air born, we nearly rolled-over, but the weight of my warriors on the left side helped the tires return to the road. Our screamer scraped the left guard rail hard, pulverizing the driver side-view mirror, but Mary guided us onto and down the ramp without further incident. More screeching of tires behind and above us on the highway, but no sound of a crash. I ordered Mary to wait and see whether Jet was able to avoid Razpudin's cowcatcher and take the exit ramp.

A firefight on the road above us gave me five long minutes of concern before our second screamer followed, partly on-fire. Jet's excited voice on the radio followed. "We took out two of theirs, but Cheyenne didn't make it, boss. That cowcatcher damaged the back of out chassis. We need five, maybe ten, minutes to effect repairs and pound the metal away from the tires."

"Status report on their transports? Are they right behind you?"

"One of their screamers is on fire pretty bad. Looks like it's all hands-on deck for them to save it. We should have time."

"Is it severe enough that we could mount an attack while they're occupied?"

"I don't know. I don't feel right making that call, boss. They still possess the higher ground."

"Damn, I wish I had eyes on the road above.

"Alright, follow us. I want to find a shelter nearby with a vantage point of the ramp. We don't need any more surprises."

Using the map, I directed Mary to what remained of the service road until we came to an abandoned warehouse large enough to hide two screamers and the trailers. I posted sentries with night vision to guard the entrances while repairs began and wounds were dressed.

Damage to the second screamer turned out to be worse than previously believed as the drive train suffered damage and a shell had punctured the chassis, causing an oil leak. Mary determined it should be able to make the ten-mile trip to the wall, but no farther and at a reduced speed.

As the sun neared the horizon, we set out due south thirty minutes later, under radio blackout. I had no idea how far behind us Razpudin's army was and our going seemed agonizingly slow due to the damaged screamer. Since the terrain appeared flat, I decided we'd drive off road and make a beeline for the wall.

We drove using only running lights as a guide and the trail screamer bogged down once in an arroyo. As we winched it free, the angry buzzing sound of Razpudin's screamers could be heard in the distance, growing closer.

By the light of a new day, Razpudin's four screamers exited the road and sped toward us.

We raced due south and minutes later the wall loomed before us. I broke radio silence and instructed both screamers to prepare the grapple hooks and rope that we'd need to scale the sheer wall. We parked next to the wall as the screamers bore down on us at breakneck speed and the firefight began. Mary, Jet, and I took cover behind the screamers and laid down suppressing fire so the first wave of women could start their climb over the wall. Razpudin's screamers stopped short once they received fire. Mary readied our last plasma charge and vaporized one of their screamers before all the men could exit and seek cover. Their screams of pain vanished along with them.

The first wave of women made it to the top of the wall and started shooting to cover the second wave of us who began our climb. Our numbers were down by half at this point.

By this time Razpudin ordered two of his remaining screamers to the wall and their first wave started to climb. Some were shot down and some hit my women. A bullet grazed my ear and ricocheted off the wall. I turned around to see Razpudin himself following me up the rope I was on, a dagger between his teeth.

I called for the first wave to climb down on to the Mexican side and pick off any men who followed us, but I wanted to kill the man on my rope myself. Our second wave began to climb down when Razpudin let go of the rope and tumbled onto me. His impact sent us both flying off the rope and crashed onto the ground in Mexico.

Bloody Mary and Jet were the only other ones left by the time Razpudin and me stood and faced off. They continued to shoot his men as they reached the top of the wall, until they ran out of ammunition. Chaz and Chip made it down the wall because they wore bullet-proof armor vests. Jet took on Chip while Mary squared off against Chaz.

Razpudin rushed me with the dagger which I blocked with a two-by-four and then knocked it from his hand. I began to beat him with the wood until he grabbed it and yanked it from my hands. We wrestled on the ground. He pulled my hair while I clawed his face. I fell on to him. My thumbs found his eyes and he screamed when I took his sight. I retrieved his dagger and said, "This is for every woman you hurt." I pulled his head backward and slit his throat. He tried to speak through the arterial spurt but all that came out was a wet burbling.

I looked to my friends and saw Jet chase Chip across the open plain, a whip in her hand, when a sharp stabbing pain in my back drove me to my knees. Chaz stood over a prone Mary, grinning as he began to run toward me. I reached behind and screamed as I pulled a large Ninja star from my back. I raised the star and sliced as he tackled me. My head struck the hard ground with all his weight on me. I blacked out. When I woke, my eyes stung from the blood in them. I rolled Chaz's lifeless body off me and vomited. My white shirt turned red on both sides by blood, I saw Jet return with an exhausted and bloodied Chip wrapped in her bullwhip. She hogtied him then she attended to me.

"Check on Mary," I said.

"She's dead, Hester. Chaz hit her with a Ninja star and Chip did the rest." She removed my shirt and irrigated the wound with water. From a nearby backpack she placed a dressing on the wound and helped pull a clean shirt over me. "You're going to need stitches, especially since we're now walking. I hope there's a village or town nearby. I saw a road not far from where I caught up with Chip." She looked at the struggling Chip. "What do we do with him?"

I thought of how much Chip and Chaz had changed since we first met. I handed her the star. "Will you do the honor. For Mary. Make it quick."

The deed done, Jet untied him and gathered what supplies made it over the wall while I said goodbye to Bloody Mary. We began to walk toward the road arm in arm in silence.

We didn't get far before dust rose along the southern road. The only functioning weapons we had were some knives, the star, and Jet's whip.

"Let's hope the natives are friendly," I said, wincing.

Jet felt the wetness on my back. "And that they have a doctor who can sew you up."

Two trucks pulled to a stop next to us. A man and a woman got out from the lead vehicle. The woman was fortyish and wore a multi-colored dress and sandals. "Welcome to Mexico! My name is Lupe, and this is Francisco. May we give you a ride to town?"

"Yes. Thank you," Jet said. "My friend needs a doctor."

The man looked to be in his sixties and wore jeans and a work shirt. He frowned. "You both look like you've been in a war. Are there other survivors or bodies by the wall?"

I nodded. "The women, especially the large one near the wall, are the only ones I care to bury. Do what you will with our enemies."

Jet helped me into the back of the lead Jeep.

The woman turned to us. "You are welcome to heal and stay here for as long as you wish. After our doc treats you, we will provide you with a hotel room and food. If you like our little city, you may choose to relocate here."

I leaned against Jet for support and said, "We appreciate your hospitality very much. What's the name of your town?"

We'd been driving on the road for some time and the tops of multi-colored small buildings appeared in the distance. "Felicidad. It means—"

I squeezed Jet's hand. "Something the world needs now, happiness."

Epilogue

I needed eight stitches and IV antibiotics during a three-day stay at the Felicidad Hospital. Jet rarely left my side. We filled up on enchiladas, rice, and other Mexican dishes. The hotel, though not fancy, was clean and the beds were soft. The inhabitants of Felicidad were friendly and accommodating. The women were not slaves of the men in Mexico, as far as we could tell. When strong enough, I attended the burial of our sister Bloody Mary in the town cemetery.

We went back over the wall one morning after convincing the local sheriff to loan us two pistolas, just in case. The screamers looked undisturbed while the vultures fed on carrion. I asked Jet to find clothes and anything usable while I lugged my bag and the contents of Razpudin's safe over the wall.

At Lupe's urging, all the dead south of the wall were buried in their local cemetery. I paid the padre of the church for the burial services of all the dead women and men from Razpudin's stash. The rest I donated to the church to feed the poor.

While I recovered, we listened to local ham radio operators across the border. The fighting raged on and seemed to be intensifying. The voices called for every healthy American to head west and join the upstart communities forming in Los Angeles, San Diego, and San Francisco. These cities had built walls and protection from the mutants and were forming armies to wipeout the mutants. On a more global scale, reports said it appeared that Russia, China, the UK, and central Europe were decimated by the world war and in worse shape than the US. Africa, Central and South America, and Australia remained neutral during the war and stood poised to dominate the world during the massive rebuilding once the mutants were killed.

During my recuperation, Jet said she wanted a romantic relationship with me and that we should head west together. I rebuffed her and said my fighting days are over, that I was staying. She rescaled the wall to make her way to California. Before she left I gave her half of my family fortune to help her along the journey. I told her to contact me once she made it to safety.

I'd fallen in love with the tiny town of Felicidad and Mexico. Snippets of my family life were returning and I realized that I'd lost too much in life to keep struggling. It was time to make something with the time I have left. With the rest of my family's savings, I bought a tiny house and restaurant. I turned the eatery into one that specializes in American comfort food. I learned to speak Spanish.

Every few weeks, the occasional American or two scaled the wall and made it to Felicidad. Within a year, we had a little female Americana section in town. On May 5 the next year, I received a postcard from Jet. She made it to San Diego, along with six other women she rescued along the way.

I wrote a memoir of my days as a sex slave and resistance fighter and donated it to the town library. I lived out my days alone in peace and tranquility until my heart gave out one day in my rocking chair.

The next day finds me parking my Solstice near the rundown brick house of Jamal Jones on Hebert Street. Memories rush back to my first visit here—parking between a brick fight waged between DeAndre and Ty, two young black boys who I soon added to my meager payroll; my meetings with Lakeesha Washington, who passed away two months after her son Lonnie was killed in jail; and my sessions in jail with Lonnie. I knock on twelve houses, some doors close in my face, those residents who do open don't answer my questions, and after an hour and a half the only thing I learn about Jamal is that he drives the old Bonneville I parked behind.

When I approach the last narrow brick bungalow on the block, the weathered green front door triggers a pleasant memory. If only I remembered her earlier, this would have been my first stop. I ring the bell, fully expecting to wait minutes so the pleasant elderly black lady can use her walker to open her door, but it swings open immediately and an attractive black woman maybe twenty years old smiles and says *hello*. My heart sinks. So much death has come to this street the last four years, it was too much to expect for her, the oldest resident on the block to still be alive.

"I'm sorry to disturb you, but I'm Dr. Mitchell Adams and I was hoping to speak with Miss Coretta Mae Givens."

She calls out over her shoulder, "Great grand-mama, there's a doctor here to see you!" Then to me: "Please, come in!"

She directs me toward a sofa across from a tiny woman in a wheelchair. I recognize the same simple ironwood cross on the wall behind her from four years ago. The kind, oval shaped eyes I remember no longer track my face exactly and her left leg, minus her foot, rests on the foot plate under a tiny cushion. A flesh-colored sock covers the stump.

As I approach, her face lights up. "The angel who answered the door is Georgia, my beautiful great-granddaughter!"

"She's a polite, young lady."

The smile lingers and she offers me a seat on the sofa. "And what sort of doctor are you, sir?"

I sit on the end closer to her. "My doctorate is in Social Work. We met about four years ago when you invited me in to discuss Lonnie and Lakeesha Washington. Do you remember that?"

A pained look crosses her face, and she pauses to close her eyes. I notice the essential tremor in her hands while she fingers a set of rosary beads. "My memory isn't what it used to be, sir. Everything that happened to that young man and his family was a tragedy." She turns to her great-granddaughter and says, "Dear, would you put on a pot of water for tea? Everyone is welcome in this home."

Georgia turns to the kitchen. "Coming up, great grand-mama."

"I met several times with Lonnie and tried to advocate for him in jail. I remember you telling me four years ago that you made sandwiches and tea every day for the homeless people and children in the neighborhood. I met

Ty and DeAndre back then, they must have been ten or twelve years old."

The pain returns to her face. "Poor DeAndre was killed two years ago in a drive-by shooting but Ty is doing well in school and hopes to go to college."

She pauses and then the light returns to her face. "I remember now! I showed you the precious gift Lonnie gave me, the title to my home, paid in full. He was one of our neighborhood angels."

I return her smile. "As are you, Miss Givens."

Georgia returns with piping hot tea.

Coretta pats her great-granddaughter's arm with an unsteady hand. "This angel here came to live with me after my sugars worsened and the doctor amputated my foot. With Georgia's help, we still make sandwiches for those less fortunate. More now than back then because the need is greater. Sun tea in the summer and hot coffee in the winter."

I sip my green tea. "I recall you brewed the tea on your back porch. I'm here to ask your counsel again on behalf of someone else on your block that I'm trying to help, Jamal Jones. Do you know of him?"

A slight frown appears and her voice lowers. "What do you want to know?"

"Do you know anything about his family and the type of person he is?"

She smiles and sips her tea. "You may or may not remember that I taught grade school here in the inner city. Jamal and Laila were students in my fifth-grade class. He was a quiet, shy boy, an average student at best, and like so many other students, there were troubles at home. Laila was more gregarious and had no qualms speaking her mind. The reasons I recall more about them than most of my former students are their circumstances were tragic, and Jamal never moved from Hebert Street. Lonnie Washington's vast economic largesse did not yet exist when their time of need occurred."

"What happened?"

She looks to the ceiling and softly sighs, as if recalling a bad memory. "Circumstance forced Jamal to grow up too soon. I didn't learn the nature or severity of the family situation until it was too late. His father was a violent alcoholic who beat his wife (may God rest her soul), and other times he took his anger out on the children. Jamal promised his mother he would protect his sister."

Cora Mae tightens her grip on a tissue. "One night the father beat Jamal's twin sister Laila. Jamal tried to intervene, but the father was too strong. The beating ended with Laila at the bottom of the basement steps. She suffered a C-4 spinal cord fracture in the fall. She's intelligent and verbal but cannot move her extremities and is incontinent. She's been a quadriplegic in a nursing home ever since. She wants to earn a counseling degree and help others like her."

"How awful. When did this occur?"

She pauses to collect her thoughts. "She was fifteen. Jamal was born first and Laila a few hours after."

I follow her lead, take a last sip of tea, and place the cup and saucer on the table.

"There's a special bond between twins. They'd finish each other's thoughts and sense when something was wrong with the other. Jamal has never been the same."

"In what ways?"

"He never forgave himself for that night. He visits his sister several times a week. Sometimes he sits on that sofa you're on and cries about Laila's care at the home. He wishes he could move her to a specialized treatment facility for quadriplegic residents. I believe he slowly gave up on life after he wasn't able to save Laila."

"Did Jamal turn to crime? Stealing? Burglary? Was he ever violent toward others?"

Her eyebrows raise as if she's surprised by the questions. "He's lived on Hebert Street his entire life and I never heard of Jamal raising a fist against anyone."

"What about his health? When I last saw him, he was doubled over in pain from coughing fits. I noticed blood on his sleeve."

Her lips purse. "He has an aggressive form of lung cancer, stage four. The last time he visited, he said the doctors gave him three months, and that was a best-case scenario that included hospitalization."

"How long ago was that?"

"I reckon a month ago, maybe two." She looks at the clock on the wall and moves her wheelchair forward. "Now if you don't mind, Dr. Adams, I have to help Georgia make sandwiches and coffee for the lunch crowd. I've never missed a meal for them except when they amputated my foot, and I don't intend to start now.

"I hope you can help Jamal; he's a good-hearted man. It's a shame that he and Lonnie never crossed paths. When you see Jamal, please tell him Coretta Mae still prays every day for him and Laila."

∞ ∞ ∞

On the drive home I stop off at the St. Louis City Foundry for Greek food. Sitting over my gyro at a bench, I call in a favor from a buddy who used to be a cop for twenty years on the east side, some of that time spent in vice. I give him names and approximate time frames Alonso provided.

"That's a long time ago in street years, Mitch," Mark the former cop says. "I can't make any promises. Maybe she's still in the data base for something more substantial than the world's oldest profession."

"If she isn't a phantom, she also had a daughter who'd be mid-to-late thirties by now. You're the best bloodhound I know. Thanks, I owe you one."

"Let's do the track one night when live racing resumes. Dinner on you."

"Deal."

I work out on the heavy bag in the basement then go for a run, but neither prevents my idle thoughts from circling back to Miranda. I force her out of my head and rethink the case; about how convenient the emergence of Jamal Jones is for the defense and that Baker and Harris have been gifted a present wrapped tightly in a big red bow.

DOMINOS

As Lt. Harris predicted, next morning's Post-Dispatch leads with a tabloid-like headline: LOCAL MAN CONFESSES, WILL BLAZE STARK WALK?

My cell barks (which reminds me to change my ring tone) before I can read the article. The word *Mark* appears on the screen.

"It took a fair amount of digging and a lotta luck, but I found her with the help of a friend still on the force. Connie Hudson is the mom, born and raised in East St. Louis. She died of a suspicious overdose within the time period you provided. AKA: Candy Finch; Robin Sykes; Linda Crane; and a year before her death, Sonya Sparrow—"

"Connie must have liked birds," I say.

A brief chuckle on the other end. "Huh, I didn't notice that. Records indicate she had one child, a daughter named Hester Hudson, the right age given your parameters."

Hester. I thank him and say, "How did you find Connie?"

"Multiple data bases. Turns out she'd been peripherally involved in a large drug ring; served as a low-level runner and did short stretches in the joint followed by stays in court-ordered drug programs. Then again later, after she died."

"You said the death was suspicious ..."

I hear one of his grandsons playing in the background. "I'd say. She was a pro and an experienced junkie, so you'd think she'd know the dose she needed. The coroner report estimates she had twenty times the lethal dose of heroin in her system when she died."

"Maybe she wanted to check out permanently," I say.

"Maybe. Funny thing is ... the ME found significant bruising on her body, like she'd been in a fight."

"Still not unusual, given her profession."

"Here's where it gets juicy ... her right arm had a dozen bloody injection sites, and she was right-handed."

"That doesn't mean much. Veins break down in chronic junkies. Sometimes they inject between their toes and under the tongue."

"Then riddle me this one ... there were no prints on the syringe. Not a one. The vic wasn't wearing gloves. Plus, her apartment was wiped clean."

I have no ready explanation for that. "You said you found Connie Hudson via multiple data bases."

"DFS and Family Court. Numerous calls to the child abuse hotline for multiple counts of abuse, neglect, and school truancy involving her daughter. After Connie OD'd, DFS found Hester next door with a neighbor—"

"Tiara Washington."

"You know her?" he says, sounding surprised.

"I know of her. She has a son named Alonso. My understanding is Tiara took Hester in and raised her with her son until she left home at nineteen. Does that sound right?'

"I can't speak to that last part. DFS approved Tiara Washington's apartment as a temporary emergency shelter, given the tragic circumstances (the kid found her mother dead that night and the worker determined Hester would not leave Tiara's apartment peacefully), Ms. Washington's willingness to take Hester in, and the amount of time they'd known each other. Reading between the lines of the DFS records, it sounds like Tiara pretty much acted as Hester's parent the last two years of Connie's life. The notes were glowing when it came to Ms. Washington. She followed through with counseling for Hester and jumped through every DFS hoop. To obtain access to the DFS info, I had to promise my source two cases of Kim Crawford Chardonnay. That's on you; I hope you don't mind."

I realize I'd completely forgotten to ask Alonso about his mother during our abbreviated time together while Blaze took her MMPI2. "Consider it done. Do you have an address for Tiara Washington?"

"Way ahead of you. She suffered a bad stroke last year and is in a home. It left her without speech. She can't communicate at all."

"You're a miracle worker, Mark. One more question … do you have any record of Hester Hudson once she turned nineteen?"

I hear a brief rustle of papers. "Nope. I got nada on her after DFS closed the case."

We're about to hang up when he says, "Damn, I almost forgot. The kid—"

"What about her?"

"There's no record of run-ins with the law on this side of the river after mom's death, but she's in the St. Louis city database."

I have a sinking feeling what he's about to say. "What for?"

"After they moved to the near north side, Hester became known to SLPD as a serial confessor. No motive or opportunity to do the crimes, plus she provided the wrong details to the cops every time. Like Chicken Little or the boy who cried wolf, the cops would listen to her latest tales and send her home. Weird, but it happens. I think it's called attention-seeking behavior in your line of work. In mine, it's just plain nuts."

The twisted puzzle pieces are starting to come together, but how do I prove any of it? "You're a miracle worker, Mark. Have you told anyone else what you just told me?"

"Not a soul, why?"

"I'll add two cases of your favorite beer if you keep this between us. We'll hit the track in the spring. Thanks again."

∞ ∞ ∞

Before I can finish my bagel and process what Mark uncovered, Baker calls my cell.

"I've seen some crazy shit in homicide, Breezy, but this takes the cake."

"I had a feeling you'd call."

"The striations and imperfections on the blade of the butcher knife found in Jamal's kitchen matches the wounds that killed Lamping, so he was in possession of the murder weapon. Jamal's prints are on it, on Lamping's wallet, and the door to Lamping's suite at the Chase. A brown package addressed to Lamping on the kitchen table also contains Jamal's prints. The concierge confirms it was the package Jamal lifted from the registration desk. CCTV places Jamal in the hotel lobby the morning of the murder, as do two employees. Lamping enters the lobby alone from the street and walks toward the elevators. Ten minutes later, the tape shows Jamal grab the package while the concierge is engaged with guests and walk toward the bank of elevators." He stops and I think he's testing me.

"Were his prints or DNA inside the suite?"

I visualize the toothpick dancing to the other side of his mouth as his grin appears. "His prints were on that brown package. No prints on Lamping, his clothes, or anywhere else in the suite during the struggle. We're waiting on DNA results.

"It gets better."

"I'm listening."

"Forty-five minutes later, CCTV shows Jamal walk through the lobby and to the street like nothing happened. Nobody noticed any unusual behavior or blood on his clothing."

"Okay …" I say, expecting more.

"We also found Jamal's prints in the city library men's room. In a stall, the nearby wall, and the floor. He told the truth about his timecard; he clocked out sick and was canned the same day. Staff escorted him outside to his car. No witnesses remember him at the book signing. Lab found a partial thumb print from Golding, but in the other bathroom stall …"

He pauses for a reason. Is he fishing for my take on the inconsistencies?

"What are you leaving out?" I ask.

"There were no prints from Jamal on Sam Golding, and none on Jamal from Golding. There's almost always transfer, Breezy. Again, we're waiting on DNA results. Lab's running everything again; just to be sure."

A lengthy silence on the other end of the line, as if he expects me to add to the unfolding picture, until at last he breaks it. "You know or suspect something, Breezy. I could slap you with a felony charge of withholding information from a police investigation."

"We both know you're not going to do that. You called because you need me. What about the syringe found in his trash?"

"Trace elements of Potassium Chloride, but here's where it goes off the tracks—"

"The only prints are Jamal's."

"Bingo. Advance to the head of the class."

"Why would he lie about the struggle for the syringe? If Jamal accidentally killed Sam, why bother to bring it home and toss the syringe in the trash? Why not dump it in the river or crush it under a boot and flush it?"

Baker huffs. "You tell me. He claimed to be suicidal that day. The little brother doesn't appear to be thinking too clearly since the day we picked him up. He seems resigned to his fate; like he wants to be caught. It happens."

I take the last bite of bagel and lick my fingers. "You're taking the easy road again."

Baker sounds frustrated. "Then tell me the other road."

When I don't answer, he says, "I'm tired of this dance. We will soon have a signed confession from Jamal Jones. He admits to the murder of Lamping and his involvement in the death of Golding. We have evidence, motive, and opportunity for Lamping's murder, and we can place him at the city library hours before the book signing, where the two could have met in the men's room. I think he's good for both murders, and my hunch is the DNA will confirm it. If the Lieutenant's happy; I'm happy."

∞   ∞   ∞

Baker shuts me out for the next ten days; I receive no update on developments in either case. I surmise he's thinks I've reached the end of my usefulness since Jamal Jones entered the picture. The Post contains little but innuendo regarding Blaze and divulges nothing new on Jamal. I leave a message with Blaze's defense team, asking them when they want my completed psych evaluation on Blaze, but I don't hear back from them. I still have twenty days per the court order. I take on three new clients to stay somewhat busy and take my mind off Miranda.

On the morning of day eleven, I receive a frenzied call from Debby Macklin. "Where the hell are you?"

"Why?"

"Blaze is due to appear in court within the hour, didn't you know? Six days ago, the defense asked the prosecution for a dismissal of all charges against her. My sources say the cops have a signed confession from this new suspect on videotape. Both sides met in the judge's chambers, but the judge wants to review the new evidence in court. I hear it's just a formality; Blaze will be free as a bird soon."

I'm wondering how quickly I can get there.

She reads the silence. "This is news to you, isn't it?"

"I can be there in thirty minutes, maybe."

She sounds distracted by someone on the other end. "I'll try to save you a place. This creepy little man here insisted I call you. He says he's your friend and partner. He reminds me of Joe Pesci, not the funny one in *My Cousin Vinny*, more like the one in *Goodfellas*. He's getting on my last nerve—"

I hear her warn what must be Gianelli that: if you don't back off and shut up, I'm going to have you arrested. Then to me: What rock did he crawl out of from under?"

"He's basically harmless, but don't sit on a couch with him. If he gets too fresh, roll up a newspaper and swat him on the nose.

"I'm on my way."

Thirty-five minutes later, I'm wedged in the back row again, this time between Debby and Gianelli, of the 22nd judicial courthouse for the state of Missouri in downtown St. Louis, crammed with Blaze's fans, extra police, and reporters. Outside, the throng of Blaze supporters has doubled from her arraignment. The mood of those in and outside the courtroom is electric; they anticipate her walking free before the trial.

With no witnesses there's no need for microphones in the courtroom, so the defense plays the videotaped confession from Jamal Jones for the judge to view and highlights the preponderance of physical evidence implicating the new suspect. Blaze's dream defense team pounds home the fact that Jamal Jones has confessed to both deaths and restates their assertion that Blaze Stark's confession was coerced.

BLAZE UNBOUND

On a chilly night a few weeks before Thanksgiving, I sit alone in my office at my desk completing paperwork for third party payers for the eight therapists under my employ. The last envelope I seal is the next payment on my renovations. Going in debt again has motivated me to take on three new clients this week.

I open a manilla folder from my transcription service.

Among the pages is my typed court evaluation on Blaze Stark, completed and unpaid for, and never presented in court.

I proofread and sign it, then stare at it for some time and wonder if I could have done anything differently without breaking client confidentiality.

The answer keeps coming up no.

The most frustrating case of my career.

I played by the rules and didn't use information obtained outside the doctor/client relationship, but in doing so did I help allow a murderer to go free and an innocent man to cop to two murders? Has this happened to other therapists and if so, how many times?

I place the document in her file and lock the cabinet.

Normally I've already planned a beach vacation someplace warm this time of year, but I decide to work through the coming winter and lick my wounds. I have no desire to date again after Miranda. I reach for the phone, about to call my parents and accept their invitation to stay with them between Christmas and New Year's when the door to the waiting room opens.

The unhurried click of heels advances and when the silhouette rounds the corner, I'm face to face with my infamous client, in the same sable coat, shades, and scarf as the night we met.

"Hello, Blaze. Is Alonso here with you?"

Without a word, she slowly removes the glasses, then the scarf and coat before she takes the seat across from me and crosses those long, shapely legs. The black ankle bracelet is gone. Her eyes never leave mine.

The fiery red hair perfectly coiffed once more, she wears another low-cut green dress, and stilettos the color of gold that match her bling. The only difference is a matching green clutch purse I almost missed that rests in her lap. A Mona Lisa smile appears.

"It wouldn't be in his or our best interests. I gave him the night off."

My blood pressure rises like it never did during that first meeting.

Her smile beams. "It's a delight to see you again as a free woman, Mitch. I like you. We're meant to be together. You know me and I really want to get to know you better. You're smart and handsome and have done so much for me I want to return the favor. You won't have to work another day for the rest of your life if you don't want to. Jet-setting to premieres of my movies. We can live anywhere, have anything. I can buy our own private island."

She's not kidding.

"I don't date clients. It's unethical."

The smile turns into a pout then a frown. "I know you and that feisty nurse broke up. What about Kristin? I heard she was a client."

I want to ask how she knows these things but then remember that she vetted me before we first met. "Blaze, you've gotten exactly what you wanted from our relationship, your freedom. You paid me in full, so we go our separate ways."

"We could have it all."

I paste on a smile. "I'm happy with what I have. *You* have it all. Enjoy your island and your premiere. It seems the fans love you now even more than before, if that's possible."

Her look changes, becomes more distant. "Then I want to thank you in person."

"For?"

The smile returns. "I locked the door on my way in so we can have privacy. I was right to cast you in my little melodrama. You carried out the role I created for you to perfection."

I stir in my seat and look about the room. "What do you mean?"

A subtle shake of the head. "Coyness doesn't become you. You've always been above board. Let's have one last brutally honest talk."

"I'm going to need more," I say, confused.

Her purse snaps open and she reaches inside. "My research was flawless. You proved your commitment to confidentiality years ago; you'd rather risk jail time than betray a client or your code of ethics. Finding a man of principle is like finding a dinosaur today, modern times has destined them for extinction, but you proved to be the perfect cat's-paw."

"Especially after the botched injection of Sam with the Potassium Chloride in the city library. I trust he fought you and caused the spillage on his shirt." I slowly reach a hand under the desk.

"Hands where I can see them! Now!" She produces a .22 from her purse and points the barrel at my chest. "I can't allow you to press an alarm button down there."

"You're a smart one, Blaze."

"I have no idea what you're talking about. Surely you've heard by now that the police have a man in custody who's confessed to killing Sam and Ted."

I laugh. "The police seem happy with the confession. How much did that cost you? The man's going to be dead soon from natural causes. What was his price?"

"This is why I'm here. You know more than you let on. I never thought I'd have to do this."

I fold my hands on the desktop and look resigned to my fate. "Did you think I'd run off with you and fall victim to some vacation *accident* that you can arrange and then explain away to the local authorities?"

"Living together in the lap of luxury sounds much more fun than what you're making me do now."

"How do you plan to explain your presence here after you kill me? There are closed circuit cameras that have documented you enter the building and will show when you leave."

"I have a plan for that." She lights a cigarette.

"You're right. If Sam hadn't fought me, that pesky ME never would've thought to focus on Potassium Chloride and would've ruled his death a heart attack. Sam was always a pain in my side, even in death."

I lean back in my chair and try to avoid staring at the gun barrel, but it's almost impossible. "Sam never kidnapped, abused, or mistreated you, did he?"

"That's true, but he did far worse. He minimized me. I was merely arm candy to be paraded around social events and causes. *He* was never published, but he patronized my writing every chance he could." She nearly cackles. "I got the last laugh on him."

"It wasn't enough to enjoy half of Sam's wealth for you, was it? You wanted it all. And your freedom from him."

She smiles broadly. "Again, the police have the killer in custody."

I wonder what she did from the age of nineteen on, but let it pass. "Why kill Ted Lamping? I know he believed Sam to be the true author of the *Boundless* trilogy and that he hired a PI to prove it, but you know they found no solid evidence, so why kill him?"

She makes a sour face. "I wish I had time and opportunity to personally take care of that little PI creep, but

I have enough evidence on him to put him away for years, if need be."

I hope I'm able to circle back to Gianelli. "Back to Ted, that must have been sweet revenge. For the casting couch, wasn't it? That must have felt so gratifying. After you paid off the fall guy, you must have told Jamal what to take, where you stabbed him, and where to leave his prints and DNA evidence. So the stories matched."

The smile returns. "I don't know what you're talking about."

I shrug. "I know Sam didn't write those books."

She lowers the weapon and nods briefly. Ash spills onto my desktop. "Thank you. I appreciate that."

"It wasn't a compliment. You didn't pen the trilogy, either."

She raises an eyebrow and the gun to my face. "You have no proof, and soon it'll be a moot point."

I think of Alonso and Tiara. "Others besides me know. Are you prepared to kill everyone who knows your secret? Even those you claim to care about? You have no idea who I've told. If any harm comes to me, copies of what I've unearthed will arrive in police stations and news media outlets."

She grins. "Why don't I believe you? Because of that code of yours."

I flash my own grin. "I know the author was Karen Jackson. I know about the garage sale, that you regularly place flowers on her grave. What I don't know is whether you edited the manuscripts at all. Frankly, I don't care. It doesn't change what you did."

Her mouth falls open while I speak. "You're wrong."

"Then why are you here to kill me?"

"In part to gloat. I fooled everyone—the police, the lawyers, even hotshot Mitchell Adams. Why, I should play the lead in *Bound*!"

It takes considerable effort, but I paste on what I hope is a convincing smirk. "You may have tricked the detectives and prison guards, but I knew you weren't a multiple personality early on and suspected you of merely posing as an author."

For the first time a trace of uncertainty enters those green eyes. "You're lying! You—"

"I briefly entertained your claim that Sam kidnapped you, but your *performance* made me question it. You plagiarized your feelings of captivity from a Wilke poem about a panther and you borrowed most of the early plot from *The Collector* by John Fowles—a lonely man uses chloroform to kidnap a young art student and hold her in his basement in the hope she will eventually fall in love with him. That, your uneven talk at the library and Lamping's concern that you didn't possess workable knowledge of your own writing from the beginning helped me form an initial opinion. Your agent and others must have suspected something since he's planning to hire an experienced screenwriter for the script to *Bound*. You lack the discipline and skills to be a best-selling author."

She cocks the gun and levels it at my face. "Lies! I convinced you I was a multiple personality!"

I close my eyes and shake my head, terrified I'm about to die. Awaiting the shot, I think of my parents, but when I open my eyes, I'm still breathing. "The onset of multiple personality disorder occurs in the teen years, almost always caused by sexual trauma. You were nineteen when you claimed to have been kidnapped. You reported no prior abuse or other personalities before then or during that period of intense stress. I've treated clients with the illness; you're not that good of an actress. If you want further proof, I can show you."

She appears flustered and waves the gun briefly in the air. "Show me."

"To do that, I have to walk to the file cabinet, so don't panic and shoot me."

"Okay, but no sudden movements. No tricks."

I unlock the client file cabinet and fumble around while I search for a manila folder.

"What's taking so long? I said no tricks!"

I find her folder and read my court report on her that was never sent to the judge. The closing paragraph reads, "In summation, based on her responses to the above administered tests and our discussions, it is my professional opinion that Ms. Blaze Stark does not suffer from Dissociative ~~Differential~~ Identity Disorder, more commonly called Multiple Personality Disorder.

"Why she is posing as a fictitious DID client is currently unknown but rife for speculation, given recent events. She does possess anti-social traits, a personality disorder, a significant degree of paranoia, struggles with authority figures (both male and female), based on her answers to the MMPI 2 and Rorschach. For more specific results of the tests, please refer to pages 2-4."

I return the report to the file cabinet, lock it, and fold my hands in my lap to keep them from shaking.

"So what? The expert my side hired insists that I am a multiple personality."

"You paid Jamal Jones, a man about to die from lung cancer, to confess to both crimes. With his help and DNA that he planted at both scenes, for now you've been exonerated. Did you have him enter the suite right after you killed Ted, discuss the scene with him, and say where to leave his prints? That's sick, even for someone like you."

Her smile is a sick leer. "You have no proof."

One of my phone lines starts to flash and she sees it. "Let your machine answer it."

I do not reach for it. "Have you heard the phrase that says: *there is no honor among thieves*? When faced with murder charges, I think Jamal will turn on you. My guess his asking price to do this was the cost of the long-term transfer and care of his sister to a specialized facility that treats C4 spinal fractures instead of the pit she's in now that can't even properly care for her bedsores. I've outlined all this in my reports in the event of my sudden death."

"That's a fantastic story. You could have been a writer." She chuckles. "Too bad you have no proof."

"Jamal is another loose end. You going to kill him, too?"

Her leer returns. "In this macabre fantasy you've created, wouldn't you think there would be consequences for his sister's ongoing care?"

"Quite possible, but you were in a panic and had to do all this on the fly, which is quite impressive. Jamal's dying and he achieved his goal of obtaining better care for his sister, at least temporarily. I anticipated your reputation with your fans would take a big hit, possibly a career-ending one, but it seems you're more popular than ever. For the time being. You're wrong about one important part of life, most people still care about values and character. The real world is nothing like the one Karen Jackson created."

"That I created. If you still refuse to run away with me, find comfort that you will have those values of yours for a few more minutes. After Sam's will is read, this *bad actress* will pocket over thirty billion. His charities will receive an equal amount unless my attorneys can find loopholes. Sam was a generous, benevolent man with a fatal flaw—he saw only the good in people."

I pass her an empty soda cup to collect the cigarette ashes in, but she ignores it.

"Lamping was a whole different problem, wasn't he? He also suspected you were a fraud, but you were desperate to publish at all costs, weren't you?"

The gun starts to shake in her hand for a few seconds, then steadies. "What do you think you know?" she says, sarcastically.

"His murder was personal for you … because of the casting couch. That explains the genital mutilation. Lamping was a revenge killing."

She seems surprised and her face flushes. She pounds the table and screams, "He was a disgusting pig. The world is better off without him."

I sense myself back up in the chair. Have I pushed her too far?

She regains her composure.

"Lamping's death was revenge; Sam's was for money."

I fold my arms across my chest. "What about Mama T and Alonso? Will you kill them, too?"

From her purse she removes a silencer and starts to thread it onto the .22. "I will worry about them. This will be quick. Do you prefer two in the head or the heart?"

It's time. "I choose neither, Hester Hudson."

She freezes in her chair, her jaw falls open again for a moment. "No, no." Her voice sounds smaller now, but the gun remains pointed at my head.

"Hester Hudson was born across the river in East St. Louis, in the poorest part of a crime-infested, dying town. Your mother Connie Hudson was a junkie and prostitute most of her adult life. She used several aliases, all bird-related. The ones I heard of were Teresa Hawk, Sonya Sparrow, and Robin Stevens. During the last year of her life, she offered you to select johns for sexual favors. That must have been awful …"

She looks away, her eyes dart to the floor. "You know nothing."

"You should have led with the truth. This early history could have produced a personality schism. That might have convinced me about the diagnosis, but that hit too close to home for comfort, didn't it?"

She remains looking at the floor. "How'd you learn this?"

I could act now but want to ask one more question. "How did your Mom die? An overdose or something else?"

I see tears on the side of her face while she looks down. "I did it. I overdosed her. To finally be free of that hell. One john nearly killed me. I watched her prep syringes since I was ten. I tripled the dose. That did it. You still wonder why I kept all this to myself?"

While she continues to focus on the floor, I spring to my feet and head for the door behind me. I enter the newly built safe room and throw the locks as she stands and shots ricochet off the door. She pounds on the door and says, "You must come out sooner or later, Mitch! I will wait for you and then this will all be over."

The steel compartment doesn't allow me to use my cell, but the contractors installed a built-in phone and intercom system that works. Baker picks up my call and mobilizes a team of cops from Clayton. Then I call Gus, the septuagerian building security guard and ask him to not allow any passengers onto my floor, except for the police and first responders. I tell him I'm okay but ask him to call back on this number the second the cops arrive.

From the closed circuit tv, I watch Blaze search my office for any telephone wires that could lead to the safe room. She rips out ones she finds near my desk but doesn't find any near the safe room walls.

I press the intercom button and say, "Blaze, you are needlessly destroying my office. The wires to the built-in phone in here go through the floor to a protected area you cannot reach. Let's talk about what your Mom did to you when you were a child. Tell me the worst of the worst. It may help you with your trial."

I watch her try and fail to break into my client files. Then she grabs as much loose paper as she can and piles it in front of the safe room door. She uses her lighter to start a fire.

I say, "You can't smoke me out. My air in here is independent of the office and something else you can't impact. Tell me about your birth Mom. It can only help your case. You're in desperate need of legal and emotional sympathy points."

She's worked herself into a frenzy now. "What did Alonso tell you? My real name? That Mom was a hooker?"

"I learned this from a retired East Side cop who did the research. All Alonso ever did was express concern for you and your well-being. He thinks you're sick and that you need help."

The safe room is quite small, large enough for two CC-TVs, a small table and chair, a phone, and a box of supplies that include a first-aid kit, food, water, and a blanket. I see smoke rise on the screen that shows the area in front of the safe room door and then the water sprinkler system in my office turns on to douse the fire.

"Hear the alarm? The fire department is on their way, Blaze."

She panics and starts to fire at the outer door of the safe room."

"You better be careful about the ricochets, Blaze. The door is solid steel and fiber glass. You can't get in that way, either. Your best recourse is to run."

She puts in a second clip and concentrates on one area of the latch. The last bullet from this round ricochets and Blaze falls to the ground directly in front of the safe room door. She remains unmoving. I can't see the arm that holds the gun in my CC-TV. Smoke rises from the bits of burnt and now soggy paper in my office. I call Gus and tell him to call for an ambulance crew to my office, STAT, that the fire department is also coming, and that the door to my suite is likely locked. He's full of questions but I hang up.

I didn't think to place a weapon in my supply box for the new safe room. I don't know how fast help will be here, and I don't want Blaze to bleed out, so I unlock the door, which swings out into my office, but her body prevents me from opening it. "Blaze! Are you hit? Can you hear me?"

She doesn't respond, so I keep pushing the door which gradually moves her a few inches at a time. At last I squeeze through the small opening and roll Blaze over. I kick the gun from her hand and across the floor. There's an expanding circle of blood on her dress just above the waist. I reenter the safe room for a second so I can wrap the blanket around her waist and keep pressure on it. I root through the first-aid kit and find gauze and an Ace bandage. She starts to moan and reaches for something behind her.

"Help is on the way. You're going to be okay, Blaze!"

Footsteps hurry down the hallway and in rushes cops and firemen, followed by two EMTs and Detective Baker, gun drawn.

I tell the crew about the bullet wound while I try to rise from the floor and get out of their way when Blaze screams and swings her right arm toward me. I back away as quickly as possible but feel a sting.

Baker roughly knocks her down and places a boot on her hand. She grimaces. He calls out, "Breezy, you okay?"

"I think so. I'm glad this is over."

The look on his face concerns me. 'What?"

"Look at your shirt." He bends down and picks up something from the floor.

His gloved hand clutches a bloody scalpel while my right hand is covered with blood.

More people enter my office. Gus, the building security guard, tries unsuccessfully to restrain Gianelli from entering, who claims he followed Blaze here, but was not allowed access to the floor by Gus. The two exchange heated unpleasantries until Gus says, "I had no proof you were working with Dr. Adams!"

"It's okay, Gus. He can stay."

Two EMTs place a moaning Blaze on a stretcher after Baker searches her for more weapons. Another EMT helps me to a chair. My chest stings worse once my shirt is removed. There's a foot-long slash wound an inch above both nipples that the EMT irrigates and cleans.

"Man, that looks like it hurts," Gianelli says. "I didn't know what else to do, so I staked out her apartment and followed when she drove here."

I turn to him and grimace. "You can stay, Gianelli. If you're quiet."

"You're lucky you backed away when you did," the EMT says. "It's primarily a surface slash, but some places are deeper than others. This area above the right nipple is still oozing and will require a few stitches. After we're done here, you will need to follow up with a doctor for wound regimen and skin care. Even with that, there will likely be some scarring."

Responding to my wincing, he adds, "You're going to be okay."

"I know. Thank you."

The other EMTs rush Blaze down to a waiting ambulance and Baker issues instructions to another cop to follow her. The firemen inspect the offices and rule out any further chance of fire.

Baker sits across from me while I get patched up. "Looks like the safe room saved your ass. That and your quick thinking to get there."

Once the EMT leaves, I recount today's talk with Blaze, which I have on tape as Missouri allows one party to record a conversation without permission from the other. I also bring a bottle of bourbon and two glasses from a desk drawer.

Baker laughs. "First she wants to run away with you and fuck you, then later wants to kill you. She's a real-life praying Mantis. I seen that a lot with dudes when I used to respond to home disputes, but not with women. Sorry that I thought at one point you might've been hitting that."

I wave that away. He's doing his job. "I was a loose end to her. If I'd been reckless enough to accept her offer, I would have been the victim of a drowning, a poisoning, or some such vacation misadventure that resulted in my death." I pour us each two fingers and we walk out to the waiting room while crime scene techs start their work. Baker takes my statement and when finished he asks about Miranda.

"She was afraid I was in danger once she learned I was Blaze's therapist. She was right. Her concerns and a few past episodes in the office were the rationale I spent money on the safe space in my office."

The toothpick returns to his mouth. "That don't mean she should break up with you."

"You don't know the whole story. I didn't like it, but I understand her reasons and can't argue with them. No hard feelings."

I ask what will become of Blaze and Jamal.

The toothpick travels to the other side of his mouth. "For her, surgery in a hospital then recovery in a prison hospital while the cops investigate everything she said. That checks out, then Jamal gets released.

"There any way Jamal's sister can stay at the fancy new hospital, as part of their deal?"

He shakes his head. "Dunno. Only if Blaze agrees to keep footing the bill. Perhaps you can suggest that to her, as a sign of good faith."

Now I shake my head. "I'm done with her. I'll be happy to discuss the case with the cop therapist who will deal with her from here. I'm going to lick my wounds, see some clients, and take a vacation. Spend time with my parents. Take a break from dating, bike, hike, and read."

"Remember, we gonna need your testimony at some point. So don't travel too far just yet."

We shake hands and I begin to clean the worst of the mess in my office after the crime scene crew leaves until the pain in my chest tells me it's time to go home.

EPILOGUE

The tragic story of Blaze consumes more local and national headlines during the next weeks. I'm hounded for interviews by personalities from CNN and Fox News, as well as reporters from People Magazine and Entertainment Weekly among many others I've never heard of but turn them all down. Local and national authors want to pick my brain to collaborate on a true-crime or a tell-all book about Blaze's personal life, but my code and common decency prevents me from considering this. The financial offers start small and double each week. I hear Gianelli is trying his best to sell what he knows about the Blaze case to the highest bidder, but that he isn't getting far.

Baker eventually convinced Jamal Jones to admit to the bizarre murder deal he struck with Blaze in exchange for his sister's transfer to a competent long-term care facility where her needs could be met. He admitted he entered Ted's suite after Lamping was dead, to leave his DNA evidence and coordinate their stories. The encounter with Sam in the bathroom at the city library was conceived and fabricated by Blaze, but once again Jamal made certain to leave evidence that he'd been there.

A week later, I haven't heard any firm news from any source (not even Baker) of how Blaze is recovering after the self-induced gunshot wound.

I receive a certified letter the next day that reads:

> My Dearest Mitch:
> The hole in my stomach has been repaired and they say I'm making slow and steady progress, but I have my doubts.
> O how I wish I'd been able to convince you to come away with me so we could have started a new life together! I would have bought us a private island to live on, we could do anything your heart desired, go anywhere at any time, buy anything we wanted. I can make you insanely happy and only you can drive out the demons inside me. You can still join me after this little police misunderstanding gets resolved.
> The place I'm in is a dreadful hell hole. Not much better than the places in Out?!? where Hester rescued and gathered her group of female followers before their march southwest.
> There is no one smart to talk to here. Certainly no one nearly as qualified as you. Nobody here realizes that the Midnight Man is getting stronger, and I fear he plans to kill me this week (he just killed Sarah and I'm next).
> I need you to save me from him.
> I need you to save me from me.
> I don't know what you think about me, but I love you.
> Help me, please, before it's too late!
> Don't abandon me! You can't leave me like this!

Name your price, I will exceed it!

Yours forever,
Blaze Stark

She's one of the most memorable and bizarre clients I've seen, but this attempt at manipulation won't work on any level with me. Her days of island hopping, and buying are done as she faces two murder charges that appear to be open and shut cases. Her D.I.D. is fictitious. She did research on it and acted the part well, but Alonso helped confirm the timeframe was out of whack. Had she led with the truth about her real childhood history of being sexually offered to her mother's johns, that may have convinced me this could be a true case of DID, but since she intentionally overdosed her mother I assume she didn't want to go down that slippery slope and potentially be caught. Given her history, it's amazing she turned out as well as she did, yet even as I say the words, I see the errors in my thinking.

I contact Dr. Stone, the prison shrink assigned to Blaze and I answer his questions about Blaze. He tells me when she heard his name she decompensated and now is certain she's Hester in her trilogy and does her best to escape the hospital prison walls. The call lasts two hours until I end it by recommending that a female doctor and therapist work with this smart, charming, borderline personality disorder.

When I exit the driveway to go to work the next day, Miranda's Prius pulls up alongside. Barney sits in the passenger seat secured in his harness, howling and wagging his tail. She powers down her window and says, "I read the articles in the Post. Are you okay?"

"I am. How are you?"

"Did she really kill Sam and her publisher?"

"There will be a trial, but it looks like it."

"And did she fire a gun at you inside your office?"

I nod. "And the ricochet hit her in the abdomen."

She looks confused. "Ricochet?"

"I had a safe room installed in the center of the offices this year in case a therapist needed to retreat from a situation. I was safely tucked in there before she tried to blast her way through the door, which is impossible."

"You never told me you added a safe room."

I look at her and say in a calm voice. "It wouldn't have changed your decision to leave. You still would have dated that other man."

Her face clouds over for a moment. "Oh, him. He's… You're right, I still would have gone out with him. You want to have breakfast somewhere and talk?"

"I can't. I'm late for a work meeting with my staff."

"Okay, then. It was good to see you, Mitch. I'm glad you're okay." She looks as if she wants to say more but doesn't.

I power up my window and know it will take some time for all things Blaze to flush out my system and to feel back to normal again. Which is why after the staff meeting, I scheduled an appointment with Dr. Peltzer, who helped me come to terms with Kris's murder several years ago.

Time heals all wounds—from murderous borderline clients with hidden agendas to estranged girlfriends, even to missing their adorable dogs.

ACKNOWLEDGMENTS

This is the fourth installment of my Mitchell Adams suspense series, the only series in all of bookdom, to my knowledge, with a social work protagonist. I enjoyed creating Mitch's multi-layered antagonist Blaze Stark, having her barge her way into Mitch's life and create such havoc. A graph of her life might have more ups and downs than the stock market before a crash.

I wanted to write an embedded narrative book, or a book within a book, after reading Minette Walters' novels and chose to set this story in the backdrop of the business of fiction publication and what the life of a mega-bestselling writer (?) with a rabid and radical fan base could look like in the near future. I cannot imagine what the real author would have felt like had she lived long enough to see her work published around the world by someone else.

Having never written a courtroom scene before Boundless, I asked my friend and attorney Mike Schaller for procedural clarifications about arraignments, as well as my friend and psychologist Dr. Felix Vincenz questions about various psychiatric diagnoses and diagnostic tests for certain behavioral traits. Their help, as always, is immensely appreciated. Any mistakes are mine.

I remember the fun I had when an initial version of the first chapter was reviewed and critiqued years ago by a panel of writers at a seminar (and a future editor, redheaded Meghan Pinson, who kindly chided me for having an antagonist with bright red hair)! I enjoy all feedback of a work in progress, for it's how you learn and grow.

I took a few liberties with St. Louis locations but they weren't major ones.

My thanks go to staff at New York Book Publishers, specifically Lisa Smith (aka: Toyko), editor James Stewart, Logan Walsh, Jessica Cohen, Emma Becker, and Jeremiah Hofsted. Plus, everyone else who worked on Boundless to get it formatted and ready for print. Another thank you to those who created and kept improving my website scottlmillerbooks.com.

I hope you enjoyed reading this tale and the best way to thank, or provide feedback to, an author, is to write a review. Short or long doesn't matter. You may do that on my website or on Amazon or other sites.

Namaste!